Secr

Voyagers

A magical fantasy series

Volume One

Close to an end---
     and a beginning---

Ron Haseman

Published in 2014 by FeedARead.com Publishing –
Arts Council funded

With loving thanks and gratitude to my wife Jo for her extreme patience and help during the years of my literary voyages

Sometimes the answer lies right there
Unseen whilst we strain and stare
Until we utter a little thanks
For the allowance of earlier pranks
On this acceptance then the door
Will open wide to our life store

Ron Haseman

Chapter One

Late winter, many centuries ago---

The growing commotion of men bellowing to each other above the noise of their horses trampling the hard frosted earth not far behind him seemed nearer with every thump of his racing heart.

On recognising the ominous sound of their approach the old man had instantly grabbed his outer fur covering and fled from the small huddle of dwellings on the hillside down into the cover of the valley, leaving all his other equipment behind.

These were the 'Searchers'. A gang of four armed thugs rewarded by those in power to roam the country and seek out any such as he for execution or imprisonment. He had lost a dear friend to them recently and now it seemed someone had claimed a reward in reporting *his* whereabouts. This time *he* was their target.

Other than the fur and a pair of well-worn animal skin slippers, all he had on was a smock tied at the waist with an old worn leather strip through which he tucked the end of his long grey beard.

Wind temperatures through the valley were below freezing. Striving to remain ahead of his hunters he hid and dodged quickly between sparse patches of bramble and bush, constantly having to unsnag his smock from vicious thorns whilst attempting to control his vaporous breath from visibly ballooning in the cold air.

Mercifully the wind dropped a little and snow began to fall heavily, muffling the noise of his pursuers and restricting their vision, yet these were known to be relentless once they had the scent of a reward and *they* were on horseback. As they drew ever nearer a more strident shout penetrated the snowfall.

"Over here you damned fools. He came in this direction."

Peering through a gap in the frosted thicket of brambles currently screening him, the hunted man could make out the lead rider a mere fifty paces away and heard him bark out a new callous order.

"Bowman! When you see him, loose an arrow into him and let's be away from this accursed place!"

With intense cold and fear coursing through his whole frame the old man muttered determinedly through his beard, "I *have* to get back, my work is so near completion."

With barely a movement of his fingers in front of his eyes, he instantly became invisible, yet his cold weakened state caused him to gasp at the mental strain required for this normally simple task.

Knowing he would still leave tracks and that any movement of the scrub might give his position away, his preferable escape would be flight, but that would take more effort than he had left and whilst the snow was helping cover his retreat, the same gathering on his invisible smock by taking to the air might render him an easy target for the bowman. Instead, he began to stealthily continue on foot towards the familiar rocky hills in the distance, when he heard another voice unexpectedly shouting.

"Hunters? Hah! You wouldn't find me if I was crawling up your nose. You're all a waste of space!"

This sudden new outburst caused him to glance back and trip, making a considerable disturbance to the frozen growth around him. Stealthily regaining his posture and despite his invisibility half expecting an arrow to embed itself in him at any second, he was surprised to see that most of the riders were heading off in a different direction. Their leader, keeping his horse reined nearby, stood high on his stirrups directing and shouting fresh evil encouragement to his men.

"Get him. Bring the brat here and we'll take it in turns to beat it out of him."

A youngster in strange brightly coloured attire had emerged from the scrub behind the riders and was yelling and gesticulating at them, establishing himself as their new target before making off speedily. The old man was not the only one to make little sense of what he was seeing. The lad was moving down the slight gradient across the snow at high speed with arms held out as if for balance, yet his legs though slightly bent at the knees, appeared still.

Pondering this and resting briefly whilst the men chased their new prey, he happened to glance again in the direction of their pig-faced leader just as a snowball thwacked with a ring against the man's helmet. Before the man could recover, another snowball hit his horse on its rump causing it to rear up, almost throwing him off. A second lad dressed similarly to the first stood brazenly close with more snowballs held in the crook of one arm whilst preparing to pitch a third and shouting,

"Cowardly pig! Go and chase your own kind."

The rider shouted and swore angrily in his struggle to maintain control of his startled mount, whilst the lad increased the man's fury by calmly calling out more insults before hitting him with the rest of his icy ammunition.

Thankful for the diversions but now concerned for the youngsters' safety, the old man began to command the little strength he had left, almost certain he would have to somehow attempt their rescue. Then whilst clearly in his sight, both boys simultaneously disappeared as if melting into the snowfall, much the same as he had himself a short time ago.

"Oh well done," he muttered to himself with a wry smile. He watched on with some amusement as the dumbfounded horsemen began to ride around the area uselessly searching, whilst their snow pelted leader sat there spitting and snarling with a look of sheer hatred and disbelief across his contorted features.

Abruptly, realising the youngsters had given him a chance for escape, the old man shook the collected snow from his smock and began to lope off invisibly across the valley on his long tired old legs.

Eventually reaching the safety of his small cave, he squatted just inside the entrance to regain spent breath while peering out warily in case of followers. There were none. The heavily falling snow was quickly obliterating his tracks and covering the bushes that screened his entrance.

He had managed to evade his hunters, albeit having had the benefit of some unexpected help. Nevertheless, his life was becoming ever more perilous. This was a tide of time when the mere *rumour* of magic being used could be taken as a threat to those in position of power.

Why? What was going on? It seemed in his limited view, as most others he had been able to converse with, that many of those in religion had teamed up with the largely self-appointed powerful leaders of the country who were out to make every man, woman or child bow to their preference and pay them taxes. Any such as *he* that wanted to investigate natural world elements and their possibilities, were to be hunted down and slain, or imprisoned under the weak excuse of allegiance with the devil or of treason to the crown. Of the few others he had known in his line of work, most, whether men or women, had simply ceased to exist.

He fervently hoped his young rescuers were aware of the dangers they were committing to and that if there was a God as claimed, then He would soon put in an appearance and put things to right one way or the other. If as an inventor and wizard he was seen by God Himself to be at fault, then so be it, he would accept his punishment. Until then, he would not give up on his quest to improve life for the innocent and the worthy.

Now returned to visibility and resting astride an upturned dry log within the depths of his cave, he recounted the sight of the two young lads using a craft similar to his own. For many years past he had felt in sore need of an apprentice, but youngsters in the nearby villages had either been warned off the Lore or had simply lacked interest. Nevertheless, he was extremely pleased to witness such a happening. It gave him a new zeal in his late years to have now visibly acknowledged he was doing the right thing. But where had these youngsters come from?

He stroked his beard while in thought and enthused about his more recent experiments.

"Could it possibly be that—no, it is too soon." He shook his head in a weak attempt to clear his tired mind, then chuckled to himself. "There again, with time, what *is* 'soon'?"

As he had no apprentice, throughout the long cold winter months he had ingeniously encapsulated his lifetime learning into a small self-driven machine to prevent his skills from becoming lost to the world.

Following a minor adjustment or two, he would arrange a secretive passage of the machine for the use of future young descendants in a suitable time window, some centuries on from these dire times.

Looking down past his feet he admired his small working invention on the cave floor through discerning grey-brown eyes

"Near done my children," he said to himself whilst running his fingers through his long grey beard. "Given time, things might change. *All* shall not perish." His quietly uttered words echoed eerily off the ancient rock walls of his cave.

Soon he could rest, somewhere new or perhaps forever-----

... ...

Chapter Two

Spring 2004 – The Learning begins….

The brothers, Toby at nine and Ben just thirteen, had enjoyed a very warm welcome from their grandmother on their arrival in England with their mother Cassie for a month's holiday.

"Where's Grandad, Nan?" asked Ben.

"He's in the loft. He has been fiddling around up there most of the morning."

Toby, already part way up the stairs, asked excitedly, "Can we go up and find him?"

"Of course you can. Wait a second though." She reached for a small torch from the hall shelf. "Here Ben, the two of you might need this in that dark old place. Be sure to be careful on the ladder."

"A ladder as well as stairs? Wicked!" This was something completely new to Toby as most houses where they lived in Australia had only one floor level.

Above them, the boys could see the shining aluminium ladder leading from the landing into the dark void above as if into another world. Ben had been given the torch and went first. Creeping up the ladder quietly until his head was level with the loft floor, he paused to let his eyes grow accustomed to the poor light conditions. A small light bulb hanging from the roof trusses dispelled some of the gloom in the nearer reaches of the loft, yet there was no obvious sign of his grandfather.

The ladder suddenly wobbled alarmingly. Toby, in his impatience had climbed up behind him whispering, "Don't stop there, I want to see him too, you know."

"I don't believe he's there. Just give me the chance and I'll make sure."

Returning his attention to the loft, Ben immediately saw the back of his grandfather crouched low not far in front of him and wondered how he had not seen him before. Never mind, he was there. Ben switched on the small torch and played the beam into the loft.

"What the devil?" His grandfather straightened up and turned quickly. "Ouch," he caught his head against one of the roof timbers whilst momentarily blinded by the torchlight. "Oh it's you, Ben" he said.

"Hi Grandad, Nan *said* you were up here somewhere."

"I'm sorry, I never heard you arrive. More than sorry in fact," he said gently touching the bruise already swelling on his bald head. "Come on up. Oh good you're there as well, Toby"

The loft seemed even darker as they stepped into it from the ladder.

"Wow!" Ben said. "This place could be full of ghosts and gremlins."

"Shut-up, Ben, you're just trying to spook me," Toby accused him.

"Well guys, now you're here," their grandfather intervened, "I'll show you around. Firstly, have a look at this and see what you think." He threw a switch on the wall beside him and a row of lights came on illuminating a part of the loft they had not seen until now.

"Oh wicked, a model railway. What a brilliant place to have it."

"Ben, it has roads with houses, bridges, trees, everything," Toby said in awe.

"There's a station too," Toby. "It has a platform with little people on it as if waiting for a train. One of them even has a dog on a lead. Did you make the scenery and everything, Grandad?"

"Your Great Grandfather made most of it, bless him. I simply moved it here when the old house was sold and added a few details. You like it, do you?"

"Of course," they agreed. "Who wouldn't? Can we see an engine running, please?"

The railway was built on a large raised area supported at a comfortable working height off the loft floor. Their grandfather crawled underneath it and suddenly popped up in the middle of the layout by the controls near the station.

"Right lads, just behind you against the wall you'll find two folding fishing chairs. Grab one each and sit along the track wherever you fancy. I'll start the engines." He threw some switches and two trains began to move with their lines of carriages rolling steadily behind them. The boys were fascinated to see him use the controls to change track points and send the trains in different directions, or cause them to speed and slow around bends and pull into stations or sidings.

"Fantastic, Grandad. It's all so real"

After around fifteen minutes in the same position their grandfather began to suffer leg cramp. "I think it's time to give the engines a rest," he said by way of an excuse. "We'll get them going again once we know what the girls want to do. Oh Lord, I haven't been down to see your Mum yet." He hastened off down the ladder.

"Hallo Cassie, it's good to see you. I'm sorry I was so long in coming down, we all got a little involved up there in the loft."

Cassie flung her arms around her stepfather and gave him a huge hug. "Never mind, Tom. I was pleased the boys went up there so soon to see you. Mum and I have had a good old chat in the meantime. It's just brilliant to be here with you both."

Cassie's mother Maggie, had divorced whilst Cassie and her sister Anna had been teenagers. She had met and married Tom a year or so after Cassie's own wedding to her husband Jack.

"It's a great shame Jack couldn't come with you," Tom said.

"I know, we are all going to miss him terribly, the boys especially. He hurt his leg at work a little while ago and his doctor advised him against the trip. He sends his love and regards and says he'll get to see you as soon as he is able."

"Poor Jack. Mind you, nearly twenty-four hours in those economy flight seats is almost unbearable when you *do* have two good legs."

Ben had been born in England and had often spent time with his grandparents until nearly three years of age when his parents had taken him to live in Australia. Tom and Maggie had last flown out to see them just after Toby's birth.

Wanting to see how much he might remember of his early times and places, Ben gained permission to take Toby to the local park that was situated beyond their back garden. Whilst having a good sense of humour, Ben was an intelligent, often serious youngster who liked to look into everything around him, having every intention of eventually becoming an inventor or a geologist. Toby, well aware of this, often mischievously called him 'Prof' or the professor.

Towards the end of the small path leading into the park, Ben stopped and pointed. "Hey, I remember this. The swings are down the hill just past those trees. Race you?"

They took off like horizontal rockets, each trying to beat the other to the big slide they could see in the distance.

Cassie stood with her parents at the end of their back garden and watched her sons charge across the park.

"It's nice to see them together like that, Cassie. I remember you were having some problems not so long ago?" her mum enquired.

"Yes, they really used to argue and upset one other, but thankfully most of that seems to have passed. They still enjoy ragging each other but it rarely gets serious." Cassie linked her arms with her parents. "So, what do you make of them?"

"We love them to bits," they both agreed.

"Those coats they have on are really good," Tom observed. "We can see them a mile off in those bright colours."

Walking back from the park the boys saw a black cat outside the front door.

"It's Biggles," Ben cried running ahead.

"Biggles?" Toby said, speeding his pace in curiosity.

"Yes," his Nan said, now holding the door open for them. "Ben knew him well when he used to visit us. Biggles is nearly seventeen now, quite an age for a cat."

Enjoying the big fuss made of him the old cat rubbed against Ben's ankles purring, almost as if saying, 'Where have you been all this time, I've not seen you in ages.'

'Jet-lag' set in early evening, forcing the small Australian contingent to their beds. It was quite late the following morning when the travellers finally roused themselves.

"What are we going to do today, Nan?" Toby asked excitedly.

"We made no plans for today as we thought you would all be tired from the long trip over."

"*I* am," said Cassie. "But these two seem full of beans."

"In that case, if you feel up to it, lads," their grandfather suggested, "Perhaps we three 'Men' should go and have a rummage amongst my treasures in the loft?"

"Oh, yes please," the two lads shouted as one.

Within a few minutes the three were again inside the loft.

"Now, be my guests and have a good look around. If you see something you are not sure about, just ask. If I know anything about it, which is unlikely, I won't hesitate to tell you."

With no second prompting necessary the boys began delving into dusty old boxes and pulling out various things to examine. The questions soon began.

"Whatever is this, Grandad? It looks like three different-sized feet joined together and it's *very heavy*," Toby grunted as he struggled to move it.

"That *is* heavy, Toby. It's cast in solid metal and is known as a Foot-last."

"Whatever is it for?"

"Well, in the old days, shoes were repaired using nailed-on leather soles. The shoe would be put on one of those suitably sized metal feet while the sole was nailed into position. The nails or lasting tacks, would go through the sole and base of the shoe and bend over flat on the inside when hitting the Foot-last to prevent them from working out again and, just as importantly, from sticking into the wearer's foot. There was then a kind of loose leather sole fitted inside the shoe to cover the bent nail ends."

"Crikey, the idea of a nail sticking up inside a shoe sounds awfully painful."

"It certainly could be! My dad repaired my school shoes on this very tool. Shoes and soles these days of course, are mostly stitched or moulded together like your trainers, so luckily there isn't much cause for nails in shoes, or for Foot-lasts I suppose, come to that."

"So why do you keep it then, Grandad?"

"For memories sake really. My dad used it and it was his dad's before that, so I don't like to part with it."

"That's nice," Ben said thoughtfully. "Now we are talking of our Great-Great-Grandad," he worked out. "That's amazing."

"Wow! That thing must be nearly a thousand years old," exclaimed Toby.

"Whoa, not quite that old," his grandad said, "Less than two hundred years actually."

"Is it the oldest thing you have up here, Grandad?"

"No Ben. There is one that is much older that I want you to see," he answered. "You'll find it as you go around I expect."

"This little box seems to be full of old photos," Toby said. "Can we have a look through them some time?"

"Yes of course. Put it near the entrance, then you can take them down whenever you want."

"Oh look at this, Toby! A pile of comics. The Beano, Dandy, Superman and others I've never heard of, Captain Marvel, The Eagle…"

"You can take those down too," their grandfather said. "But treat them with care as they've been around for a while. I had those when I was a boy."

"Wow, *real* antiques then? Oops, sorry Grandad," Ben said as he carefully gathered them.

"That's alright young fellow, I'll let that go. It will be your turn to be an antique soon enough," he added, poking him in the ribs with his finger.

"That old covered chest they were stacked on looks ancient," Ben mentioned.

"Yes it is and it's also very dusty. It's too late in the day now to get involved but if you'd care to drag it out and clean it in the morning, I'm sure you will love and make good use of what's inside."

"Oh yes, gladly," Ben replied as Toby lifted a corner of the covering and peered interestedly at the old chest.

"Fine, now we had best get ourselves down with the others ready for tea, then afterwards I might join you to read some of those old comics."

The loft ladder suffered yet again as six feet attached to various proportioned bodies rapidly descended in the general direction of food.

Next morning, following considerable effort to drag it out and clean it, the lads were admiring the old chest. "Even without the dust and cobwebs it looks ancient. Who did the chest originally belong to, Grandad?"

"I reckon it's a pirate's chest," Toby interrupted excitedly. "Captain Hook's perhaps?"

His grandad chuckled. "I'm not at all sure when Hook was supposed to have been around, Toby, but it is certainly old. The contents are believed to have been made by one of our family forebears, many, many centuries ago and handed down for the use of the children as a legacy ever since."

"Why is it for the family children, Grandad? Is there something special inside it?"

"Very special indeed, Ben."

Toby by now was becoming extremely fidgety. "Can we open the chest now?"

"You guys are at the right age to look into its mysteries, so yes, I'll go and get the key."

"Wow, *our* turn to open an ancient chest. I can't wait. What do you think *is* inside, Ben?" He knelt down attempting to peer with one eye through a ring of tiny vent holes.

Ben shrugged negatively. "Knowing Grandad, it's likely to be a huge Jack-in-a-box trick that will suddenly move when we open it. Then again, if it really *is* that old, it could contain something quite frightening. We had better watch out when we open it."

Toby instantly sprang away from the chest as if something lurking inside might grab and pull him through the vent holes into the dark unknown.

Their Grandfather was soon back and handing them the key. "You will find the contents immaculate and they need to be kept that way, as well as intact for future children. Most likely they will be your own offspring at some time," he said with a wink. "There are other reasons too, but you'll learn about those once you have seen and used what there is inside. As current guardian for the chest and all its contents, I am responsible, so please don't let me down."

"We'll look after it, Grandad."

"I'm sure you will. Keep the items on the shelf separate from those below and see what you make of it. You can tell me if you're interested when I come back." He swung a leg over the top of the loft ladder and glanced back. "I know you will be, as *I* was the new grandchild myself a long time ago," he added with a wistful smile.

···   ···   ···

Chapter Three

"Right it's unlocked, I'll lift the lid slowly just in case of tricks. Ready?"

"Yep, okay," Toby answered from a distance.

Ben looked round to see Toby crouched and peering from behind a stack of boxes.

"Oh come on, Toby. If anything happens it will only be a joke thing. I shall probably need your help to open it anyway. Those lid hinges appear to be well rusty."

"Oh alright," Toby murmured warily. "I'm coming."

With the extra effort, the lid lifted on its creaking hinges and finally swung back fully open. Both boys kept well clear of it for a few seconds hoping to avoid anything that may have jumped out at them. Luckily nothing did and they soon plucked up enough courage to both peer over the top and inside.

"No wonder the contents are clean," Ben said. "The inside of the chest is all cloth lined. I remember seeing a *coffin* like this in a Vampire film I once watched."

"Urgh!" Toby sprang well away from it immediately.

Though he admitted nothing, Ben found *he* had to steel himself to take a second look.

"There doesn't appear to be anything frightening in it," Ben said somewhat relieved. "Nor exciting either! It seems to be chock full of bits and pieces made from some kind of black stuff - old wood probably. I'll get a few out and we'll have a closer look at them. Oo-er! Look at these, Toby."

Toby edged nearer and stood alongside him.

The first things he removed were two pot-like containers that had been cut and carefully hollowed out from part of a tree sometime in the distant past. One was empty, the other absolutely full with very fine, dry sand. A hole at the centre of each pot base was covered by a small disc of wood held at one edge by a wooden pivot pin. The disc itself had been part of a small tree branch cleverly cut across either side of a shortened twig which had been left as a lever and forming a crude but effective valve for the exit of the sand.

Ben's inventiveness became aroused. "Clever, but what on earth are they for?"

The boys spent the next few minutes lifting out other objects of varying shapes and sizes, all carved beautifully from the same ancient black ebony.

"These seem to be wooden gears."

"You're right, this must be some kind of machine."

"Well, let's see if we can put it together," Toby suggested. "Grandad did say, 'See what you make of it'."

"True," Ben said, "I'm not so sure that's *exactly* what he meant, though it seems a good enough excuse."

"This should be fun, Ben. It will be something like Meccano." Then his small forehead creased into a frown. "Come to think of it though, we haven't seen any screws yet, nor anything else to hold it all together."

Once they had cleared the shelf in the chest, Toby made ready to lift it.

"No, hold on and stop being so impatient, Toby. We are supposed to keep the shelf parts separate from those below. Let's deal with these for now. This big bit is probably the base. Hey, there are markings or words carved around this. Perhaps it will tell us when it was made. Can you pass me the torch please."

"Yep, here you are."

Ben shone the torch on the markings and peered at them. "No date, just a few words - *'Make me-feed me'*- Do you have your notebook and pencil with you?"

"You have to be kidding. Does it really say *that*?"

"No you great loon," Ben said laughing. *"I asked* that. I thought we ought to make a note of the words in case they are instructions or clues."

"Clues? Wow! Hang on a minute." Toby streaked down the ladder and was back within seconds, hopping from one foot to the other in his excitement and scrabbling through his notebook for a new page. "Okay, start again and I'll write them down."

Ben read, *"'Make me-feed me-watch me speak-should you light the torch to seek'."*

Toby chewed the end of his pencil in thought. "How can you watch a machine speak?"

"Search me! It all seems a bit odd," Ben answered, then began to show the imaginary professorial mantle he sometimes wore when getting serious.

"Quite honestly I can't see how this can be as old as Grandad says. Any written language in those days would have surely been different from that we've just found. Oh well," he shrugged, "The clue says *'Make me'*, so pass some parts over and we'll give it a try."

Toby obliged, then tried putting a few pieces together himself. "These curved bits just seem to lock together somehow, but they hold very well. It seems to be part of a wheel of some sort. What do you think it is, Ben, this thing we're trying to build?"

"There's no telling what it is, if it will work, or what it will do if it does."

Toby chuckled. "You sounded just like Grandad then."

"Cheeky devil," Ben retorted. "But yes I suppose I did come to think of it," he added. "You're dead right about

23

the fit of these parts. They only seem to hold together when they are in the right place and it's a job to get them apart again then, almost as if they are magnetised. But how can that be, wood isn't magnetic?"

"Oh come on Prof, you're worrying too much about detail. Just get on with it."

Despite their differences the brothers worked well together. Before long, a strange contrivance began to emerge on the loft floor. It resembled 'The Eye', that huge popular Ferris wheel built recently as a city viewing attraction on the London Thames Embankment, though on a much smaller scale.

The wheel of the loft version was near sixty centimetres in diameter and had a series of small hollowed out wooden buckets swinging from it, rather than the plush people accommodation cabins that the 'Eye' offered. The wheel shaft was supported either side by wooden frames held together by two platforms, one mounted high above the wheel, the other at base level. A hollowed area in the base platform formed a kind of tray, whilst the top platform had a thumb-sized hole at each end along its centre-line, positioned towards the left and right of the wheel diameter.

"Hmmm, I wonder what all this means," Ben asked peering at a deeply carved v-shaped groove running almost the length of the top platform and ending with arrow heads pointing in opposite directions towards the holes.

"One arrow has been left black with a small moon carved below it, the other has a gold tip and a sign like a radiating sun."

Having absolutely no idea what they might be for, they carried on with the main assembly.

"What else do we have left?"

"Just this little stack of grey bits."

The 'grey bits', almost transparent, were a child's palm size, slightly thicker than a modern compact disc and carved from a whitish-grey stone or bone of some kind. Each had two tapered pegs along their bottom edges that proved to fit and lock securely in the holes provided on one of the drive shafts. Once assembled, when the big wheel was turned gently, the second shaft turned much faster, similar to a small fan-wheel.

Ben sat and looked at the assembly lovingly. "This is very like that water wheel we saw recently, except it must use sand instead of water. The full sand pot apparently sits over that top platform hole allowing the sand to fall through into the buckets. I'll put that in position now, Toby if you'll put the empty one at the bottom as the collector. We'll use the mounting positions to the right of the wheel for the time being, near the 'Sun' markings. I really can't see a reason for those others." He paused and peered intently at the framework. "There *has* been something else fitted here but it seems to have mostly been burnt away?"

"It might not matter, Prof, let's see if it works," Toby said impatiently.

"Alright here goes. I'll open the sand valve."

Sand began to flow from the pot directly into the bucket swinging below. Once nearly full, the weight of it caused the wheel to turn a little, bringing the next bucket below the sand flow and gradually adding to the wheel's momentum.

"That's it," the boys shouted. "We've cracked it. The wheel is beginning to turn."

But once the first full bucket reached the bottom everything stopped. Everything that is, except the sand which quickly overfilled the top bucket and began to spill into the base tray.

"Oh no, now we're in trouble." Ben hurriedly turned off the sand valve.

"Why did that happen?" Toby sighed disappointedly. "It started off so well."

"We've obviously made a muck-up of something somewhere," Ben replied looking quite despondent. "We had best pick up all that spilt sand before we do anything else. If it gets in the works it might damage the gears or something and we shall need to be very careful not to lose any of it. It seems much finer than ordinary sand and we have yet to find a spare supply in the chest. I'll"--

"Argh!" they both cried out in fright. A head had suddenly appeared through the loft opening.

"Sorry I didn't mean to make you jump," their grandfather chuckled. "I came to tell you there are pork pies and lemonade on offer downstairs in case you are interested."

They were soon clattering and chattering on their way back up the small metal loft ladder.

"Those pies were good" they agreed.

"Now, what do you think happened to make the machine stop, Ben?"

"I know what the problem *is*," Ben replied, "but I'm not sure about an answer. The design of that water wheel we recently saw, allowed the water to pour out just before the containers reached the bottom. Our sand doesn't. The buckets at the bottom are full and too heavy to allow the wheel to go round any further."

Toby sighed. "But what can we do about that?"

"We'd best get that sand cleared away first before we—Hey! There's no sign of it now?"

"Grandad has been up I expect while we were finishing our lunch."

"That's strange, I'd have sworn he went straight down to the garage after the break. Oh well, it's great that it's done. Now let's see, are there any bits left over?"

"Just one," Toby answered peering at it. "A kind of paddle shaped thingy on a shaft. I never noticed it before but I can't see it making much difference. Here," he said passing it over.

After peering at it and the machine closely, Ben said, "Well, there are only a couple of frame holes left where it might fit, so let's give it a try."

Fortunately, with no dismantling necessary, they were soon ready for a second trial. But now, as soon as the first full bucket neared the bottom of its travel, it bumped up against the newly fitted paddle.

"Damn, I thought that might happen," Ben said, sighing. "That thing is right in the way."

He reached over to turn off the sand-valve and then paused as he watched the weight of the filled sand buckets above causing the snagged one to slowly tilt and tip its contents into the pot below before swinging free of the paddle. The boys were overjoyed to see the wheel keep turning and the now empty bucket soon followed by others, returning to the top for the refill sequence.

"Result," they both yelled, punching the air with their fists.

"The wheel itself turns fairly slowly but look at that fan go," exclaimed Ben. "I have no idea what it's for, but it's so fast those grey blades are almost invisible."

"This is the best thing we've ever built," Toby said excitedly. "It doesn't need screws, nuts, or glue, not even clockworks or batteries. It's a *wicked* invention."

"It really is awesome. Let's stop it now and have a look at the other stuff in the chest."

They were about to lift the shelf out when they heard someone on the ladder again.

"How are you getting on fellers?" Their grandfather climbed into the loft and looked the assembly over. "You've done well, you'll have it running before long I expect."

"We already did, Grandad, it's brilliant."

"We found some clues and I've written them down in my notebook," explained Toby excitedly. "Do you know what they mean?"

"I do, Toby, but by the chest rules, children wanting to use the sand wheel have to use their *own* intelligence. You've done very well so far."

"Rules! We have enough of those back at school," Toby complained. "Why *must* there be so many rules?"

"They are generally for people's safety, Toby. In this case, if children can't assemble the wheel or solve the clues without help, then it would be dangerous for them to use it at all. In any case, too much help would spoil the fun. Have you not enjoyed finding out how to put it together?"

"We certainly have," Toby admitted. "Though we wouldn't mind a teeny bit of help."

"Alright," his grandfather replied with a grin, "Just one tiny nudge. Amongst the clues you will find the word 'Torch' mentioned. That was of course the torch of long ago made from strips of old sacking or clothing attached to a stick and then soaked in Pitch or"--

"Pitch? *Whatever* is that?" Toby interrupted him. "That sounds more like something to do with football?"

"Toby, you do ask the most difficult questions, but then that's good, other than for the person who has to answer them," he added. "Never be afraid to ask questions. Pitch used to be found in natural pools a long time ago, I believe. Nowadays it can be obtained from the Tar process manufacturers for waterproofing and the like. It's thick black sticky stuff, similar to tar or natural crude oil and inflammable—it burns well," he explained. "You would be best looking it up in a dictionary young fellow. Once set alight, people would carry those torches in the dark or use them as fixtures on walls for general illumination. You may have noticed a few burn marks on the machine framework where the original torch used to stand."

Ben's face lit up as if that very torch had suddenly been shone on it. "Ah so that's what caused them."

"When using that first clue, you will find your Nan's torch will do the job very well *and* without risk of causing a fire," their grandfather advised.

"Thanks, Grandad. By the way, you mentioning oil a moment ago reminded me, is it alright if I use some of your train oil on the chest hinges, they are rusty and really stiff."

"Good idea, Ben. Please do that. But now, a quick explanation. Our unknown ancestor obviously had skills which these days would be considered totally unobtainable. Apparently, he wanted them to be passed on to future family descendants by allowing the children access, but cleverly including a means to ensure that only those capable would be able to make use of them."

"How could he do that?"

"Simply by supplying the sand machine in pieces with no instructions and only simple riddles to tell them how to use it. You've already passed the first test by constructing the machine and getting it to run. You would be surprised how many children have failed to get that far, sometimes simply because of a lack of interest or enthusiasm."

"Ah I see. We've really loved doing that, but I still find it all a little odd."

"Why is that, Ben?"

"I never thought machines of any kind *existed* before the sixteenth century, least of all made from wood?"

"It was far from unusual actually, Ben. You'll find wind and water mills were mostly made from wood, including the gears. Another ancient wooden machine or engine, were Trebuchets. They are known to have been used during battle in the tenth and eleventh centuries. Records *are* said to have been unearthed of them having been used during the first century BC."

"Wowee! That certainly squashes my doubts about early machines."

"How on earth did they use tree bushes in battle?" Toby interrupted.

"I'm sorry, Toby," his grandfather answered with a chuckle. "I must have voiced it wrongly. The 'e's' should be pronounced as 'a's', so I should have said '*Trebuchets*'. They were enormous wooden Siege Machines, or 'Catapults' as we would now know them, that soldiers would operate while lying siege to a castle or fort belonging to an enemy. The ammunition used would normally have been large rocks in an attempt to breach the fortress walls to gain entry for their attack. It is said that they would also launch rotting cabbages, or even the removed heads of their enemies, in an attempt to cause discomfort and stress to those inside or defending the fort."

"Urgh- yuck," Toby muttered.

"I'm sorry little fellow. Perhaps I should have kept that fact to myself. Generally though, people had more time on their hands for invention then, but not of course the materials we have available these days, hence the use of wood. There would have been plenty of that, as

Britain was heavily forested then. As far as inventions go, *you* are both very useful with computers. Have a look on the web sometime for Leonardo da Vinci. He was very famous, largely as a painter. He lived in the late fourteen hundreds. Apart from painting, he produced various mechanical invention designs, including sketches that resemble a helicopter, way ahead of his time. How can we explain that? Futuristic dreams or time travel? I was always taught there is a reason or explanation for everything. It's just a matter of finding it. So never be afraid to question anything."

"Yes, I suppose you are right," Ben agreed showing interest. "So, why then, a sand wheel machine? What is it actually for?"

"One could say it has many purposes, but for now consider it largely as an adventure machine. As an ex-adventurer myself, I can tell you it's capabilities are almost beyond belief."

"You've used it yourself? Then how?"--

Grandad put his hands up. "Hold up a minute. Firstly, I must give you a couple of very important rules," he said giving Toby a wry grin.

There was a huge sigh and a groan from Toby.

"I know but bear with me, you'll both find it well worth it. Firstly, the chest, its contents and results must be kept a very close secret. No mention of it to friends or even family unless you check with *me* first. Secondly, the sand wheel must only be used in the loft and must be locked in the chest when not in use. These rules are essential to *all* adventurers, as well as for the family itself."

"Fair enough, Grandad. Secrets are different," Toby allowed.

"It's a pity you are only going to be able to use the chest if you happen to be here in England on holiday, but then there are no other children in the family near a suitable age at present to take over, so at least it will be available to you for several years yet."

"That sounds good anyway," Toby said.

"Everything else you will find when you start to use the wheel. Ben, you had a question?"

"How can we possibly have *adventures* using it?"

"That's for you to work out," he said. "You've already found the first clues. Look at those and work them out to find others. *Then* your adventures will begin."

"What kind of adventures?" Toby asked excitedly.

"You'll be able to make them as funny, exciting or even as frightening as you wish. Just help each other along and you'll find you will be able to do almost anything you can imagine - probably more in fact."

"That sounds almost *too* good to be true," Ben said a little pointedly.

"You'll see. Right now, it has to be decision time. If you don't believe in it or you don't like the rules, we'll take it apart and lock it away until the next grandchildren come along, 'No worries' as you Aussies say. Would you like to be the new family adventurers?"

"Yes-s-ss," the two brothers chorused simultaneously. "And we promise to keep it a secret."

"Good! I'm sure you'll never regret it."

Toby pulled at his Grandfather's sleeve. "Can we start now?"

"I'm sorry but I have to say no, as tea will be ready soon. Then this evening we had all best spend some time with your mum as it's her holiday too. We'll get some games out to play later." Seeing the disappointed looks on their faces, he grinned and added, "But there is always tomorrow. Lock the sand wheel in its chest for now, Ben."

"Do we have to dismantle it first? I doubt it will go in as it is?"

"It will, Ben. You won't need to dismantle it until it has to be handed on. You *can* remove the sand pots if you like so that it's not quite so heavy."

"Okay. Ah, that reminds me. Thanks for clearing up the spilt sand for us. It's so easily spilt. Do you have any spare sand for it?"

"No need to thank *me,* I didn't touch it. The sand *is* easily spilt, yes, but *never* lost."

Feeling extremely puzzled by his grandfather's answer, Ben lifted the machine and gently lowered it into the chest to find there was room to spare.

"That's surprising, I guess it just *looked* bigger when it was standing on the floor."

Toby looked shocked. "But Ben, it *was* bigger!"

"What do you mean?"

"The machine, as you put it into the chest it seemed to get smaller. You must have noticed."

"Don't be silly, Toby." Ben turned to his Grandfather again. "I think he's overdue for some grub, it's as if he's beginning to hallucinate."

"Well yes, he could be I suppose, but then it could be a case of someone *not* seeing things."

"Are you trying to tell me it really did get smaller?"

"Ah, that's for you both to decide. Was it magic or just imagination? That's all part of being an adventurer. One last thing before we go down, I expect the pair of you will be itching to get back to the machine tomorrow?"

"Oh will we ever!"

"Rain is forecast yet again so at least the weather is on your side. I will have to see if I can assist it in some way," he said with a wink. "Come on guys let's go down and be with the others."

The weather forecast had been right. Rain was teeming down when they woke in the morning making the outlook very gloomy. Their grandfather announced that the car would be out of action as he had some urgent work to do on it in the garage.

"Ah, then I'll grab an umbrella and walk down the road and see my friend Laura this morning," said Cassie. "I want to catch up with the latest news on our old drama club and friends. Will you boys come with me or would you sooner stay here with Nanny?"

"We'll stay here please, if it's alright with Nan."

"That's fine by me," said Nan. "But you will have to amuse yourselves this morning. As it's raining I am going to have to put all the washing through the drier."

"If we are careful with them, could we play with the trains please, Grandad?"

"Yes of course you can. I'll come up and explain the switchgear."

"Thanks for all your help, this is exciting," Ben said as he prepared the machine.

"I'm almost as excited *for* you," his grandfather replied. "I can remember when I was first allowed the machine myself."

Once he had showed them how to operate the engines in case they should have visitors to the loft or really *did* want to play with the trains, he left them and went off to the garage.

"Right, Toby, what were those words we found?"

Toby fumbled through his notebook. "Here they are. *'Make me - Feed me'*. If *'Feed me'* means fill me, we've already done that," he exclaimed. "This next bit is odd though, *'Watch me speak, should you light the torch to seek'*."

34

"Ah, Grandad was telling us about the torch," Ben said, hurriedly pulling it from his pocket. "I guess we'd best have the machine running first."

Once the wheel was revolving again, the boys turned on and positioned the small torch on the old burn marks, finding that when 'watched', the beam of light playing on the revolving fan blades made them look mysteriously transparent whilst producing a smoky grey stroboscopic apparition which seemed to hover above them, altogether eerie in the gloom of the loft.

"This is an awesome machine but as for adventure-?" Ben stopped short in amazement as darker greys above the whirring fan-blades gathered in places, then gradually manifested into shapes, slowly forming shaky letters and words:

'Greetings Friends
Adventures free be so like mine
Should you turn the sands of time.'

... ...

Chapter Four

The stunned boys remained rooted to the spot for a few seconds, realising the machine had sent them a clear but silent message.

"Oh my God, **'Watch me speak'**. It happened, Toby."

"Spooky," said Toby his eyes and ears still partly covered with his hands.

"No worries, Toby, it seems friendly enough. Almost like an ancient computer."

"Yes, I suppose you're right," Toby said grudgingly. "You know now I think about it, it's quite funny."

Ben looked perplexed. "How is that?"

"We've spent all that time building it and getting it to work properly, scratching our heads over a riddle, then finally it 'Speaks' and frightens the socks off us."

"It makes me wonder what we're getting into, Toby. This has to be magic. I've never believed in it before!"

"I guess I've always believed in it, so this is well wicked. What do we do next, Ben?"

"I don't know. I suppose we'll have to wait a while and see if it says anything else."

Almost as if the machine sensed the lads had recovered from their initial shock, the message began to fade. Toby hurriedly got his notebook and pencil at the ready and the two wide-eyed boys watched as shadows again merged into sentences.

'Used I be for good or fun
Cease else shall my wheel to run
First seek those that still be hidden
Then one's wishes can be bidden.'

"This is incredible," Ben said excitedly. "It looks as if we have a lot to learn and more to find yet. Are you getting it all down okay, Toby?"

"So far, but this pencil is not that good. It depends on how much more there is."

Another message began to form.

"Perhaps we could stop the machine while I go down for a sharpener or another pencil."

"Hang on if you can, Toby. I'm not so sure we should turn it off while it er- *'speaks'*. It can't have much more to say surely?"

Luckily the machine appeared to agree. It formed a short message this time.

'Farewell my friends.'

The grey smokiness seemed to level again, then nothing more.

"That seems to be it for now, I think we'll give it a well-deserved rest," Ben said as he closed the sand valve. "I'm having a job getting my head around all this. It's like having a strange day-dream."

"Day-dream! You must be kidding," Toby said. "My pencil is blunt and my new notebook is full of scribble."

Ben grinned. "Is your note book really full?"

"No I was just fooling, but this pencil has had it. I'll nip downstairs and use my sharpener."

"Okay, I'll put the machine in the chest for a while in case Mum should get back and come up to see us. It's going to be awfully difficult to keep this a secret."

"It sure is," Toby answered as he went down the ladder.

While he was gone, Ben took the torch and the pots from the machine, then carefully lifted and lowered it into the chest. This time he flinched in shock to find Toby had been right. It was a smooth, hardly noticeable process, but the machine was definitely decreasing in size as it neared the chest. He closed the lid and sat down on the fishing chair he had used earlier and attempted to calm his nerves. He was certainly believing in magic now.

Shortly afterwards a small head popped up through the hatch. Toby was back with a freshly sharpened pencil at the ready and carrying a small plate of sandwiches.

"Here, Ben, Grandad made these for us, cheese and onion. Are you all right? You look as if you've seen a ghost." Then abruptly his jaw dropped and he looked around the loft nervously. "You haven't have you?"

"Well, yes and no," said Ben. "Yes I'm okay. No I haven't seen a ghost. But I do owe you an apology. I said you were seeing things yesterday. I'm really sorry, you were quite right, the machine did get smaller. It just happened again as I put it back in the chest."

"I knew it," Toby said with glee. "I'm so glad you've seen it happen. Incidentally, there's no sign of Mum yet, so shall we get it out again?

Once it was out of the chest they watched with fresh awe as the old machine steadily grew to its former size.

"That's quite amazing," Ben remarked, "but I just can't see a reason for it."

"I can't either but I suppose there must be one. I expect we'll find out as we go along. I know one thing for sure, these sandwiches are good."

"Mmm are they ever? While we're eating perhaps we can solve some of the riddles. I think the first part of that clue simply means we can have adventures when we run the machine. I'm not so certain about the *'Like mine'* part, but one thing is for sure, our ancestor must certainly have been a wizard or someone extremely skilled in the use of magic."

"Wow! Our ancestor a wizard and we're allowed to use his machine," Toby said excitedly clapping his hands. Then calming down again he looked at his notebook. "I suppose in this last clue, if *'Cease'* means stop, then that's what Grandad already told us. Unless it is used for good reasons or for fun and adventure, it will stop working."

"Yes that's about it I reckon. Then it seems we have to find *'Something hidden'* before we can expect to do much else. Never mind, if we find those, we'll be able to sort out the others. Now we've finished eating we ought to have a look under the shelf in the chest. It should lift out easily, so we can start looking through the remaining contents."

"Here we go then. Ben these are all carvings from pieces of that old black wood again. This one's an elephant, it has wonderful ears."

"That's *some* carving, Toby," Ben said appraisingly. "Take a look at this lion, he's beautiful. There is a small cat here as well, just like my Cass at home," he said stroking it. "I do miss him."

The boys found other exquisitely carved animals and birds, then a canoe, a small ladder, a machete and even a carved coil of rope.

"This is strange, I've found a little car."

"It looks good. What's strange about it?"

"Only that the chest is supposed to be ancient. Most of the stuff we've found so far could easily have come from those times, but a car?"

"Look at these then, an aeroplane and a motorboat," Toby said as he held them up. "They are old and look

39

as if they are out of a history book, but they're obviously not from ancient times."

"That's true. The carving detail seems to vary a lot too. The animals and the canoe are beautifully carved as if they have had an awful lot of time spent on them. The vehicles are quite crude in comparison, although they are still very good. I doubt if I could carve anything that well?"

"You might get the chance yet," Toby answered with some amusement, "Have a look at these, they all seem to be blank blocks."

It was true. The bottom of the chest was almost covered with unused blocks of the same strange black wood. Piece by piece Ben and Toby emptied the contents of the chest not really knowing what they were looking for. They shook each block and carving as they removed them in case they rattled, suggesting something hidden inside, but to no avail.

"We're not having much luck here," complained Ben. "Is there really something hidden?"

They busied themselves in their frustration by replacing the blocks and carvings and after a close look at the shelves, replaced those too. Toby proceeded to close the chest.

"This lid takes some moving even though you've oiled the hinges," Toby remarked. "Perhaps it's just heavy?"

Ben abruptly jumped to his feet. "That's the one thing we haven't looked at closely." He studied the lid inside and out, then gave a sudden cry of excitement. "Look, these hinges are fixed on the outside with three rivets, but inside the lid this one has four. Is it possible this is a--?" He pressed the end of the extra rivet and there was a loud click as the entire inside covering of the lid swung down to reveal a big wallet-like pocket fixed to its uppermost surface.

"Yes," shouted Ben. "*Something hidden.*"

"Sick," said Toby.

"Here we go," said Ben. "I hope to God there are no spiders or anything like that in here." He gingerly pushed his hand into the lid pocket up to the wrist before his fingers encountered and extracted an old leather pouch with a long gold necklace attached to it. "Wow! Take a look at this, Toby."

"Awesome! Whatever is there going to be in there I wonder. Pieces of pirate gold perhaps?"

"It's certainly fairly heavy," Ben said drawing the contents out. "Not gold though. Just a few pieces of old flat stone or bone by the look of it. They're about the same size as the fan-blades. Spares perhaps? Wait a second though, this thicker one seems to be two fixed together somehow, back to back." He turned it over, studying it closely. "There is a small carving on both top corners. One side has a little moon, the other a sun."

"They are the same as those on the machine, Ben."

"Yes, you're right." Ben was now looking curiously at a small pocket formed at the bottom of the leather pouch. "There is more yet," he said pulling out something wrapped in a small piece of gold coloured soft leather. Inside the wrapping were two small cubes apparently made from bone of some kind. He carefully laid all the new findings in a row on the floor for further examination.

"Hey, these are dice," Toby said picking up the grey cubes. "Well this one is," he said as he had a closer look at them. "This has the numbers 'One' to 'six' carved on it in words instead of the usual spots, but the other one is completely blank."

After a quick look Ben agreed. "There's more mystery here too, Toby. This single flat stone from the pouch has tiny words carved all the way around its edge. It looks as if we might fill your notebook yet."

"Okay then, Ben, I have my pencil ready. Fire away."

"It reads:

*'Toss my bone squares from the gold
then adventures shall unfold.'*

While Toby was busy recording it in his notebook, Ben was punching the air again with his fist. "Yes! It sounds as if we're away. Can it be that easy, just throw the dice?"

Toby hurriedly put his pencil back in his pocket. "I guess there's only one way to find out."

"You're right. Hey, why don't we give the machine a name? It would seem friendlier somehow, instead of keep calling it 'It', or 'the machine'?"

"Great idea but what can we call it?"

"It's a sand machine, so why don't we call it Sandy?"

"I love it, Ben. Sandy it is."

"It will help us keep it a secret too. If anyone should ever hear us talking about Sandy, we can easily explain Sandy as being a friend of ours."

"Talking of easily, Ben, how are we ever going to remember all these clues so that we can make use of him?"

"Well thanks to you, we'll have them all in your notebook."

"Yes, that's okay with me but what if there are loads more yet?"

"I think if there are, most of them will be 'one-offs' anyway. Once we've begun to actually use Sandy, we'll remember most of them I expect. You know, like using a computer or most other things. We already know without looking how to fill, start and stop Sandy, and now we've found '*those that are hidden*'."

Ben turned and switched on the already positioned torch, then opened the sand valve.

The very second the wheel began to turn Ben was startled by a loud shout from Toby.

"Ben! Quick, come and have a look at this."

Something was happening to the bonded stone slab lying on the floor near Toby. At first its surface seemed to shimmer as if molten, then changed.

"Wow! It's become a mirror," exclaimed Ben. He carefully picked it up. The whole surface except for the small sun carving was now a mirror. "That is simply amazing. But what would we need a mirror for?"

Toby shook his head with raised eyebrows. "Perhaps it's for the girls."

Ben's interest suddenly accelerated. "Girls?"

"Whoa. Settle down big brother. I should have said for any *girl adventurers* - perhaps grand-daughters in the family. Girls can't seem to exist without a mirror."

"Mmm good thinking. I wonder how many of our aunts have been introduced to Sandy in the past?"

By now Toby was keen to get back to the mysteries of the chest and all but ignored Ben's ponderings about relatives. "Has the stone changed on both sides, Ben?"

"No," Ben said turning it over in his hand. "The moon side is still stone. I suppose that must be because we are using the 'Sun' position for the pots?"

"Yeah I guess so."

"Go for it then, Toby, you have first throw."

"Thanks Ben," he said, but showing a slight hesitance. "Urgh," he muttered as he picked up the dice. "Sorry but I can't help wondering if these *are* bone, what kind of creature they have been carved from." He shuddered a little as he cupped the dice in his hands, then shook them for a prolonged period before finally lowering his hands and allowing them to roll out and settle on the loft floor.

"One!" Ben said chuckling. "After all that shaking, you managed a *one*. Remind me never to take you out gambling when we're older. But it seems to have worked nevertheless. Sandy's fan is doing something already."

Words were beginning to form.

> *'One must wear*
> *Hands held to share*
> *With sun or moon please set my urn*
> *Should I stop then you return.'*

"Oh here I go again," said Toby reaching for his notebook. "Hey look, the words have appeared on this single stone slab too. Maybe Sandy keeps his own notes?"

Ben was too involved thinking about these latest clues to answer his brother. "It seems that one of us has to wear that pouch thingy around our neck and we have to hold hands to share adventures. That all seems fairly straightforward. We've already set the urn in the 'Sun' position. I'm not at all sure about that last line though. Whoops, there's more," he said.

> *'Speak the place and show a wink*
> *I will take you in a blink*
> *Should one need to turn back home*
> *Open pouch and kiss my stone.'*

"Wowee! That takes some believing? Say where we want to go, wink and we'll be there in a blink. I can't see that happening, can you?"

44

"I sure like the sound of it if it does," Toby exclaimed happily.

Ben's excitement was beginning to set in too. "That really sounds like an adventure. Shall I try it on my own or do you want to come with me?"

"What! You're not trying anything without me, let's get that straight, right now. In any case it says to hold hands."

"Okay, okay. I was only kidding. I'd sooner have your company anyway, I must admit, as it's all a bit scary."

"It sure is. I wonder how long this will take. I expect Mum will be back soon," Toby said worriedly.

"Yes, we'd best pull that old box across so Sandy won't be seen from the ladder, just in case. I'll put the pouch around my neck with the small bits in it, then I can hold the mirrors."

"Yep okay, Ben I'll bring the stone slab. Hey this is good. The latest riddles are still showing on it even though they are no longer showing on Sandy. I'll bring the notebook too though, in case of problems."

"Where shall we try for? It will have to be quick, it's nearly one o'clock already."

"How about the park?"

"That will do fine I reckon. Here grab my hand. Ready?"

"Yep," said Toby nervously trying to sound brave.

Ben braced himself and said, "The Park please." He gave a wink. Nothing happened.

"Oh what," he exclaimed disappointedly in spite of his shown disbelief.

"Perhaps you have to wink at yourself in the mirror," suggested Toby.

"Okay I'll try again." He looked in the mirror. "Urgh, that's horrible!" he said.

With a look of sheer terror, Toby was away and on the loft ladder before Ben stopped him with a cry of wonderment. "Toby, where are you going?"

His brother maintained a firm grip on the top of the ladder ready to move if needs be. "You just scared the hell out of me, Ben. Whatever did you see in the mirror?"

"I just noticed I have a huge zit growing on the end of my nose."

Toby relaxed and burst out laughing. "You great idiot, is that all it was? I nearly died of fright thinking you had seen some enormous monster. But looking at that," he giggled and pointed at Ben's nose, "I guess you did."

Ben was at the age when he hated having spots on his face but he cracked up with laughter all the same. Then his face abruptly straightened again as he remembered their lack of time. "Come on, give me your hand again. The Park, please." He looked in the mirror and gave himself a huge wink.

On opening his eye he was amazed to find himself still hand in hand with his brother but in the middle of the park not far from the back of the house.

"Sick!" Toby shouted happily. "Absolutely awesome! It's a good job the rain has stopped."

Ben, just into his first teen-age year was having trouble believing any of it. He simply stared at the park open-mouthed for several seconds. It was what Toby said *next*, very loudly, that brought him out of it.

"Ben! It's Mum. She just walked round the back alley and saw us. What are we going to do?"

"Oh no, what makes you think she saw us?"

"She waved to us before going into the back garden. What do we do? We should have had Nanny's permission to come to the park in the first place and we are supposed to be keeping this all a secret. Oh Ben, what a mess we're in."

"Come on, we'll have to go back and hope we can beat Mum to it. Er—how do we do this?" He glanced quickly at the words still showing on the stone slab in his brother's hand. "Kiss the stone? Quick, grab my hand again and kiss that stone. Let's hope this works as well the other way around."

...　...　...

Chapter Five

Cassie had enjoyed a lovely chat with her friend and collected addresses of others she wished to contact.
There was no answer when she rang the doorbell so she walked round the alley to the rear entrance.

"Oh that's nice," she said to herself as she saw her sons standing in the park holding hands and gave the boys a quick wave as she turned into the back garden. She had a quick peek in the garage for her father but he had apparently taken the car out to test it following his maintenance. When she entered the conservatory she found her mother fast asleep in the armchair. 'So that's why no-one answered the front door' she thought.

Taking her paperwork up to her bedroom, she noticed the loft ladder down and lights on in the loft. "Those little monkeys should have seen to that before going over the park," she muttered to herself. "I expect they slipped past their Nan without even asking to go. I'd best go up I suppose and switch everything off myself. Just wait till I see them later."

She climbed the ladder and was thoroughly shocked to see her boys in the loft seemingly fully absorbed in playing with the trains.

"Oh! You *are* here!"

"Sorry Mum, what did you say?" Toby turned from the trains to face her, managing a look of innocence.

"I thought I saw you over the park," she said, "I even waved. I guess I should have known it wasn't you as they didn't wave back. I'm about to make us some lunch boys, so come down in about ten minutes."

"Okay, thanks Mum." Then, once they knew their mother was out of earshot. "Phew, that was a close one," Ben said. "It's a jolly good job you never returned her wave when we were in the park."

"I was so worried about us being caught out, I never *thought* about waving back."

Ben was looking at the loft floor. "We've been even luckier than we thought," he said. "If Mum had noticed those we would have had to come up with some quick answers." He pointed down at their trail of wet footprints. "Poor Mum. She was quite right. She did see us-- in both places. This is all so totally incredible!"

"Come on, we'd best get this lot all packed away for now and get down for our lunch," Toby said. "Despite we've not long finished eating those other sandwiches."

"There you are boys," Cassie said as she gave them their food. "Now to warn you, I shall need your help in around an hour to go and do some food shopping. I'll give you a shout when I'm ready."

"Okay, Mum, Thanks."

Eventually, feeling somewhat stuffed after eating their second round of food together with the salad she had prepared for them, they somewhat more slowly than usual climbed up to the loft again. With the recent excitement still fresh in their minds they had a fierce desire to try it all again, but first decided to get the trains running again as a cover in case of more unscheduled visitors to the loft.

"Now, do we try for the park again or roll the dice and try and find more clues?"

"The park again I think. We hardly had time to realise we were there before."

"That's true. Okay, grab a hold again," Ben said, extending his hand, then giving the mirror a wink as he asked for the park.

"Wow that's so quick it's unbelievable," he said, lowering the mirror and looking across the park grass. "It's unlike any other form of travel we know. There's no sense of time, movement, or anything."

"Amazing," agreed Toby. "Sandy is certainly a fantastic invention. Grandad said we would be able to do almost anything we wished. I wonder what other surprises we are in-"

Abruptly they found themselves back in the loft.

"-for?" Toby finished asking. "What did you do, Ben?"

"Nothing," exclaimed Ben. "It was as if the magic had been switched off."

"Oh no, we haven't done anything really bad. Only a few small fibs. Besides, we've only just begun to"--

"Hang on, Toby, it might be alright after all," Ben announced looking down at the machine. "I never thought to check the sand pot before we went and it's empty now. That's why Sandy stopped."

"Oh, that's a relief, but that seems to have run out very quickly," Toby commented.

"Yes, but on thinking back, I suppose we've probably used most of the pot-full while we were listening to him run and looking through the clues."

The boys quickly swapped the full and empty sand pots over, opened the valve and the wheel started to turn again.

"I'll just check it out to make sure," Ben said. He picked up the mirror and winked at it, said something and simply disappeared. Within seconds, the machine stopped and Ben reappeared. "Good, that proves it's all okay again," he declared with a smile.

"Thank goodness for that," laughed Toby. "I worried though when I saw the machine stop again. Watching you come back was awesome. One second you were nowhere to be seen, the next you suddenly were."

An expression of wonderment fleetingly crossed Ben's face at Toby's statement and Toby quickly picked up on it.

"What's up, Ben?" he asked with a frown.

"It just crossed my mind that Grandad was like that when I first looked for him in the loft. Nowhere to be seen, then suddenly there? You don't think--?"

Toby gave a gasp but then quickly pointed out, "No, he couldn't have been using Sandy, the chest was underneath all those comics and cobwcbs at the time."

"Yes, I suppose you're right. Grandad would have had to have been a wizard himself to accomplish that."

They both turned and stared at each other for a long stretched out moment.

"Hold up," Ben said. "I think our imagination is beginning to run away with us."

"No worries. By the way, you were ever so quick, where did you go?"

"Only to the bathroom." Ben answered with a grin. "But that other thing you mentioned, about Sandy stopping again, is very interesting. Kissing the stone returns *us* but it obviously stops Sandy as well. I think that has just answered that odd riddle."

"Which one?" Toby asked looking in his notebook.

"Er, that one," Ben said pointing over his brother's shoulder. *'**Should I stop then you return**'*. "Now we know if Sandy stops for any reason, the magic stops too and we return to the loft. It's probably just as well. I guess we could end up being stuck almost anywhere otherwise, once we begin to experiment."

"Geeps that could be frightening." Toby turned and patted the old machine as if it were a family pet. "Thanks Sandy for looking after us."

"We need to look into solving more of those riddles now, Toby, but there's something I'd like to do even *before* that, if it's okay with you. I want to try using those other pot positions that Sandy has. I'm certain it will cause Sandy's wheel to run the other way, but why it should need to I can't imagine, yet the more we can find out now, the better, for safety's sake."

"Yep, okay then," Toby said somewhat reluctantly.

Ben knelt to work on the machine and gave a cry.

"Oh heck, I never thought of the sand continuing to run when the stone stopped Sandy just then. It's all over the base tray now."

He quickly turned the sand valve off to save any more spillage. "We could do with a brush and dustpan or something." He paused, then suddenly gave a gasp of astonishment. "Oh what?" he yelled. "Quick, Toby come and see this."

The accumulation of spilt sand had begun to move. The two boys watched in utter silence as the spilt sand gradually formed a neat circular shape, its centre becoming ever higher until a very thin stream of particles rose vertically through the air and poured itself back into the supply pot. Soon, not a loose grain of sand could be seen anywhere on the machine.

"Absolutely amazing," exclaimed Ben. "So that must be what happened before. Now I can see what Grandad meant when he said the sand is not easily lost. The sand itself is magical. Unbelievable!"

Once they had recovered from their astonishment, Ben removed and repositioned the feeder pot and found it fitted just as perfectly at the moon end of the machine.

52

Toby quickly followed suit with the base pot and opened the valve again. As Ben had thought, Sandy ran quite happily but in the opposite direction.

"Wow, the mirror has shifted now to the moon side of the slab," he cried out. "That solves that problem then, but we still don't know *why* Sandy should need to run in reverse." He glanced at Toby's notebook. "The riddle doesn't seem to tell us much either. '***With sun or moon please set my urn***.'"

"No you're right, it doesn't," Toby agreed.

"Never mind, let's try and go somewhere else," Toby suggested, picking up the dice ready to throw again.

"We can't just yet, Toby. We're supposed to be going out shopping with Mum at any moment now."

"Oh come on, Ben," he said excitedly. "She said she will give us a *shout* when she's ready."

"Yes, but if we're out, we won't hear her?"

Toby's impatience ran riot. "Come *on*," he shouted as he grabbed his brother's hand. "Let's at least *try* something else." He threw the dice high in the air in his excitement but with his free hand only managed to catch one of them.

The other die dropped with a loud crack directly on to the moon mirror stone which was on the loft floor. Everything instantly plunged into utter blackness and the ambient temperature plummeted to freezing.

··· ··· ···

53

Chapter Six

"What on earth?" Toby found himself shivering violently, both from the cold and from a fear of what he might have caused. As his eyes began to make some sense in the darkness he realised there was now a thick eerie fog swirling around, almost clinging to him and that he no longer had hold of Ben's hand. He peered around worriedly. Though he could *see* very little he thought he sensed a movement close to him.

"Ben?"

The answer he received was not from Ben but the terrifyingly close loud roar of an obviously huge creature. In uncontrolled fear and almost matching the volume of the creature's roar, Toby screamed. As he drew breath for another, he heard Ben's voice quiet but firm. "Shut up, Toby, for God's sake."

Immediately there was another almighty roar from very close quarters which seemed to make everything vibrate.

Somehow Ben managed to find his younger brother's hand and squeeze it to calm him a little, though he felt far from calm himself. "Stand still, Toby, and make as little noise as possible," he whispered directly into Toby's ear now that he had found him. "I don't know what's happened to us, but that sounded like a bear or something equally as big and I would sooner it knows far less than we do as to where we are."

"I-I'm sorry, this is probably all my fault."

"What do you mean—probably? It *is* your fault," Ben said ungraciously, then gave his brother's hand another squeeze and added, "But this is no time to worry about stuff like that."

They stood stock still for several minutes, both craning their necks and peering into the foggy gloom. Though nothing seemed to be moving, the stillness and silence itself was totally menacing.

"Over there," Ben said suddenly moving a little and pointing. "The fog parted a little and I saw trees and the ridge tiles of a small roof of some kind. Let's head in that direction and see if we can get some cover and perhaps find out where we are."

Hand in hand the two boys were approaching the 'ridged tiled roof' when it suddenly moved and appeared to drop in height at one end whilst accompanied with a loud crunching sound.

"What the hell was that?" With shattered nerves the boys stood staring, their eyes trying desperately to penetrate the murky gloom.

"Aargh!" Ben had to shake his hand free somewhat irritably as Toby increased his grip in fear.

"Ben! Those ridged tiles you saw were the back bones of a huge dinosaur!"

"Don't be stupid, there *are* no dinosaurs these days."

"*It is*," Toby riled insistently. "We've been learning about them at school. Some of the plant-eaters are enormous. It seems to be eating something on the ground there. I can see its neck and part of its head and one eye, but I can't quite see yet which kind it"--

This time Toby was interrupted. With an horrendously loud threatening squeal, something a third of the size of the first creature sprang out of the disturbed rolling fog depths and clamped its massive jaws across the other's neck. With a 'crack' like a whip the big dinosaur flicked its huge tail round in an arc in an attempt to ward off the attacker. Some of the dense fog moved as a result, revealing the action of the opponents. This was obviously not play and looked as if it was about to become a gruesome fight, possibly to the death.

The noise became almost unbearable and the boys began to slowly back off whilst looking around them in case of other creatures being attracted to the sounds of battle. Then completely unexpectedly, Toby doubled up with a scream holding his hands tightly against the sides of his head and ears.

"Toby! What's the matter?" Though it was the last thing Ben wanted to do, he had to *shout* to make Toby hear him. "Toby!"

Luckily there was more than enough noise still issuing from the fight just a few metres away to absorb Ben's shout. He put his arms around his brother protectively but completely unsure what he could do about the situation. "Toby," he shouted again. "I can't help unless you tell me what the problem is?"

Toby tentatively moved his hands from his ears, sobbing as if terrified. "I heard laughter, so loud and *really* evil."

"Laughter, I didn't hear any laughter. All that noise has affected your ear drums I expect. I felt as if it was going to *burst* mine." He looked down at his little brother's white terrified face and drew himself up tall.

"I've had enough of this. A joke is a joke but this is taking things too far. Dinosaurs scrapping that don't exist anymore, both of us half deaf and terrified, it's just not on. I don't know if we have somehow arrived at some odd natural history show, or if someone has set up an elaborate trick especially for *us*, but it's all too much. I'm going over to take a closer look at those dinosaur models and find out just who is operating them and having a laugh at our expense."

"No Ben, please don't," Toby pleaded while clinging on to his brother's arm. "I feel sure they are real."

"No they are *not*," Ben said in exasperation. "They can't be real, dinosaurs have been extinct for millions of years. They might *look* very real and I've no doubt they are very cleverly made, but enough is enough."

He broke free of Toby's hold and strode off in the direction of the on-going fight. Once closer he found himself almost wincing at the spectacle in front of him. 'Certainly very clever and impressive' he thought.

The onslaught had been so violent that it appeared to have cleared most of the fog in that area. The bulk of the large creature he had partly seen through the gloom was sinking fast, the other having torn its throat open using one of the big sickle claws on its hind feet. Ben could see blood and mess scattered about all over the place. Whilst he stood there directly in front of the carnage wondering why on earth anyone would stage such an elaborate trick for two ordinary unsuspecting lads, the head and eyes of the victor slowly turned to view the possibility of a new opponent.

Ben could not but admire the fantastic detail in the face, neck and eyes of the creature now looking directly at him. Still utterly convinced that this was all part of a sick though clever set-up, Ben went to put a foot nearer to see if he could spot any of the working mechanism. He never got to put his foot *down*. The movement was so swift there was no time to react. Massive jaws clamped down on the end of his right trainer. Now, with a scream, Ben leapt back in fear, full realisation finally hitting him. This *was* no joke. This was for *real*. With a mighty pull of his right leg he spun around and ran, limping seriously for his life.

The dinosaur bit down hard on its easily obtained mouthful but it was not quite what it had expected. It tasted quite bitter and even more annoyingly it was now stuck on one of its huge teeth. It shook its head madly in its frustration and the unwanted mouthful eventually took off on a flight of its own.

In the midst of his terrified escape whilst hurtling half blindly across the dark foggy undergrowth, something hit Ben hard on the back of his head. A flying Pterodactyl immediately registered in his now terrified imagination. He went down in a heap quite convinced he had been struck on the creature's first pass, then immediately curled up trying to pretend he was dead with the dread it would soon be back and that he might become its latest meal. For a minute or so he laid completely still, his eyes screwed tightly shut. Just as he began to think he had fooled it and was safe, something nudged against his shoulder and he cringed yet again. The creature must have flown back and was now deciding where to begin eating.

"Ben? You're hurt. What can I do?" Toby pushed at Ben's shoulder again. "Please-"

For a split second, Ben wasn't sure about anything.

"Ben," the insistent voice pleaded."

Ben felt something warm and wet drop on his face and risked opening one eye. As it focussed he saw his brother's white, tear stricken face looking down over him.

"Ben. Oh thank goodness, you *are* still alive."

"Toby? What happened? I thought I had--?"

"I saw you coming out of the fog limping horribly, then when you suddenly fell over in an unmoving heap I thought the dinosaur had bitten off one of your legs or something and you had finally bled to death," Toby sobbed.

Ben began to struggle up somewhat amazed he *was* still alive and could move, when he saw something covered in bright red blood lying immediately behind him. He almost lost consciousness at the recognition of his shoe believing his foot might still be inside it. On managing to recover his nerve and look down past the end of his trouser leg he all but passed out again, this time with relief. His foot was still there and he immediately wriggled his toes to prove it. On picking the trainer up he could see the blood was from the attacker's earlier victim but it now had an enormous hole right through it where it had been stuck on one of the dinosaur's teeth. The thought of the creature's tooth having passed between his toes and then what might have been had his shoe not come off so easily, all but made him throw up. Even so, he was unbelievably happy about his non-compliance with his mother's instructions over the years to tie his shoe laces up more tightly, not that he was likely to ever brag about it.

Toby was staring at it too. "Not real, eh prof," he commented. "Now do you believe it was a--?"

He broke off at a sudden stealthy movement close to them. The thinning remains of the fog parted slightly to reveal the massive, blood dripping jaw and rows of sharp teeth belonging to the shoe taster closing in on them, now roaring in expectancy of its reclaimed meal.

"Aargh! No more," Toby screamed. "We must get out of here." He stared at the small stone cube in his hand and from more of a prayer to it rather than any conscious thought of its possible use, he raised it to his mouth.

Instantly there was utter silence. The fog had gone and more importantly the dinosaur was nowhere to be seen. It was warm again and the boys found themselves still open-mouthed, screams having died in their throats, now shielding their eyes from the dim light bulb inside the safety of their Grandfather's loft.

"Oh God," Ben said shaking his head. It's so good to be back here, though I'm having trouble telling myself things might *stay* normal now. Whatever happened?"

"Ben, Toby, it's time we were going," their mother called from downstairs.

"How lovely it is to hear Mum's voice again, too." Toby murmured appreciatively.

"You're right," Ben agreed. "Okay Mum, we're coming," he answered. "We'll just clear away and switch everything off."

"Please don't be too long," she replied.

"Okay."

"Phew. Before we go down I guess it's time I said thanks, Toby, for getting us out of there."

"You shouldn't really be thanking me. After all it was *me* that got us in there in the first place, besides which I don't have a clue what I did to get us out."

"Never mind, thanks anyway. I wonder where the hell it *was* that Sandy took us. So much for me not believing in magic or adventure!"

"I've no idea where he took us. Not a very friendly place that's for sure. But I can tell you one thing, Ben. Having caused all that I am determined to get my impatience under control from now on."

"I'm pleased to hear you say that. I'll try and help you whenever I can."

"How can you do that?"

"Quite easily I think." Ben looked at him with a wry grin. "If ever I notice it coming on again I'll just shout out, 'Dinosaurs!"

They had a semi-nervous chuckle between themselves, then Ben looked at his little brother and suggested, "You had best nip into the bathroom before going down, Toby. Your eyes look terrible. Are you feeling okay?"

"Yep, I'm fine now thanks. I will give my face a quick rinse though." He looked Ben over. "Cripes, you'd best lose that horrible looking thing, Ben and wash your hands, otherwise we'll be facing some really awkward questions." He pointed at the blood-soaked trainer.

"Oh God yes, I must dig out my other pair before I go anywhere. Thanks again, Toby. We'll have to try and find out what happened to cause all that when we get back from shopping."

They never got back in the loft that evening as their Nan and Grandad took them out and treated them to a Pizza followed by a huge ice cream dessert.

... ...

Chapter Seven

"Morning everyone," Ben said the next morning as he walked into the kitchen. "What's for breakfast, Nan?"

"You *really* want breakfast after all that Pizza you polished off last night?"

"You bet I do, but that *was* delicious thanks."

Nan laughed. "I'm glad you enjoyed it and I knew full well you would still want breakfast. You have a choice. You can have bacon and eggs, or a bacon sandy."

"*What* fell on Sandy?" Toby came in rubbing the sleep from his eyes.

"Bacon sandy," said Ben giving Toby a warning look. "Or bacon and eggs."

"Yes please, Nan. I'll have one of those."

His Nan chuckled and ruffled his hair. "Come on sleepyhead, one of which? An egg, a rasher of bacon, or a bacon sandwich?"

"An egg please. No sorry Nanny, perhaps I'll have a few cornflakes first and then a sandwich please."

"And you Ben?"

"Oh yes, just a bacon sandy please."

"Morning guys, it's lovely out there today," their grandfather said as he walked in via the conservatory. "Perhaps we should all go out somewhere today, unless you and the boys have anything planned Cassie?"

"No, that sounds fine to me, Tom."

"How about our favourite spot by the river? We could take some food with us and have a picnic," Nan suggested.

"Great idea," they all agreed.

The destination was situated along a beautiful stretch of the River Wey near Guildford. The river wound a little erratically through fields and trees while the canal, the Navigator Wey, ran a fairly straight course in a similar direction just north of it, often within a stones' throw distance.

The family walked along the canal towpath before taking the overgrown path they had discovered many years before. This led to a bend of the river with a grassy bank, ideal for picnics and play. The bank dropped away at one point to afford an easy entrance to a small area of shallow water, should anyone feel the need for a paddle.

"I remember this now," Cassie said. "Jack and I came here with you years ago. We all went for a pub lunch nearby."

"Yes, you're right Cassie. We all had a really lovely day here."

The adults began to spread the blankets out ready for the picnic while reminiscing about past times as the boys slipped away and wandered back up the path to the canal.

"Now we can have a talk about what happened last night," Ben started to say, but then he stopped and pointed. "Oh, look at those."

They were delighted to see three long narrow-boats gliding serenely past, one after the other, all beautifully painted with shining aluminium framed windows or bright brass portholes and having sign-written names on their sides.

The boats were gently chugging past as if there was all the time in the world to reach their destination. As the boys waved the people on them there was a wonderful smell of cooking bacon drifting back in their direction which reminded them of their imminent feast back at the riverbank. As one they turned around and headed back towards the clearing.

Toby seemed a little quiet and thoughtful about something as they walked along. Ben asked, "Are *you* thinking about Dad *too* by any chance?"

"Yes, I'm really missing him now. The smell of that bacon reminded me of him cooking our barbies out in the back yard at home. I do wish he was with us. It's so unfair we had to leave him behind."

"Yes it is. I hope his leg is getting better by now." Ben then seemed to go off into thought himself. "I suppose we've hardly used Sandy enough to know yet, but-"

"What do you mean, Ben?"

"I was wondering if there is any limit to where he can take us when we wink-wish? It just *might* be possible we could nip home to Melbourne and see Dad."

His brother's head lifted slowly like a sunflower at dawn, eyes gleaming with a new bright intensity at the exciting images running through his mind. "Wicked idea, Ben and you never know, it just *might* work."

"I'm sorry, Toby. I really shouldn't get your hopes up. Two trips to the park and one to the bathroom is not much to go on is it? Sandy might only work over a set distance and in any case Melbourne would probably take far too long, we could be missing for ages. Perhaps we should find out a bit more about using him first."

"Oh please let's try when we get back to the loft."

Ben looked Toby full in the face. "Okay, we'll give it a try, but don't get your hopes up too much - Dinosaur!"

Toby's face coloured up. "Sorry Ben."

The subject then had to be dropped as they had arrived back with the family.

It was a perfect day for a picnic. While they sat munching quietly through their food, nature provided them with some wonderful entertainment. A beautiful Emperor dragonfly flew lazily above the water displaying wonderful lace-like wings as it hovered almost unmoving in the air like a tiny helicopter. Seemingly large fish jumped for insects every now and then in the calm water under the big tree opposite them, while a robin sitting above gave his best ever rendering of his favourite song. All this, while the river slipped past gurgling and almost chuckling as it speeded up on the bend, then slowed beyond it, forming small whirlpools and eddies.

Ben finally broke the contented silence. "Could we swim here Grandad?"

"No. It's too risky. That's why we never mentioned swimming gear. The current here is quite deceptive and the banks downstream are much higher than here making it difficult to get out again."

"It sounds as if you've had experience of it, Tom," said Cassie.

"Yes, or I should say I was *with* someone who had a bad experience."

"What happened, Grandad?"

"My Dad and Mum used to bring us here sometimes, together with my foster brother Luke and my friend Michael."

"What *is* a foster brother, Grandad?" asked Toby.

"For various reasons people are sometimes unable to have their children live with them as a family unit and have to make other arrangements. Foster parents, usually a married couple, will often take on a child as their own until events change sufficiently in the true parent's life that they can have their child back to live with them.

My Mum and Dad fostered Luke when he was a baby and brought him up as one of ours until he was old

65

enough to make up his own mind about his life. He was my younger brother, like Toby is to you Ben.

We were in this very spot having a really fine time. We boys, except Luke as he was only six or seven at the time, joined Dad for a bit of a splash about in the river. The water is fairly deep here. Michael and I were about your size Ben and the water was over our waists. What with large rocks on the river bottom and having to be careful the current didn't take you with it, trying to swim was not really on. But Dad had brought an inflated car tyre inner tube along with him for us to float on. We would take it in turns to wriggle into the tube up to our armpits and use it as a kind of all-round water float. We would slide or jump into the river shallows there, lift our legs a little and hurtle round the bend with the current. We were only allowed to do it when Dad was in the water around this side of the bend to catch us. We had some great fun I can tell you."

"It sounds wicked," Toby said.

"It was, but Luke, being smaller than the rest of us, was not allowed to do it and he threw a bit of a strop. While we were sitting talking and eating we suddenly realised he was no longer with us. We had just begun to call and look around for him, when there was an almighty splash upstream. Luckily, Dad recognised the sound for what it was and jumped into the river on our side of the bend. It was a good thing he did, for within a few seconds my little brother came whizzing round the bend. But it had all gone horribly wrong. Instead of wearing the tube under his armpits, Luke, finding it was too big for him, had jumped into the shallows and simply *sat* on the tube for the ride. Because he was small, his backside slipped and wedged him into the centre of the then wet tube causing his feet to leave the river bottom. He immediately became top heavy. The tube flipped over with him stuck in it and the river current obliged him with his ride, but all that we saw of Luke when he shot around the corner was his bum stuck up in the air!"

There was a roar of laughter from the family and then he continued.

"It really *did* look funny but it was extremely dangerous for Luke, as his head of course, was under water."

"Oh my God," said Cassie quietly. "Poor kid what happened?"

"Dad somehow managed to grab him as he went past and more or less threw him up on the bank and jumped up after him. He had to get Luke out of the tube and pump the water out of his lungs. Luckily Dad was an ex-fireman and knew what he was doing, so Luke was okay. In a sense, Luke became a bit of a hero over it afterwards because none of us could stop talking about his adventure."

He stopped and looked towards Ben. "So I guess the answer to your question about swimming here, has to be no."

"You're too right it has to be no," said Cassie. "I had my doubts before, but not now."

"I suppose your foster brother is a grown up now, Granddad. Will we get to meet him someday?"

"Yes I'm sure you will."

"Does he remember it happening?"

"Yes, some of it. He was over here recently from America where he lives now with his wife Gillian. He told us that once he sat in the tube all he could remember was that everything turned green."

While the boys, together with their Mum and Nan played Piggy in the Middle, their grandfather decided to have a quick look at a boating brochure sheet he had brought along from the car. When the others returned, they found he had made a passable paper boat with it.

"Hey that's good," said Ben. "Would it float Grandad?"

"See if you can find a long stick and we'll give it a try."

The two of them rushed off into the undergrowth and soon returned brandishing part of a dead broken tree branch. "Will this do Grandad?"

"I'm sure that will do just fine lads. If one of you wants to launch the boat where the bank dips a bit and float it around"--

"Bum corner," suggested Ben laughing.

"Mmm, okay. Bum Corner it is," his grandfather said with a wry grin before continuing. "Then I'll attempt to fish it out with the stick when it comes round the bend. But be careful, I don't want to have to fish you out as well."

The boys, while hanging on to one another, carefully pushed the little boat from the side of the bank. Then they watched as the boat picked up speed and ploughed round the bend.

"It's on its way Grandad," Toby yelled out as it went from their sight. Then they both rushed across the picnic area to watch as the boat came level with him and he somehow managed to catch the bow of the boat with his stick and flick it up next to him on to dry land.

"Brilliant, Grandad," exclaimed Ben. "It reached one heck of a speed."

"It was certainly travelling when it got to me, I was lucky to get it out so easily."

"That was good, Grandad," shouted Toby. "Can we do it again please."

The boys really enjoyed their boating play until a time came when the boat managed to evade their grandfather's earlier skills at catching it. All the three despondent boys could do was to stand and watch their beloved paper boat sail proudly down the river and disappear in the distance.

"Oh well," their grandad sighed. "The boat's keel was becoming soaked, so it would have gone to the bottom before long anyway, I expect."

"Can you make another for us, Grandad?"

"I'd love to, but I can't I'm afraid Toby. We don't have any more paper. I'll show you how to make one yourself when we get home."

Finally they all had a pleasant walk back along the towpath to the car and a leisurely drive home.

"*Can* we try and see Dad later?" Toby asked Ben cautiously out in the garden.

"We will, Toby but if we succeed it will have to be the fastest visit ever. Here's what we'll do. We'll hop up to the loft to fill and start Sandy, then drag the chest in front of him. Then we'll take the mirrors, slab, and everything we need with us to our bedroom."

"Why the bedroom, Ben?"

"If it works, we will need all the time we can get. We'll say we want an early night for once. If everyone believes we are in bed asleep, it will give us all night to get there and back. As you know, it's an awfully long trip, so even that might not give us enough time. If not, we'll have to chance they think we are sleeping on for a while in the morning. It will be great to see Dad and our cat, even if it is only for a minute or two."

"Oh yes I can't wait. Perhaps we should we put our seat cushions in the beds to make it look like us, in case anyone peeps in?"

"That's a brilliant idea," Ben answered.

Once evening had arrived, the boys feigned tiredness and announced they were off for an early night.

"I'm not surprised. We've all had a good long day," their Mum agreed.

The boys said goodnight and toddled off up the stairs yawning just at the thought of it. They quietly crept up to the loft, set Sandy running and closed the trap-door. Once they were in the bedroom, they quickly set up the beds to make it look as if they were in them.

"Are you ready, Toby?"

"You bet."

"Grab my hand then."

Ben looked in the mirror, said "Melbourne please," and then winked, but nothing happened. "Melbourne, Australia," he winked. Nothing happened. "Our home in Melbourne, Australia, please," he asked again. But they were still in the bedroom in England.

Toby grabbed the mirror and said, "Our house to see our Dad, please," almost pleadingly but still nothing happened. He handed the mirror back. "Damn, I was so looking forward to seeing Dad," he sniffed.

"Me too," Ben said trying hard to stop his own eyes welling up. "Perhaps Sandy was made before Australia had been discovered. Don't get too upset, Toby. Sandy is doing some other great stuff for us, isn't he?"

"Yes, you're right, perhaps we'll be able to think of something *new* to try tomorrow," he half-joked trying hard to get his thoughts away from his Dad.

"Yes, we might at that. Come on, let's get some sleep."

When their Mother looked in on them a little later, it actually was the boys she saw all curled up and fast asleep, not that she would have had any reason to suspect otherwise.

Their grandfather met them at the foot of the stairs the following morning.

"We had an incredible coincidence last night after you guys had gone to bed. My foster brother Luke rang. He is over from America on business. He has a few more hours in London this morning to finish and asked if he could pop in and see your Nan and I before he flies home. When he heard you were here, he managed to change his flight for tomorrow so that he can meet you all this afternoon and stay overnight," he explained.

"Oh good it will be great to meet him. Will his wife be with him?"

"No not this time," his grandfather answered.

"Do you know, Ben I have a feeling we are going to get on well with Luke," Toby said.

"Yes, hopefully anyway," Ben said. "I know he's not really an American, Grandad, but does he talk like one?"

"Yes he does, Ben. But then he has been living in America for an awfully long time. You've only been in Australia for about ten years and you already sound like a true Aussie most of the time."

"He still sounds like a Pom to me," his brother said but making sure he was well out of reach. "I'm a *true* Aussie," he shouted as Ben chased him out into the garden.

... ...

Chapter Eight

As the house only had three bedrooms, Cassie and her boys decided they would sleep in her bedroom for the one night to free the other room for Luke's visit. As soon as breakfast was over the adults began the task of shifting and remaking beds, whilst the boys made themselves scarce playing Frisbee over the park.

Luke managed to complete his business in London early morning and arrived at their door having narrowly avoided the rush hour.

"Luke it's so good to see you," Tom said giving him a hug. "You were meant to ring. I would have driven down to the station to collect you."

"Hell no, the walk will have done me some good," he said with a deep Americanised voice. "I've been on my backside all day."

"Let the poor man through the door," Maggie said. "Hello Luke, this is really good, getting to see you like this," she said, receiving a kiss. "It's a pity Gill is not with you."

"She would have loved to have met these guys," he said as he looked past Maggie at Cassie and the boys.

"This is Cassie, Maggie's eldest," said Tom introducing them. "Cassie - Luke, my brother."

"It's nice to meet you, Luke. Tom was only telling us about you the other day."

"Aw gee, it's happening already. Look, there is no doubt he will have given you a false impression of me. He always used to do his best to get me into trouble when we were young."

Luke looked around as he heard the boys chuckling at this last remark.

"So this is Ben and Toby. Now I've seen them I can't believe they're as bad as you made them out to be, Tom. They look good kids to me. So I guess you must be Ben, and this little guy I guess is Toby. It's nice to meet up with you at last. Oh and please don't start calling me Uncle. Luke will do just fine."

"G'day then, Luke, it's good to meet you."

"Yeah, G'day, Luke," said Toby.

"Oh, I like it. G'day guys. I can see we're gonna get along just great."

"Excuse us for a moment, Luke, I believe we have something to sort out." said Ben.

The two boys walked across to their grandfather. Ben with his arms folded asked, "Now what's all this you've been telling Luke about us?"

"Don't take too much notice of him, Ben," his grandfather warned him. "Perhaps I should remind you that Luke is my younger brother - *like Toby is to you*, Ben," he added with a wink.

"Oh of course. Okay, no need to say more," Ben said smirking.

"What do you mean by that?" Toby tried to look upset, but broke into a laugh instead.

"You see what I mean," his Grandfather said with a chuckle. "Luke is hardly inside the door and we have trouble already."

"I can see what you mean, Tom," said Maggie. She looked at Cassie. "It means, dear daughter, that instead of three, we now have four kids to deal with," she said with a hearty laugh.

The six had a very nice evening together, drawing comparisons between their different countries, governments, television programmes and schools. Then the boys got the entire set of card and board games out and they all joined in playing anything and everything into the late hours.

Despite their late night the boys were up early the next morning. They could hear someone moving about downstairs and thought they might as well join them. It was Luke.

"Hi guys, I hope I didn't wake you. I never sleep too well when I'm over for just a few days."

"No worries, Luke. Toby and I are up fairly early *most* mornings playing with the trains."

"You have trains with you?"

"Oh no, they belong to Grandad. He has a wicked model railway in the loft. Once the rest of the family are up we will show you if you want."

"Yeah I'd like that. The last time I played with trains, I was only a few years older than you are now, Ben. Dad had just started to build a set in his loft."

Ben looked thoughtful for a second. "That would have been our Great-grandad, I suppose?"

"Gee, yes. I never thought of Dad being your Great-grandad. He was a lovely guy, it's a shame you never knew him. You would have loved Mum too, your Great-grandmother. She was a wonderful lady, real special."

"I wish we *could* have met them both," Ben replied, I'd have loved that. Grandad was telling us just the other day how most of the set upstairs had been built by his Dad and was brought here from the old house."

Luke put his head in his hands for a second or two, then wiped a dampness from his eyes.

"Sorry guys, that thought took me right back. I would have dearly loved to have seen the old house before it was sold. I guess your Great-grandad must have carried on building the train set after I left for America?"

"Yes he did, Luke," Tom said as he and the others came from the stairs and into the living room. "Sorry I never meant to eavesdrop, I heard your question as we came down."

"Why did you go to America?" asked Toby.

"Toby you shouldn't ask about that-" Cassie began.

"He's okay," Luke interrupted. "It's high time I explained myself to someone in the family. You see Toby, I loved both my foster parents dearly and we had some wonderful years together as you can imagine. But as soon as I realised I had a *real* Dad somewhere, it ate into me. I'd never met him, seen him or talked to him, but whoever or wherever he was I knew I had to find him. I guess that took over even more as I grew older.

I found out all I could about him from my real Mum and she helped me as much as she could and accompanied me to America to find my Dad."

"Did you find him?" Ben asked "I can't imagine being without a real father," he admitted, thinking how much he was missing his own after just a few days.

"Yeah I did. He was good to me and introduced me to his wife and family, so it turned out I have quite a lot of relatives in America. But as nice as they are to me, it's somehow not *my* family, though it's difficult to explain. It was an important thing I had to do in my life and I did it, but I messed up. I'd left the only *real* family and Mum and Dad I'd ever known."

"Did you ever get back to see them?"

"No, that's my biggest regret. I was drafted into the American Army for three years and when I was released I was so busy trying to make a new life I had little time for the old one. After I met and married Gill and became comfortable in life with time to dwell on it, twenty or more years had passed by and I was full of doubt. Should I visit? Would they even *want* to see me after all that time? Then Gill finally convinced me I had to and she came with me. But I'd left it too long. I had never thought of Mum and Dad being over sixty when I left them."

Tom put a hand on Luke's shoulder. "I'm very glad Gill did convince you to come over. It's great to have a younger brother again."

Maggie made breakfast for everyone and whilst they were reminiscing, their day out at the canal was mentioned. Luke asked Tom if this would have been the same place he remembered and the whole story was brought to life again by him, except that he could only remember the 'Green' ending. When a certain young fellow casually mentioned the new name recently given to that particular bend in the river, Luke thought it hilarious and said he could not wait to get home and tell his wife.

Following breakfast Grandad and the boys took Luke up to the loft.

"Geeze, I remember some of this train layout. It's all so much bigger and better now. I remember helping Dad to paint this station and that tunnel. It doesn't seem possible. All those years ago. It's wonderful," cried Luke. "I feel like a fifteen year old again." He was looking across the rail track when his eyes settled on something in the corner.

"Aw heck," he exclaimed. "Is that the chest that Dad had in *his* loft?"

Six eyes instantly turned in his direction.

"Er, yes it is," Tom said. "Did dad ever get to show it to you?"

Luke looked a little awkward. "Yes he did and I guess he must have shown you long before me, but"-- he angled his head towards the boys.

"It's okay they know. Tell me one thing about it you remember?"

"I can give you two words to do with it that have always stuck in my mind. '*Greetings friends*'."

"Ye-e-ss," the boys shouted excitedly. "Luke's an adventurer too."

"Well done, Luke, the two ideal words. So when did Dad introduce you to the chest?"

"A short time after you went in the army to do your National Service. Once I'd proved I could build it, he said I could use it until you came back, with the idea we could share it until the next kids came along. But of course you were still in Germany when I decided to leave you all and look for my Dad."

"Yes, I remember that, all too well."

"I must confess that you being away meant one less bit of opposition to my plans at the time. Sorry Tom."

"It's okay, I quite understand your reasons Luke. I guess I'd have done the same."

"So with things as they are, I suppose you're the guardian for the machine now?"

"That's right."

"And I guess we are those *next kids*," Toby said.

"Good for you boys, it's a fantastic machine. I hated leaving it, but at the time, finding my real Dad was my biggest interest. You know it seems really strange being able to talk about the chest now after keeping it a secret all these years?"

"It's unusual for us too, isn't it boys? But outside of us four here now, it *still* has to remain a secret."

"Could I see it run while I'm here? I remember I often used to sit in front of it and just listen to it. It was almost hypnotic."

"We love doing that too," said Ben. "Did you get to use it much, find out all about it?"

"No unfortunately, I was too busy trying to track my Dad's address and everything. I managed to get to a few places and once even sorted out a school bully with the use of it, but not much other than that. To be honest I lost interest in it when I found I couldn't get it to take me to America or help me to find my Dad."

The boys glanced at each other but said nothing.

Their grandfather sighed. "That's a great shame as it's such a capable machine. But listen, I have to get the car out ready to run the girls into Epsom to do our food shopping. I'm sure the boys here would love to show you the machine running. Do you mind us leaving you to it, you three? We'll probably be gone for quite a while, knowing the girls and their shopping."

"I'm happy with that providing the boys are?"

They both said they would love his company. "Could we show Luke some of those old photos we found the other day, Grandad?"

"I think they were mostly before Luke's time but you can certainly show him."

Luke was in awe of the machine once he saw it out and running. "Sandy," he repeated when the boys told him they had named it. "Great idea, wish I'd thought of it." He crouched on his haunches staring at the old machine. "For the second time this morning I feel as if I'm a fifteen year old watching this," he exclaimed. "It's exactly the same as I remember it and that sound it makes is wonderful. Even the layout of this loft is similar to the old one." He suddenly looked a little puzzled. "Actually, something about the er- Sandy, seems different. I could have sworn the wheel used to turn the other way"

Ben laughed. "You have a very good memory Luke. It did, but we changed it around yesterday to see what would happen."

"I never got around to doing anything much like that. What did happen?"

"Well, it seems to have made no difference yet, other than the wheel direction."

Toby spread the contents of the pouch on the loft floor to show Luke.

"Gee, I remember this stone tablet," said Luke. "It's the one the messages show on." He paused, looking worried. "Oh heck, talking of messages reminds me. I was supposed to ring my wife last night to tell her my new flying arrangements. I won't be able to do that now as she'll still be asleep. Our local time in America is five hours behind yours. I shall have to send her an e-mail on my laptop. Excuse me lads for a couple of minutes, I'll be back shortly," he called over his shoulder as he climbed down to the ladder.

"You were right again Toby," Ben said, once Luke had left the loft.

"Right about what?"

"Us, finding we get on so well with Luke. He's a very nice guy and isn't it brilliant he knows about Sandy."

"Yes it's really good we don't have to keep it all a secret from him," Toby agreed. "While we wait for him I'm going to have a look through some of these old photos I found," Toby said standing in the light near the loft-trap door.

"Okay," Ben said while busily setting up the torch on the old machine.

"Oh, you should see the old swim suits they are wearing in these shots, they're hilarious. This old guy looks as if he has braces holding up his bathers. Hey, how about we copy some of these on Grandad's printer and put them in our school scrapbooks?"

"Awesome idea for a laugh," Ben agreed. "Our friends will love them."

Having been made aware of the family's intended holiday trip to the UK before the event, their school teachers had requested that they put together a scrapbook each, showing places they visited and special events during their holiday, so that the other pupils could see something of England.

Toby enjoyed looking through the old photos, even though most were old family shots of a bygone age. Several of the other photos depicted old local scenes and then he came across something a little more unusual.

... ...

Chapter Nine

Luke clicked 'Send' on his e-mail, signed off and shut down his laptop. Leaving the bedroom he began climbing the small ladder leading up into the loft.

"I'm on my way up guys," he called through the entrance above him. "I've mailed Gill to tell her I'm staying with you overnight."

There was no reply. It was only when he had stepped on to the boarded floor inside the loft that he sensed he was alone. On still remembering his own youth he assumed his nephews had likely gone down to the kitchen for a glass of lemonade, or to raid their grandmother's sweet jar while waiting for him.

Out of curiosity and to kill time until their return, he picked up a small cardboard box from the floor near the entrance. He found it nearly full of photos that someone had apparently rifled through recently and he began looking at them, holding each one into the bright daylight streaming up through the loft opening from the window on the stairwell below. The prints were mostly all sepia toned and very old, depicting faces or places of the past that meant little or nothing to him. Becoming disinterested he put them down and bracing himself with his hands while kneeling with his head through the loft entrance he called out again for the boys. "Ben. Toby. Where are you guys?"

There was no response. He thought it unlikely they would have gone out without telling him, as they had all been enjoying each other's company prior to him having to send his e-mail and that had only taken him a few minutes. Beginning to suspect mischief, he turned back to peer into the depths of the loft half expecting them to jump out of the shadows there to play tricks on him. Sensing movement of some kind a little further in the gloomy loft, he waited a second or two until his eyes became more adjusted to the lack of light. Soon with some surprise, yet slight annoyance, he could see that the movement was only that of the old adventure machine busily turning over quietly and efficiently on the loft floor having apparently been left abandoned whilst still running.

"So much for secrecy and companionship," he grumbled to himself. "It looks as if the little devils have used it to go off somewhere as soon as I turned my back." Then following another random thought he immediately asked out aloud, "Or have you already found out how to make yourselves invisible?"

Mildly amused at his own question he waited, expecting a spontaneous burst of laughter, but it never happened. Perhaps they had not yet acquired such levels with the old machine he thought, and finally had to accept the fact he really was on his own in the loft.

Being unsure of what he should do about their disappearance, he thought about how he had used the machine himself for a short time during his early teens. A part of one of the machine riddles popped into his brain from the past. '*Should I stop, then you return*.'

"That's it boys, a little fun is one thing, but if you play around with me when you're in my charge then I shall have to show you I'm not that easy to mess with," he said with a grin.

He stooped and closed the valve on the machine and as the wheel stopped he quickly went into hiding behind some of the big storage boxes hoping to shock the boys when they unexpectedly returned to the loft.

The wheel stopped turning, but strangely there was no reappearance of his nephews.

"Now that's odd," he muttered, "I'm sure that should have brought them back." He glanced around the loft yet again. "Oh hell," he said aloud, his mind beginning to race. "The stone and the mirrors are still here on the floor where they had them out earlier to show me. How could they have gone anywhere without them? What on earth is going on?"

Picking up the tablet and mirror stones he examined them in the forlorn hope they might give him an indication as to what the boys might have done. Then acting on a long distant memory he placed the objects in the old pouch and automatically placed the attached necklace around his neck. He was becoming very anxious. He had after all, been left with a certain new responsibility for the boys while their parents were out. Now they were missing and it was down to him to find them.

Liking the machine to his computer if it 'crashed' he immediately restarted it in the hope he might clear the glitch and cause the return of the boys. But to no avail, nor did it give him any visual sign as to their whereabouts. Then he spotted the pair of old stone dice almost covered by a photo the boys must have dropped. On picking up the photo he saw it showed a big house on fire, huge flames having reached the roof at one end. Luke picked up the dice in his other hand instinctively aware that these had something to do with the mystery. He vaguely remembered the dice from the past; one die plain, the other carved, and wondered again despite the years gone by, why one was plain and what it was for? Transferring the dice to the palm of his hand still holding the photo, he turned the unusual lettered die over with his free index finger to read 'Three'. With an adult approach and marvelling at the ancient carver's expertise on such a small area of stone, he rolled it over to 'Four', and then to 'Five'.

Luke's mental focus was instantly drawn from the dice to find he was now standing outside somewhere on grass. A large arrow sign near his feet apparently hastily formed of something yellow, pointed off in a direction to his right. Feeling completely unreal, Luke slowly raised his area of vision to find he was at the edge of a huge lawn near the front of the big house he had seen in the photo, one end of which was on fire and blazing seriously. The sign at his feet seemed to point towards the end of the house as yet remaining unaffected by the fire. Luke stood stock still for a second or two in stunned shock and disbelief. Earlier, he had thought of the old machine 'crashing' like a computer. Now, believing he was hallucinating, he began to wonder if his *brain* had 'crashed', and he was having serious doubts as to how he could ever affect a restart.

Suddenly all thoughts of the computer world were roughly thrown aside, reality abruptly triggered by the shrill urgent screams of young voices.

"Help! Fire! We're trapped. H-e-e-l-l-p!"

··· ··· ···

Chapter Ten

"Wow!" Toby strode across the loft floor to Ben. "Look at this photo. It's really unusual. It's a picture of a house on fire. A real big fire too, nearly half of the house has burnt away."

Ben put his hand out to take the photo but it slipped through his fingers and landed in amongst the pouch contents they had been showing Luke. He bent over to pick it up, then was shocked to find there was no sign of the photo nor of anything else now on the rug.

"Rug? There was no rug on the loft floor," he said to himself. He looked up quickly at a sharp intake of breath from his brother, as he too found they were no longer in the loft.

"What happened?" Toby asked. "What did you do?"

"I was about to ask *you* the same thing," Ben said turning to look around. "We seem to be in someone's bedroom, but how?"

"It has to be Sandy. We *had* started him running, but we never did anything else or did we?"

"No! We had begun to show Luke everything before he went to use his laptop and I was just putting the torch in position. This is all very odd. I thought the idea of using Sandy was to be able to make adventures for ourselves, but once again it seems as if Sandy is doing his own thing. I wonder which kind this is going to be. Perhaps we should have a look around to try and find out where we are first."

"I'd sooner not." Toby looked somewhat pale and strained "I am having the weirdest feeling we are being watched. I'm sure we are in danger of some kind." he said with a shudder. "There is something very odd about this place. I feel we need to get out of here and now please."

"Okay Toby, I believe you. We'll go straightaway."

"I'm sorry to whinge."

Ben put his hand up to his neck and gave a cry of disbelief. "Toby! I don't have the pouch. It was all on the loft floor, the mirror, the stone-" and as the truth dawned "-everything. We can't *go* back!"

Toby took this terrible news calmly as if he had other worries. "I'm sure we'll be okay outside, but there is some kind of threat in this house, I can feel it." He suddenly flinched and covered his ears.

Ben quickly put his hands on his little brother's shoulders. "Hey, it will be alright. We'll find a way to get back, don't worry."

"It's not that, Ben, I just heard that evil laughter again didn't you?" Then before Ben could answer, he cried out, "Whatever we can or can't do, we have to get out of here. Now!"

"Come on then, let's go," Ben agreed quickly. Once again he had not heard anything out of place, but he could see that this was not simply his brother's impatience breaking out and that Toby was really nervous.

They hurried across and opened the bedroom door on to a landing at the top of a stairwell but then instantly shrank back into the room and slammed the door tight shut. The whole of the downstairs floor was ablaze and fire was already consuming the staircase.

"Oh my God, you're right, we *are* in danger. Quick, we'll have to get out through the window."

The boys quickly slid the net curtains out of the way and unfastened the catch on the old sash-style window, but no matter how hard they pushed and shoved at it, the window refused to slide open.

"It has to open somehow," Ben muttered. "Even if we break the glass we won't be able to get through those small holes." He looked around and picked up an ornately carved bedside chair. "Oh well, it looks as if it is all likely to be burnt anyway." He swung the chair above his head then smashed it down on the floor breaking two of the legs off. One of these he picked up and with Toby's help used as a lever across the bottom of the window frame and under the first glazing bar. With their combined effort and leverage, the seal of paint holding the window released with a loud cracking noise and the window slid up and opened. "Thank goodness for that," he cried.

But when they went to clamber through the opening they saw for the first time that they were three floors up. There was nowhere to go. The only thing to climb on to was the outer window sill and that was an awfully long way from the ground.

"*That* looks as if it might be our only chance." Ben pointed to a huge old tree close to the house with a big branch almost touching the roof above the window. He climbed through on to the sill in the hope he might be able to grab hold of a part of the branch, but even while dangerously balancing at tiptoe on the sill and stretching to his limit, the branch was still out of his reach. He worriedly climbed back into the room to his brother. "We have to get help and now!"

With their heads through the window opening they screamed as loud as they were able, "Help! Fire! We're trapped. H-e-e-l-l-p! "

After shouting themselves almost hoarse with no evidence of any help from outside, the brothers knew they would have to look after themselves as best they could. Smoke was now beginning to creep through the gap under the door. Luckily, they both managed to keep panic from their minds.

"This might at least help to keep some of the smoke from us," Ben said quickly stuffing the pillows from the bed along the gap at the bottom of the door.

"Ben, could we make an escape rope by tying the sheets together like they did in the old black and white movies?"

"It's well worth a try," Ben answered. "But it will need to be a long rope. You start on the sheets. These long curtains might help too if I can get them down somehow."

He got hold of the curtain one side of the window and swung all his weight on it. With a loud tearing sound all the old fashioned brass hooks ripped out of the heading and he landed on his backside with a grunt and the curtains fell on top of him. Without hesitation he repeated the procedure on the other curtain. Then the two boys set about trying to tie them together with the sheets and blankets to make as much length as possible, still continuing to shout through the window for help at regular intervals while they were busy.

In the rest of the house the fire was rapidly gaining intensity, crackling greedily as if it were a living form that was sweeping along gobbling up carpets and furnishings on the landing while heading towards the bedrooms.

Sticking their heads through the window, the boys screamed again, "Help! Fire! He-e-l-l-p!"

... ...

Chapter Eleven

Luke ran towards the house, leaping over borders and scrabbling through rose bushes and shrubs, first following the direction of the yellow arrow, then the cries for help. He felt certain it was the boys shouting from somewhere high up at the far end of the building.

"I'm coming guys," he shouted at the top of his voice, then knew he was wasting his much needed breath. They were hardly likely to hear him above the steadily increasing noise of the fire now breaking out all along the house frontage at lower levels.

He cleared the corner of the building split seconds ahead of a deafening 'Boom' and 'Swoosh' of intense heat as a window exploded with a lethal shower of broken glass shards. Flames broke though the smoke with the renewed oxygen supply and began to lick greedily at the windows of the next floor behind him as he ran.

Luke considered climbing up the old metal rainwater pipe situated near the house corner but there were no windows within reach from it. Looking up at the huge old oak tree near the house he noticed that some of the big uppermost branches were almost touching the roof near the open window on the top floor. Knowing the tree might be his only chance to get to the boys, he quickly pulled himself up on to the lowest branch and began to climb. The lower branches proved to be a long way apart vertically and twice he had to balance on one, then jump and grab the next and pull himself up solely by the strength of his arms. Luckily the higher branches were closer together vertically but by now he was rapidly weakening and gasping for breath. His heart beat was pulsing alarmingly through his ears and skull, reminding him of the sound of the bass notes from a car with sound systems on at full blast, 'boom-boom-boom-boom'.

"I have to keep going - I must get to them - I have to," he kept repeating to the blood pressure rhythm inside his head.

He was almost on the point of collapse when teenage memories flooded his mind. He had loved to climb trees then and used to play and swing in them for hours.

Reaching up high he grabbed the next branch with one hand and was about to place his other when one of his feet slipped from the supporting branch. His body twisted violently about his established arm until he managed to regain his foothold and posture. The pouch around his neck swung precariously and he grasped it with his free hand thinking it was going to fall.

"Ye Gods!" he exclaimed loudly and infuriatedly. "That was a close thing. Come on, I *have* to get to them." Gritting his teeth he prepared himself for another huge effort. "I used to be able to do this so easily. If only I could be young again."

At this his vision seemed to blur making his hands appear to shrink. His legs felt weird almost as if they were shortening, while at the same time the hanging weight of his body on his remaining anchored arm seemed to decrease. He suddenly felt a surge of renewed power through his limbs. With hardly an effort he began to climb up the tree like a monkey, swinging from branch to branch.

... ...

Chapter Twelve

After struggling to tie all the available material together, Ben and Toby were desperately trying to anchor one end of their made up rope around the leg of the bed that they had dragged and jammed against the wall beneath the window. Smoke was now coming in around the sides of the door. As soon as the rope was secure, Ben flung the remaining bulk through the open window and jumped up on the sill to watch it descend. With fear and bitter disappointment he could see now that it was nowhere near long enough for a safe escape. The huge knots they had been forced to make had used up a lot of the available material length.

Ben glanced behind him at a strange noise from the bedroom door. It was almost as if something was scratching at it trying to get in. He was horrified to see the paint beginning to bubble on it from the heat of the flames on the stairwell.

"Quick Toby we have to get out of here-Toby?"

Toby was standing very still, looking ashen faced with glazed eyes.

"Toby," he shouted again with little or no response. Then realising that any shock might work he grabbed him by the shoulders and shouted "Dinosaurs" directly into his face.

This time Toby's eyes returned to near normal looking back at Ben. "I heard that evil laughter again," he said looking all around the room, his expression still distant and really terrified. "It seemed to be taunting me."

"It was probably just the noise of the fire. Come *on*, we have to get out of here. *Now!*" he screamed at his brother while climbing up on to the window frame and extending his hand. "Quick get up here. Our rope isn't long enough but it's our only chance. We'll have to climb down it one at a time and swing on the end and try to land in those bushes to cushion our fall when we let go."

Feet on the windowsill and hanging on to the frame with one hand, Ben had just helped Toby up to join him when he suddenly heard a shout from somewhere outside seemingly directly behind him.

"Ben, Toby, hang on I'm coming."

On looking out Ben saw a teenaged boy crawling towards them along the big tree branch above the window. The closer he got, the more the branch lowered giving Ben a fresh hope for their escape. He had little time to wonder who the teenager was or how he knew their names. "Quick," Luke shouted. "Help Toby lean towards me so I can grab him."

Toby balanced himself bravely with his hands outstretched while Ben with one hand holding the window frame and the other grasping his brother's trouser belt, gradually leaned him out over the void.

"Now," shouted Luke.

Ben gave a final stretch, all but pushing Toby towards Luke, who somehow managed to lock on to Toby's wrist with one hand and swing the terrified screaming youngster safely on to the branch behind him. Luke then had to help the trembling Toby crawl along the branch and get him to hold on tight to the tree trunk before going back for Ben.

Ben was already into a bout of serious coughing. Smoke was pouring out of the window now and engulfing him. Luke knew he had only seconds left. Ben, being taller than Toby, had the bonus of a longer reach, but by now his eyes were streaming with the effect of the smoke and coughing and could hardly see his would-be rescuer. Holding on to part of their made up rope and partially blinded, he could only lean out as far as he dared from the window-sill and wave his outstretched arm around in the pure hope that Luke could reach him. Luke had to go out further along the branch than intended and the end of the branch dipped worryingly as he stretched his arm towards Ben.

There was a sudden loud splintering 'Crraack'---

... ...

Chapter Thirteen

The bedroom door had finally burnt sufficiently for it to split and burst wide open with the pressure of heat building behind it, allowing a huge surge of flame to blast into the room. The massive heat force from the landing literally *blew* Ben from his lonely dangerous perch and with a desperate lunge Luke caught hold of him and hauled him across the gap. The branch dipped alarmingly with the sudden extra weight as the two boys clung on for dear life. Amazingly it held, and as soon as it steadied they carefully manoeuvred themselves along it until they were at last clustered around the tree trunk together with Toby.

Although in near exhaustion and trying to recover their breath, Luke did his best to explain who he was and that something extremely strange had happened to him during his climb, whilst trying hard to put the pieces of the puzzle together in his *own* mind. Ben, still trying to get some fresh air into his lungs simply watched with smoke stung streaming eyes as flames from the bottom window billowed out to catch the floating end of their intended escape rope and ran extremely quickly up the full length of it. Toby looked as if he had had more than enough of the situation already, so Ben, although shuddering at the sight, kept quiet about what he had just witnessed. Once or twice above the horrendous noise of the fire crackling and spitting they heard what they thought might be the sound of bells ringing in the distance. Eventually they heard a vehicle screech to a stop on the drive.

"Thank God," Luke said. "It sounds as if the fire trucks have arrived."

Although not in sight from their position, they could hear the sound of firemen shouting to each other and the sudden welcome noise of high pressure water gushing from nozzles accompanied by a loud hissing, as cold water met the red-hot embers that used to be a splendid house.

As soon as Luke thought the lads were recovered enough, he helped them begin their descent. This time, the difficulty was reversed. The branches steadily got fewer and the distances between them longer. Eventually, partly due to his own now decreased personal height and with yet several metres to ground level, Luke knew they were stuck. Although he kept the thought to himself his biggest worry now was of the tree itself catching alight at its top. If they were forced to jump it would be at the risk of broken limbs or worse.

As daylight began to fail there was an enormous violent crash like thunder as part of the roof collapsed falling into the bedroom from which the boys had recently made their escape. The falling roof took the bedroom floor with it and part of the windowed outer wall, leaving the remainder extremely insecure. The resulting cloud of dust and smoke engulfed the tree and the small group in it for some time while they crouched watching helplessly. A fresh threat of danger now posed itself to them. If the rest of the wall were to collapse it was all too close to the tree in which they were trapped.

During the brief quiet lull following, the boys were at first startled by Luke abruptly shouting out "Help, help" at the top of his voice. But they soon shouted with him in the hope someone would hear their combined efforts.

When they eased up to regain their breath they heard someone directly below trying to locate them.

"Hallo-o, where are you? Are you up there in the tree?"

"Yes," shouted Luke, "we are, but we're stuck and can't get down any further."

"How many are you?"

"Three."

"Stay put for a second or two."

A few seconds later, a strong torch beam probed the branches of the tree until it picked up the three boys sitting huddled together.

"Right, now I know where you are I'll put up a ladder. See if you can grab the top of it and steer it to a safe location."

Peering down into the increasing gloom they soon spotted the top of the ladder waving about precariously. Grabbing it they positioned it firmly against their branch.

"Okay we've got it," they called out.

"Well done, I'll be up straightaway."

Soon a friendly face in a helmet appeared from below. "Right lads, let's get you down from here. I'll start with the smallest." One by one they were nervously each given a fireman's lift down to the ground and safety.

Only now could they see the full extent of the fire damage. Despite the fact they had only heard one arrive, there were three fire engine crews being kept busy. The far end of the house was almost at ground level with just a few charred upright timbers left. Firemen were still directing their water jets through the remains of the black scorched hole that had been the bedroom they had found themselves in earlier. Ben shuddered again at the thought of what might have happened if it had not been for his brother's 'feelings' or for Luke's daring rescue. Both brothers flung their arms around the young Luke and thanked him profusely for getting them out.

They then thanked the fireman and he led them over to be confronted by the Chief Fire Officer heading the operation.

"You were extremely lucky there boys," the officer said. "Frankly I'm amazed you managed to get out unharmed. This place is well away from the road or any other housing, so at the first report of smoke we sent one fire truck out to investigate. Obviously once we knew the extent of the fire we backed them up with others." He then scrutinised each of their faces and said sternly, "But-- I am wondering what you were doing in the house in the first place. We were informed the house was empty and the owner abroad. I have a lot of questions I must ask you." He looked them up and down and could see they were shivering with the shock of their ordeal. "In the meantime we'll first get you out of harm's way and comfortable."

He then instructed the men to see the three boys were all wrapped up in blankets and put inside one of the vehicles for warmth and safety.

After stowing his ladder, the leading fireman walked back over to the officer. "As you have the fire under control now chief, perhaps I could take these guys in the tender and get them some fast TLC?"

"Yes you can, Dag but do you realise there is no-one on duty in the canteen today?"

"Actually I was thinking of taking them back to my place and let my missis sort them out."

"Good idea," the chief agreed. "I wish I was able to come along. Go with Dag lads. He'll look after you." Then taking the fireman to one side he said quietly, though Ben overheard him, "I shall obviously need their personal details and information as to how they got in the house in the first place and what they were up to in there. See what you can find out and bring them to the station later."

Before long they were racing through the streets in the small fire vehicle each wearing a spare fireman's helmet in an attempt to relax them. As Toby was the smallest he was allowed to give the fire bell a clang every now and then to help take his mind off the dangerous situation they had been in.

Luke found himself staring at his small hands and legs feeling incapable of rational thought. 'This can't be happening, it has to be a dream, I'm not a teenager any more'. He mentally questioned himself. 'How did we all get there in the first place?' Questions and ideas were turning around in his head faster than Sandy's wheel.

He tried pinching himself hoping to wake from the dream, but to no avail. 'Why are the firemen using such antique vehicles? There are hook ladders stowed on this one which I'm sure were taken out of the service during the mid-eighties. They're using bells instead of sirens. Even their uniforms seem out-dated. Whatever is going on? Perhaps it's just that I've been in America for too long.' Then his thoughts changed direction slightly. 'There's another thing that seems odd. This fireman is so like the dad I remember when I was a kid around the age I seem to be now. Even the brass helmet he's wearing looks like the one I remember him in. Hell! I used to polish one similar to that for him with Mum's Brasso.' He shook his head and shoulders as if to clear his mind. 'No it's just not possible. Yet the Fire-chief did call him 'Dag' and that was the name most people knew Dad by. I don't know whether I'm still dreaming or going completely mad but I'm thankful that at least the kids seem okay.'

He felt the engine slowing down and turning and then a bump as it went up the kerb from the road into an alley. A short distance later it turned left and stopped by the side of an old corrugated steel garage. Climbing out, the three were led down a winding back garden path that Luke strangely felt he knew even in the dark, then into the back entrance of a small terraced house, through a tiny scullery and into a living room. A small kind-looking lady with a familiar face and greying hair got up from an armchair in front of a roaring fire as they were shown into the room.

"Look who I've brought home to see you love."

"Oh wonderful, Daggle," she said giving the boys a welcoming smile. "So you are Ben and Toby," she said, without any introduction. "It's wonderful to meet you." She gave them both a huge long cuddle. "Sit down and warm yourselves by the fire my loves."

She turned to Luke who was still standing as if asleep on his feet. "You Luke, I know very well of course. Come here and give me a hug. I can't tell you how good it is to see you. It seems I've been waiting for ever for you to come back over the ocean and see me and Dad." She enfolded him in her arms. "You are nearly out of time now Luke, but there will be others. Just remember this- we knew you had to go, so don't feel bad. We never stopped loving you. You're still our son."

Luke's thoughts and emotions were already running wild. After all his previous exertions and excitement this was all too much. His consciousness gradually slipped away.

On opening his eyes Luke found himself sitting on the fishing chair in the loft. The boys seemed to be playing with the trains as if nothing unusual had happened. Looking down at the floor he saw the photo of the burning building. He hurriedly picked it up and put it amongst the photos as if it was hot. Then, beginning to remember other things that had happened, he looked closely at his hands. They were scratched and filthy but at least they were back to normal size. But then, had they ever *really* changed in the first place? The pouch was no longer around his neck. He panicked for a second or two remembering it swinging whilst climbing the tree and began to think he had lost it, but almost as if Ben had read his mind the boy removed it from around his own neck and placed it inside the chest and locked it away.

"Luke's awake," Ben said to Toby and they both started to move over towards him, but just then there was a noise on the ladder and Cassie's head popped through the hatch.

"Hi guys, we're back. I'm sorry we've been so long. Everywhere was so busy. Thank you for staying with my sons, Luke. I hope you guys have looked after him and have been good."

"It's been more a case of Luke looking after us Mum," Toby said.

"They've been great," Luke answered quickly. "No worries' as you say in Australia. It's been quite an adventure,"- he paused, very briefly looking at the boys and wondering about his own appearance and then continued -"for me not having kids of my own but I'd look after these two any chance I can get," he said putting his arms around their shoulders.

"I might hold you to that sometime," Cassie said laughing. "I'm glad you all get on so well together.

Now you'd all best get downstairs soon as Mum has started to prepare lunch."

As soon as she had gone downstairs the three hurriedly exited the loft extremely thankful for the poor light there having screened their full appearances from Cassie.

Following the boys, Luke in turn quickly slipped into the bathroom to have a quick clean-up and a check on his age and general appearance in the mirror before collecting his laptop and suitcase from the bedroom ready for his oncoming departure.

After lunch, Tom brought the car to the front of the house. They all said their goodbyes which the boys found hard to do as they had not had a chance to talk to Luke or to show their real gratitude to him for saving their lives. Instead they both thanked him for looking after them and said how much they had enjoyed his company. Luke managed to press the stone dice he had just found in his trouser pocket into Ben's hand while shaking it goodbye.

At the same time he quietly joked, "Whatever have you been up to? You smell as if you've been having a bonfire."

"It's probably from all the dust on that old box of photos," Ben replied with a wink and a big grin.

Tom and Luke said their goodbyes as the train slowly pulled in. "Thanks for everything, Tom. I feel I've lost all that sadness about not getting back to see Mum and Dad. I know now they never stopped loving me after all."

He looked around to see the last passengers boarding. "I've gotta go. I'll try and explain sometime," he said as he climbed into the train.

"You don't have to explain anything," Tom said. "You know we're always here for you. 'Bye mate, take care," he shouted, waving as the train pulled out. "Give our love to Gill."

Luke nodded and waved. He settled himself back in the carriage seat more relaxed and comfortable than he had felt for at least thirty years. He could not begin to understand what had happened to him and the boys a few hours ago, but it *had* happened as he could still smell the smoke on himself and although he no longer looked a teenager, he felt much younger knowing he had shed many years of worry and sadness.

It was early evening before the boys managed to get back in the loft to discuss their latest hair-raising adventure. Neither of them could come up with any explanations as to why they had suddenly found themselves in the strange house, though they knew it had to be something to do with Sandy. As to how Luke had known where to find them or what had brought about the changes to him during the rescue was utterly beyond them. They knew they had a lot to learn yet about Sandy's capabilities and that it might be some time before they would be able to find answers.

"One thing I *must* remember is to always put the pouch around my neck before starting Sandy in future," said Ben. "That might help to keep us out of trouble and I'm going to take more notice of the way you seem to sense danger, Toby. You're a bit like Sandy yourself with those magical senses. Neither of us know how any of it works, but there is no doubt it does."

"Perhaps if we get to see Luke again he might be able

to give us some answers Ben?"

"Yes, he might, but I have the impression he was as mystified as we were, or perhaps even more so."

The more Ben thought about what had just happened to them, made him appreciate how lucky they had been to escape the danger they had been confronted with. He began to worry a little as to how it might have affected his younger brother and purposely put the question of the laughter Toby thought he had heard to one side at the moment. Instead he said, "I hope that fireman didn't get in too much trouble for not taking us to the fire-station afterwards. Well, I don't know about you, Toby, but I could do with a change of scenery. Shall we have a play with the trains until bed time?"

"Yep, good idea," came the surprisingly relaxed reply as Toby switched the lights on above the track. "Can *I* use the control this time?"

"Yes, of course you can. Are you still happy to go on with our adventures? I know Grandad originally said we could make them as exciting as we wished, but we don't seem to have had much of a say in the last two. They were both positively dangerous."

"Yes they were, but you bet I want to carry on," Toby answered gamely. "This is turning out to be one heck of a good holiday. Let's see what happens with the 'Two' on the dice tomorrow."

... ...

Chapter Fourteen

Ben was stretched out on the floor supporting his head with his hands, watching as Sandy's buckets filled and emptied continuously. It was an efficient little machine and ran very quietly. Apart from a very slight clanking from the buckets as they emptied, the only other noticeable noise came from the fan blades buffeting the air as they spun around at high speed.

As he laid there it seemed the level of sound from the fan was strangely increasing in volume and for some odd reason a roughness in the sound appeared to increase and pause, increase and pause, at regular intervals. He moved his head nearer the old machine in an attempt to determine what was causing this unusual variation in case some maintenance was due. The noise was louder now, yet still slowly pulsing.

Listening intently, Ben moved a little *too* close. A long strand of his hair caught in the fan gearing and suddenly began to wind, tugging his head towards the blades. He could not turn his head to see what he was doing but had to grope about desperately in the vain hope he could find the sand valve and stop Sandy before it was too late. With his face almost into the fan blades, he strained back so hard against the pull of the machine he felt he was going to pull all the hair from his scalp and was about to scream when he abruptly woke from the dream he had been suffering.

His fright had not been caused by Sandy at all. Biggles was paying him an early morning visit. The old cat had gradually moved closer to Ben's face and was making himself comfortable, purring loudly while pumping and pulling at the pillow and Ben's hair with his claws. Awake now, Ben burst out laughing in relief that it had only been Biggles when he heard someone else chuckling in the room.

Nan had let herself in while they were asleep and over the other side of the room was attempting to wake Toby by gently tickling his feet that were hanging out of the bed.

"That was so funny," she said. "Here I am tickling Toby's foot to wake *him* and it was *you* that happened to wake and laugh first."

"I was laughing because the machine-er, the gnashing noise I dreamed about turned out to be Biggles purring," he explained. He had managed to recover himself, remembering he had to keep the machine a secret.

At that moment the tickling sensation got through to Toby and he woke with a start, shouting. "Hey! What's going on? Oh, it's you, Nanny."

Cassie abruptly strode into the room, "Come on you pair of sleepy heads. Get yourselves downstairs. Breakfast is waiting for you. Once you have eaten, get yourselves washed and dressed and we'll be off to see your Great Nanny Flo before she goes to her social club this afternoon. I am so looking forward to seeing her. It doesn't seem possible she is ninety years old already."

"How do we get in, Nan?" Toby pushed hard at the outer door of the block of flats. "It seems to be locked?"

"Yes it has to be for security," explained Nan. "Most of the people in these flats are elderly like your great Nana Flo. They all have their own separate flats with their own front doors inside the block. But to save them hassle with sales people or strangers getting in, they also have these locked doors on the outside. The entrance panel there has a row of buttons for the flat numbers and another one marked call. You can operate the door for us if you want, Ben. I told you the flat number earlier. Do you remember it?"

"Yes, I do, like this?" Ben asked, as he pressed the appropriate numbered buttons.

"That's it," answered his Nan. "Now, just wait a little while."

Toby shoved the door impatiently. "It hasn't worked, Ben. You must have done it wrong. The door is still locked," he muttered, pushing at it again. "Let me have a try," he said, pushing past Ben to get at the panel of buttons.

Ben was about to shout out 'Dinosaurs' but realized it might ask for a lot of awkward explanations. Luckily their Grandfather came to his aid.

"Hold on a minute, Toby," he said. "We have to tell her who we are first."

A small speaker on the panel crackled and a female voice said "Hallo-o, who is it?"

Ben moved to the control saying, "It's me, Ben, Nana Flo. We are all here to see you."

"Who? Oh, Ben," their Great Nan's voice answered. "This is a lovely surprise, I'll let you in."

There was a loud click and another voice that of the recording machine in the pane, which said, "The door is now open. You may enter. Please close the door firmly, behind you. Thank you."

"Cool!" Toby exclaimed.

Once in, as they approached the lift door, their grandad said, "Go on then, Toby. Your turn. Press the call button first."

Toby happily obliged. There was a clanking noise from somewhere well above them, and a second or two later the door opened to reveal a tiny lift compartment.

One by one they all squeezed in and Toby pushed the buttons to make the lift climb its weary way up to the next flat level.

"Wow," said Toby. "I think it will just about make it, there are so many of us!"

Ben was sitting down behind him. "This is the first time I've seen a lift with a seat. What a great idea for old people."

"It looks as if you are feeling your age already, Prof, sitting there," Toby joked.

Their Great-Grandmother was waiting for them along the corridor with her flat door open. She was really excited and pleased to see them. Cassie had to wait a while to give her Nan a cuddle as the boys beat her to it and were very slow to relinquish theirs.

"You are simply amazing Nanny," Cassie sighed as she finally enjoyed her moment. "You honestly don't look a bit different since I last saw you three years ago."

"She does to me," Ben interjected to his mother's worried astonishment. "She looks a lot shorter than I remember."

"That's because you've grown so," said Flo laughing and taking it all in her stride. "You are as tall as me now. But then I was only ever a little-'un. Four foot, eleven and a half inches exactly."

"Ah, you know what they say Nanny? Good things come in small packages and you are very special to us all. I really love you and it's so good to be with you again," said Cassie as she squashed her Nan to her again.

"So, what do you think of my little home," Flo asked as soon as she recovered her breath.

The boys said they would love to live in a flat similar to it themselves when they were grown up, especially if it had a lift and a talking door.

"You have a lovely garden Nanny," Cassie said looking out from the window.

"Yes it is nice. The best of it is I no longer have to work on it to keep it tidy. That is all done for us. I sometimes go out there and sit and read when the weather is good."

Ben being a keen reader himself promptly asked, "What types of book do you like to read Nanny?"

"Oh, mostly historical or geographical I suppose, probably boring to a young fellow like yourself."

"Not necessarily, Nanny. I quite enjoy English history. May I have a quick look through your bookshelves?"

"Of course you may Ben. You are very welcome to borrow any of them if you wish, other than the one sitting on top there. That's a library book."

"It's really nice to know you are so comfortable here Nan," said Cassie.

"Yes, it's good" Toby agreed. "When we talk to you on the telephone in the future we'll be able to imagine you sitting here looking out the window."

"It's Me," Ben said out loud reading the title of something he had found on the bookshelf. "What's this Nanny? It looks almost handmade?" He held up the small sheath of printed papers bound together with two tiny squeezed metal clamps.

"Oh that's something my children have put together between them. Your aunt Tania, Uncle Paul and your Nan here. Many years ago they asked me to write down any bits and pieces that I remembered or had already told them about my early life. Since then they have typed and printed it and included some of my old photos."

"So is this *your* photograph on the front cover then, Nanny?"

"Yes, I have to admit it is."

"You were really beautiful Nanny."

"Thank you Ben," Flo said, looking both pleased and slightly embarrassed at the same time.

"What made you call your book 'It's Me' Nanny?"

"It was something that stuck with me all my life, Ben. As a youngster I used to always say 'It's me' whenever I called any of the family on the telephone.

"I like that," Ben said. "Would I be able to borrow this and read about you?"

"Yes of course you can. When you've read it you can either give it to your Nan or, if you want you can bring it back yourself as it would be lovely to see you at any time."

The boys loved the flat all the more when their Great Nana Flo came back from the kitchen with lemonade, heaps of 'Jammy Dodger' biscuits and a block of her special toffee together with a tiny silver toffee hammer.

... ...

Chapter Fifteen

Later that day Cassie's parents asked her to check through some bits and pieces she had left in the garage several years ago before moving to Australia, as they were having a tidy up.

"Of course I will," she said, soon beginning to rummage through it. "But I dare say you can dump it if I haven't missed it in all this time."

Tom looked around at the boys. "When you go to the loft, can you take a small box full of bits and pieces up for me lads? It's not heavy," he added as he saw Maggie's eyebrows rise.

"I wasn't thinking about the weight of it so much as the fact you are taking even more junk out of the garage to put in the loft," she exclaimed.

"It's not junk. It's all quite useful," he argued.

The boys asked, "Can we have a look at it when we get it up there?"

"Yes of course Ben, then you can let your Nan know that it *is* all good stuff."

Once the boys had put their Grandfather's box up on one of the shelves, they turned to have yet another look around the rest of the loft. The main wall was lined with shelves crammed with all sorts of stuff. Dusty old wooden and cardboard boxes sat on the floor beneath with unrecognisable bits and pieces protruding almost as if they had grown there. It was still very much an 'Aladdin's' cave to the boys as well as being their very special adventure place. Ben peered at a large silver and chrome object, precariously perched on the top of an old cardboard box.

"I noticed this the other day," he said to Toby. "The label on it says 'Photographic Enlarger'. I must remember to ask Granddad about it some time. It looks awfully interesting."

Ben unlocked the old chest and lifted Sandy from it, then stood for a second or two looking intently at the old machine.

"What's up, Ben?"

"Nothing really, except I think perhaps we should get Sandy running forward again, especially now we know Luke remembered him running that way. To be honest, I'm just a little concerned it might have been the reason for us having such dangerous adventures."

"I must admit I don't like watching him so much when he is running backwards," Toby said. "He seems natural—more at ease somehow the other way."

"Right we'll do it," said Ben, already starting to remove the top sand pot. "While we are at it I'll open the sand valve a little less full-flow than I have so far when I've started him. I believe it might slow him a little and give us more time with a full pot of sand. If we make some notes now on our settings, we might be able to adjust it a little more as we go on. A few more minutes could make a lot of difference to an adventure."

Soon they were sitting comfortably again in their fishing chairs and watching the old machine turning in its original direction, Toby having made various small scribbles for record in his notebook.

"Another thing we ought to try is to see if Sandy will run *inside* the chest. He runs so quietly no-one would know he was there if they happened to look in the loft while we are on an adventure. I'll stop him for a minute while I put him in, it will be easier."

With Sandy in the chest and running again he finally closed the chest lid. "That's better, I feel a whole lot happier now about keeping this all a secret."

"Do you think there'll be enough air in there, Ben, will he be able to breathe?"

"That lid is far from airtight, Toby and it has a small area of vent holes on the lid. If I remember right, you tried to peep through them before we had the key. The main worry I think is his shrunken size, but I don't believe it will make any difference to his running."

"Okay then, Ben, shall we try the number 'Two' now? I'm really excited to see what else Sandy can offer us."

"Yes so am I." He lifted the chest lid, leaned over and switched on the already positioned torch.

"Right my notebook is at the ready," said Toby excitedly.

"I'll have a go at the dice this time," Ben said looking at them as he picked them up. "I suppose there's no point in rolling the two of them if one is a blank." He placed the die with the selected carved number uppermost, but although waiting for some time, nothing happened.

"Perhaps I'm not such a bad gambler after all," Toby said with a giggle.

Ben tried rolling it and then placing it with the 'Two' showing again but to no avail. Finally he tried placing the blank die next to it. Immediately the grey smoky effect of the fan-blades began to form words. "Really strange stuff this magic," Ben muttered.

New words had formed.

'Gaze at me - twice blink those eyes

112

No one else shall you espy
Open them - both wide and clear
Once again espied back here'

"I'll put it in the notebook Ben, but I probably don't need to as it's showing on the stone slab anyway. Whatever does 'espy' and 'espied mean?"

"I'm not at all sure. At first, I thought it meant we would not *see* anyone else but that doesn't seem to make much sense. We'll just have to try it to find out." He quickly checked through the trap door for anyone around. "It's all clear, ready when you are, Toby."

"Try it on your own this time Ben, then I'll be here if anyone does show up. You can do the same for me next time."

"Good idea. Now what did it say? Look in the mirror and blink my eyes twice?"

Ben was gone instantly. Toby began to worry. What did the clue mean? Ben could have gone anywhere. Perhaps they should have gone together after all?

"Geeps what should I do?" he muttered out loud.

"You mean, what should *I* do?"

Toby looked round behind him.

"I must have got it wrong again, nothing happened," Ben said in puzzlement. He could see his brother peering into corners and behind boxes. "What are you doing? What are you looking for?"

"I'm looking for you of course you idiot. Where are you, why are you hiding?"

"What do you mean idiot? I'm not hiding. I'm here, hallo-o," Ben began waving his hands in front of his brother's face but suddenly stopping in alarm. "Oh hell, I've become invisible! So that's what the clue meant."

"You're tricking me. Stop it!"

"I'm not, Toby, honestly. I really am invisible. Put your hand out and I'll shake it."

Toby nervously extended his hand feeling quite certain this must be one of his brother's tricks and that Ben was simply hiding in the shadows. When an invisible hand grabbed hold of his and shook it, his reactions were firstly a huge mixture of shock and disbelief, but then sheer joy that Ben really was there and what he had told him was true.

"Wow! You really are invisible." His mischievous little face broke into a huge grin. "Oh boy, are we going to have some fun with this. I can't wait. Can I give it a try now?"

"Sure you can. I'll just-" Ben paused in what he was saying. He swung his eyes from side to side, then up and down and he pulled faces. "Oh of course," he said more or less to himself. "No nose in the way."

"What *are* you on about now, Ben. No nose?"

"Well, it's just that I seem to be seeing everything with super wide vision. I've just realised that being invisible I no longer have anything to restrict my sight at all. No nose, cheeks, or eye sockets. That must sound really weird to you but it's quite amazing how much more I can see. I'll let you have a go now, then you'll see what I mean—that is providing this works okay the other way around?"

"You're okay, Ben. You're back in sight again, even if you are pulling funny faces."

"Phew!" Ben gasped. "That was fantastic, but well scary. The clue says 'Open both eyes wide and clear.' I lifted the mirror to do that and found the mirror was invisible too. My eyes must have opened well wide with panic at the thought of being stuck with invisibility. Are you sure you want to give it a try?"

"You bet," answered Toby excitedly.

114

"Okay then, here's the mirror. Mind you don't drop it when you can't see your hand. Oh, and Toby?"

"Yes Ben?" His voice came as if from nowhere.

"Please promise me whatever you do don't leave the loft, anything could happen and I wouldn't know where to look for you."

"Alright Ben, I promise."

There was an eerie silence for a minute or so.

"Are you there?" Ben asked worriedly. Then again, "Toby, where are you?"

Toby's laugh rattled around the loft. "It's okay Ben, I'm here. You are right about the vision, but it's not the only thing that is weird. I just tried moving and because I can't see my feet, I don't know exactly where I am putting them, so I feel I have to look down all the time. But it doesn't help much because I can't see them anyway, if you see what I mean?"

"Now it's you beginning to sound like Grandad," Ben said chuckling.

They burst into peals of laughter even though Ben felt a little odd as he seemed to be laughing alone.

"What on earth are you two up to?" Their mother's voice called from the stairwell near the bottom of the ladder.

Toby blinked back into reality quicker than someone beamed back to the Star Ship Enterprise. Trying to move on his newly found feet he stumbled a little but by the time Cassie put her head through the hatch, both he and Ben, though still laughing, appeared to be playing with the trains.

"Whatever was all that noise about? I could hear you from the bottom of the stairs."

"Ben just came out with an hilarious joke," Toby fibbed hurriedly.

"Oh I see. Well, you certainly seem happy enough up

here. I was worrying you might get bored. We can go out somewhere if you would sooner?"

"We're fine, Mum, honest," said Ben. "We love it up here."

"I somehow thought that would be your answer," she said with a chuckle as she started off down the ladder. "That's quite okay, so long as you are enjoying your holiday."

"We sure are, Mum," Toby answered.

"Oh well, we know now what the number two brings and we seem to have proved that Sandy runs alright in the chest. I think we should get our heads together straight away now on some sort of an alarm system to let us know if anyone is looking for us while we're out on an adventure, else we'll never get to enjoy them. We've already had a couple of close scrapes with Mum popping up unexpectedly."

... ...

Chapter Sixteen

They sat in the loft for some time coming up with various ideas, but try as they might they found it very difficult to find a practical answer.

"I thought we'd soon solve this, yet the only answer at the moment seems to be for one of us to stay behind and watch out for the other, though even in that case it would be no good us shouting or whistling. If the adventure was happening somewhere as close as Grandad's shed, we still might not hear it."

Toby was highly amused. "That sounds unlikely! An adventure in Grandad's shed! But I know what you mean and in any case we need to be able to *share* our adventures."

Ben shook his head. "I was trying to think of devising something using our alarm clock but that wouldn't be any good either. What we really need is a means of bringing us back if anyone comes looking for us. Hey that's *it*! What's the only thing that could bring us back which we already have?"

Toby frowned in thought. Then his eyes lit up as he shouted excitedly, "Sandy!"

"Yes. If he stops we could be back here in a flash."

"So, we have to fix something to stop him if anyone comes near the loft."

"That's about it I reckon, but it's going to take some working out how we will do it."

"Hmm, it sounds almost as if we're going to have to make our *own* magic," Toby commented.

"If only we could. Perhaps if we have a look around Grandad's stuff again, we might come up with something useful," Ben suggested.

"No harm in looking," remarked Toby.

A few minutes later they had to admit they were still not making any progress.

"That really is quite amazing, Toby. We have all Grandad's goodies tucked up here and available and we still have no answer. Hold on a minute, we've yet to look in the box we just brought up. Grandad said we could."

They took the box lid off and pulled out various bits and pieces, some familiar, some not, placing them on the floor around the box.

"Whatever is this?" Toby asked as he pulled out a small rectangle of wood with a stiff spring wire attached to it.

"That's an old-style mousetrap, have you never seen one before?"

"No I guess not. How could *that* catch a mouse? There's no way it could move as fast as a mouse that's for sure. It has no wheels for a start."

Ben burst out laughing. "You are so funny at times but you're dead right. The only way that would move as fast as a mouse would be if you threw it at one."

This time it was Toby's turn to laugh. "So how *does* it work then?"

"Traps are cruel really but then I suppose a mouse can be a real nuisance and people have to use them sometimes. What you have to do is hold the wooden base firm while you pull this spring lever up high like this and then put this little prop under it to keep the spring from slamming down again. It's a very strong spring. If it slips while you're setting it, it will really hurt your fingers if you get them in the way. The prop has to be placed very carefully like this, so the slightest movement will set it off. You watch."

Ben carefully touched the trap with a pencil he had just found. With a loud 'BANG' the spring came down fast and hard making a big dent in the side of it.

"Wow," exclaimed Toby. "That worked well. How do you tell the mouse what to do?"

"Oh Toby, I do love you my little brother. We have such fun together," he said with a chuckle. "If you told the mouse what to do he would have none of it. Neither would I, if I were a mouse. What you do is to place a small piece of cheese or chocolate on the board as near the prop as you can get it without setting off the trap, then once the mouse smells the food, he climbs up on the board and starts nibbling."

"Ah I see, then 'bang'." Toby's forehead creased into a frown. "Does it hurt him very much Ben?"

"Yes it –er, knocks him unconscious. Then he has to be taken somewhere else, far from the place he was being a nuisance in." Ben tried to avoid the truth knowing his brother was an animal lover.

"Poor little mouse," said Toby thoughtfully.

"Never mind the poor little mouse. We are supposed to be inventing an alarm. Hey perhaps we can use the mousetrap as the alarm mechanism."

"We still won't be able to hear it, Ben."

"We won't have to," Ben said laughing. "We'll place the trap and set it - without the cheese before you ask - up against the loft ladder. With a bit of practice setting it up it should go off immediately anyone starts to climb up here."

"That's good. But I don't think I'm with you properly yet. How much help is someone setting off a mousetrap going to be to us when we're over the park for instance?"

"You're right yet again, none at all."

"But-"

119

"That's just it, *but-* if we were to tie a cord to the spring and run it high over that roof rafter-"

"Oh yes," Toby shouted adding "Then tie it to Sandy somewhere to stop him running if the trap is sprung."

"That's it! Then we would instantly return here, safe from being found out," Ben completed.

They were both pleased with themselves at having come up with a possible answer. *Now* they had to prove they could actually do it.

After all the time and concentration used in coming up with the idea, it took hardly any time to get the alarm under way. Half a blob of their Nan's blue sticky stuff covertly borrowed from her kitchen notice board was again halved. Part of this was stuck to the top of the loft ladder, the other tiny blob fixed near the bottom of the mousetrap prop. A short length of thread from the train repair box was all that was needed for the connection; this they made taut when positioning the trap. Toby became the project tester. On the second attempt the trap was sprung by the slightest movement on the ladder. They were both highly delighted.

The next problem was connecting it to Sandy. This proved to be a little trickier. It needed to be a means of stopping him easily without causing damage. They worked out between them that as the trap sprung in a downwards direction, a length of the thread tied to the trap spring and hung over a roof rafter would change the movement at the free end of the cord to an upwards direction. On having a good long look at Sandy while he was running, they came up with a possible answer. Carefully tying another short length of thread around the head of an old pencil, they then secured it to the machine frame so that it would pivot horizontally just below the path of the moving sand containers. With the trap spring thread tied to the other end of the pencil, when operated, it would pull up against the frame and stop the buckets from turning. The lucky addition to their alarm system was that any of the magic sand still flowing, quickly returned itself to the top pot.

Following a few failures mainly caused by the thread sometimes catching on the rough sawn rafter, they re-routed it over an old protruding nail head a little further along. The cord now ran smoothly with the bonus of line accuracy kept by the nail head. So on shifting the chest containing Sandy into an on-line position and sticking the mousetrap down so it's base could not move, they finally achieved success.

The only other small problem encountered, was that for secrecy, they needed to leave Sandy locked in the chest and running while they were out on adventures. Ben soon found he could slightly realign Sandy with the line position to cnable it to run straight through one of the small vent holes in the chest lid. With the cord cut to the right length, it could be simply positioned over the rafter nail each time they closed and locked the chest lid with Sandy running inside, prior to resetting the mouse trap.

Once more Toby became chief tester of the new system and soon announced they were ready to roll. Both boys were ecstatic at having overcome one of their major problems.

"That's great, now what shall we do, Ben?"

"Perhaps *now* we can get back to experimenting with our invisibility?"

"I'm ready when you are." Toby replied eagerly."

"We'll both go this time," Ben suggested. "I guess we'll have to hold hands again as before. We can't easily be looking in the mirror at the same time."

He looked in the mirror and blinked twice. "Oo-er, this is really odd. I'm holding your hand but I can't see it or you."

"It's all very strange." Toby's voice said immediately next to him. "Do you think I would become visible again if I let go of your hand?"

"I really don't know. Let go and find out."

"Okay, can you see me now?"

"Nope."

"Good, so at least we won't have to walk around *all* the time holding hands like a pair of little kids. So what shall we do now?"

"I thought if we are really quiet, we'll creep downstairs and out into the back garden for a start."

"Nice one Ben, let's go for it."

As Toby had found, they did have trouble at first co-ordinating their invisible feet and their movements. But once they accepted this was not the usual practice when owning *visible* feet, they began to walk normally. The next big problem of course was the squeaking staircase. Even though the boys were invisible, it made no difference to their weight. As soon as he heard the first stair squeak a little, Ben automatically turned to Toby and put a finger up to his mouth to indicate the need for stealth, then realised that Toby could not see him *or* his finger. They must have been about half way down when a stair tread made a really loud creak. The boys froze as they heard someone coming across the room below, towards the door.

They stood stock still in desperation. "What now?"

If they were to dash either way on the stairs they would make an awful din, apart from the possibility of getting tangled up or tripping over each other because they were invisible. If they stood still they would not be seen, but if someone decided to come upstairs they would be in the way. It was dear old Grandad who came to the rescue. Instead of opening the door, he moved across the room to the radio and switched it on quite loudly while announcing that he wanted to listen to the news. As well as the noise from the radio there was a huge sigh of relief from the boys as they both raced down the remaining stairs with no more worries. They dashed through the kitchen and out into the back garden.

"Heck," gasped Ben. "That could have been awkward. Thank goodness for Grandad and his news. We are going to have to put some practice in on those stairs, they're so creaky."

"You're right. I found myself wondering if Grandad knew we were in some kind of trouble."

"He could have I suppose," answered Ben. "It certainly seemed more than coincidence. We may never know but it's a great thought he might be watching out for us in some way."

The boys had a great time in the back garden trying out their invisibility, which included giving poor Biggles his exercise for the day. He had been enjoying a lovely quiet uninterrupted sleep under the old apple tree when the boys saw him and went across to make a fuss of him. Even above sleep and a good feed this was his real notch in life, he could take as much of this as he could get. He stretched to his full length and rolled over on his side for his tummy to be stroked, then opened his eyes to mere slits to see who was making such a lovely fuss of him. Once it dawned on him there was no one in sight, he leapt about a metre in the air and shot off at an astounding speed for an old cat, disappearing into the house to look for a safe dark corner. As there was no one else around the boys used the nice peaceful spot Biggles had left, to sit and discuss their next tactics.

"This is great fun," laughed Ben. "Poor old Biggles I hope he's still friends with us later. I've been wondering, if I were to put something on the ground, the torch for instance, yes, it becomes visible as soon as it is away from me. So, if we drop anything we should be able to find it again. Also anything we pick up should disappear like this." It did.

"That's interesting Prof, but why should it matter?"

"Only that if we were near someone and picked up something which *stayed* visible, it would be seen moving around in mid-air. Likewise, we shall need to be careful not to drop anything when there is anyone around for a similar reason. It's such a shame that we have to keep this all a secret otherwise we could have a whale of a time playing tricks on people."

"I know," murmured Toby grinning. "We could have some great fun." Then his grin faded. "It's going to be difficult now to get back in the loft without being heard? The news will have long finished."

"No worries. We can kiss the stone. That will take us straight back--" he paused. "Oh God how silly can we get? We had no need to worry about the squeaking stairs, we could have *wink-wished* ourselves out here."

"Oh of course. I had forgotten the stone *and* the mirror. This is all going to take some getting used to." He looked about them in the loft. "Wicked! I didn't even see you do it."

Ben looked thoughtful. "That was good, but there is something else we haven't tried as yet."

"What's that?"

"We ought to try using the *mirror* somewhere other than in the loft. I know we're not allowed to take Sandy out but I'm sure that if the stone works outside, then the

124

mirror should too. Let's take the stuff over the park and give it a go."

"Yep okay. It'll be good to have some fun on the slides and swings anyway."

"We'd best ask for permission first this time."

"Hallo you two, we haven't seen you for hours," their Nan said. "Are you having fun?"

"You should have heard the noise they were making earlier, Mum. They certainly sounded as if they were enjoying themselves," Cassie said.

"We just love it up there and Grandad's train set is something else. But we would like to go over the park now for some fun if that's alright Mum, please?"

"As you asked so nicely I guess I had best say yes, but don't be over there too long as we'll be getting tea ready soon. You have an hour, alright?"

"Thanks Mum. See you later."

There were only two other children in the play area when they arrived and luckily these were soon called in for tea from one of the adjoining houses.

"Oh good, *now* we'll be able to try invisibility out here with the mirror."

"Okay, I'll grab your hand."

Ben looked in the mirror and blinked twice. They both instantly disappeared.

"Great, so it does work outside. That will make so much difference to our adventures. Right, keep a hold for a minute, let's have some fun while we're here." He held the mirror up again and wink-wished them both to the top of the biggest slide.

It was as well there were no onlookers. They might have found themselves escorted to the hospital for treatment or sedatives on reporting having seen strange things going on in the park. Roundabouts whizzing around at great speed, swings swinging, seesaws going up and down, all apparently of their own accord and not a soul to be seen anywhere.

···   ···   ···

Chapter Seventeen

Having returned from the park before tea was ready, they were chatting in the back garden when their grandfather saw them and called from the shed.

"Lads, I have an apology to make to you. With all the excitement over Luke's visit, I forgot my promise to show you how to fold a paper boat."

"No worries. We've been so busy with Sandy we'd forgotten about it too, but we would still love you to show us."

"I'll show you straight after our meal if you like?"

"That will be good Grandad, thanks."

"So dare I ask who this 'Sandy' is, you just mentioned?" He looked at Ben with a puzzled expression. "A mate? A girl-friend perhaps?"

"Oh of course, we haven't told you yet. That's what we've named the adventure machine."

"Ah, I see. That sounds a jolly good name for him."

Once they had been shown how to fold a boat they soon got the hang of it and set about making a deluxe version of their own, adding two life-belts and a coil of string as a rope, a pair of oars and a stuck-on funnel. Nan watched interestedly and said she would help if she could. Toby asked her if there were any old paint boxes around that he could use. After a look through her cupboards she finally came out with several old nail-varnishes.

"These will probably be *ideal* for you if the colours are what you need. They are quick drying and have a brush inside the lid too, see?"

"Cool, Nan," Toby said looking at them. "Can we take two please, the clear and scarlet ones?"

"Here, take them all and use whatever you like. Your Aunt Anna was going to throw them out so I had them instead, but I doubt I shall ever use them."

"Brilliant, Nan, thanks."

"There is only one thing Toby, can you please be sure to use them outside somewhere? Nail varnish has a very strong smell."

"Okay I will. Thanks again, Nan."

Toby thoroughly enjoyed himself painting the boat. He painted everything that might end below the water line with the clear varnish and various other parts of the boat in bright scarlet with a few silver trimmings. He soon realised that his Nan was right about the smell.

"Urgh, this is really foul," he muttered to himself. "How can girls use something like this on their finger nails? Perhaps it's *really* to remind them not to pick their noses in public?"

Once they had finished with the boat they asked for permission to play with the trains again and then hurriedly scooted off up to the loft for the remainder of the evening.

Toby was up with the lark in the morning. He crept downstairs and found his Grandfather sitting at his computer.

"Hi Granddad, what are you doing?"

"Oh, I am just writing a little story about you guys."

"You are writing a story about us?"

"Yes. I'll let you see it one of these days." Then he casually glanced at the time on his computer. "Six-fifty! Whatever are you doing up at this time in the morning? I thought I was the only early-riser in the family."

"I woke up thinking of our new boat. I loved the time we had on the river playing with the boat you built. I was wondering if you knew anywhere close we could try sailing our new one?"

"Actually, there is a little stream in the park that should be ideal for small craft, providing the water level is not too low at this time of the year?"

"A stream here in the park? Whereabouts is that?"

"Ah I thought it was unlikely you'd have noticed it. The stream runs into the park underground below the park entrance. It comes out under a small bridge at the end of the footpath and runs right through the park in between the trees."

"Oh wicked! If I go and wake Ben, is it okay if we go over there now? Then, if there is enough water we'll give our boat a trial launch."

"Of course you can, Toby. Luckily for you the park people don't seem to close the gates overnight anymore, otherwise you would have had to wait until later for them to open it. There is one problem though, I don't think there's much of a bank to run along at the stream. You will likely have to wear your boots and run along in the stream itself. It's only ever a few inches deep anyway."

"That sounds even more fun."

His grandfather laughed. "Now why did I expect you to say that? Be careful nevertheless. Go on, be off with you."

When Toby returned to the bedroom he found Ben already up and dressed. He had woken as Toby had left the room and been busy ever since. He had even managed to quietly get into the loft and leave the old machine running.

"I knew you were up to something," he explained, "as soon as I caught sight of you creeping out of the bedroom."

Toby told him of his plans, so once they had picked up their boat and boots they crept down the stairs again and let themselves out of the front door after having given their Grandad a quick wave.

The stream was there exactly where Toby had been told and they both marvelled at the fact they had never noticed it on previous visits. They stood on the small bridge and watched the water as it tumbled out of the underground exit making small gurgling noises as if glad to be out in the daylight at last. It ran between grassed banks for a few metres then disappeared between the narrow woodland strip that escorted it down the hill and through the park.

"It looks good," Toby said, sitting on the grass bank hurriedly pulling on his Wellington boots.

"The water should be quite deep enough for the boat and probably fast too, as the park is all downhill," Ben said while stowing their shoes just inside on the dry side of the tunnel mouth.

When they tried to follow the stream into the woody area they found the entrance blocked by piles of old branches. Some of the local children had apparently been trying to build a dam, but luckily for the local residents, they were not as skilled in the art as their small expert counterpart, the Beaver that they had apparently been learning about. The water simply carried on *underneath* their new construction.

Nevertheless it did block everyone's access to the stream entrance. The boys had to enter through the trees a few metres downstream instead, while noticing the wooded banks were already gaining height above the water level. Here, although not quite as deep, the stream had spread itself out slightly, as presumably over many years of dashing and cutting its way down the hill it had encountered various big stones and rocks and made small detours to one side or the other.

"This is great down here," exclaimed Ben splashing about in his boots. "Now I can see why we've never noticed it before. It's well down from grass level and completely hidden by the trees."

Toby was too busy getting his boat ready for a sail to take much notice of what his brother was rambling on about. He carefully placed all the ropes, oars, and other parts on the deck, then made sure the scarlet funnel was still standing proudly upright.

"Right I'm ready. If you go downstream a little you can catch it as it comes past."

Ben did as he was told and waded along the stream until he came to the first bend and shouted, "Will this do?"

"That's good," answered Toby. "Here it comes." He gave the little boat a push into the current.

He stood behind it for a while arms folded, proudly watching their small creation as it gradually gathered speed, occasionally twitching and flashing scarlet reflections while changing directions to follow the current of the stream weaving its way downhill. Then, as if this wonderful thing was going to escape from him forever, he started a mad gallop along the stream chasing it, chuckling to himself with glee all the while.

Ben, standing downstream waiting for the little craft to arrive, had to laugh to himself at the funny sight of his little brother cavorting along towards him with the sunlight behind him and water splashing in all directions. He was so absorbed in watching his brother's antics he all but forgot to grab the boat out of the water before it sailed past.

"That went really well," exclaimed a very wet but delighted Toby when he arrived seconds later. "Shall we do it again? I'll catch it this time."

Without waiting for an answer he ploughed off downstream again as fast as the wake of water around his Wellies would allow. "I'll be just around the next bend," he called back over his shoulder.

Ben waited until Toby disappeared around the bend, then carefully placed the boat in the water again and released it. Like Toby, he then stood for a second or two watching the small craft as it bobbed around various obstacles on the stream bed. He had started to follow just before it reached the bend, when suddenly the boat was snatched out of the water by hands that obviously did not belong to his brother. The snatching was accompanied by a loud hoot of derisive laughter.

Toby, waiting round the bend expecting his beloved boat to appear at any second, knew nothing of this. He heard the laughter of course and the sound of somebody crashing through the trees upstream, but assumed it was someone else having fun. When the boat did not arrive he plodded back upstream to the bend until he was looking back to the point where he had left Ben. There was no sign of the boat or of Ben.

The boat-snatchers, both around fourteen or fifteen years of age, ran along the park grass outside the tree line at high speed. When they achieved some distance down the hill they had a quick look behind them and ducked back through the trees to the stream.

"I don't know why we bothered looking behind us," the bigger one said as he put the boat down near the stream. "Those two little kids were hardly likely to chase us and if they had, more fool them."

"Do you really want to play with their boat, Jess? It's only a kids' paper thing."

"No of course not, what do you think I am, a child?"

His companion simply shrugged his shoulders without answering.

"I just love to mess people around. They've probably taken ages to make and paint this. I'll jump on it now and leave it where they are sure to find it. That will be such a gag." He stopped and looked around on the bank in surprise. "Where is it? Why did you move it?"

"I haven't touched it."

"Yes you have, you must have hidden it the minute I turned my back. You want it yourself don't you? Well you're not having it, come on what have you done with it?"

He gave the other boy a sharp push in the chest and much to his surprise saw him stagger, trip backwards over something and land on his back in the middle of the stream.

"Ha ha ha," mocked Jess. "That will teach you to not to mess around with *me* in the future. Now tell me where you hid it or I'll jump on top of *you* instead of the boat."

"I told you I never touched the damned stupid boat," the other shouted, attempting to struggle to his feet.

"Right don't say I didn't warn you." Jess took one step down the slope towards the other boy, then he too suddenly tripped and fell headlong landing face down in the shallow water and lay there cursing and swearing as he tried to lift himself using his arms.

Having achieved his own slippery struggle to his feet the other boy was busy muttering to himself and trying to squeeze some of the muddy water from his clothes. With his back to him, he never saw Jess push himself half up then suddenly collapse again into the water. Nor did he notice the small wet muddy boot prints appear all up his back as if someone was walking all over him.

"Alright, alright, I never meant it. I wouldn't have really jumped on you," Jess screamed and spluttered spitting out mud.

"Oh shut up and get a life," said the other boy still with his back to Jess. "You're like some spoilt brat wanting things all your own way while upsetting everyone else. You can find some other fool to keep you company in the future. That's if you're lucky enough," he added as he stormed off up the hill.

Ben reappeared holding the undamaged boat just a short distance away in amongst the trees and watched the second sobbing, soaking, mud bedraggled creature emerge from the wood and make its way down to the bottom park gate.

"Oh well," he sighed to himself. "I don't think we'll have any more trouble with them." He replaced the stone mirror in the pouch. "Thanks Sandy."

He heard a noise in the bushes close by and re-entered the wood.

"Toby there you are. Sorry bro', I saw some blokes messing around in the stream near you and thought I had best look after the boat just in case of trouble. By the time I had finished walking -- past them, I had a job to find you again. Right we'll go through here and start again. I'm really enjoying this."

After an hour or so of fun up and down the stream they were met by their Grandfather as they approached the park gate to return home.

"Oh good, it looks as if you've already smelled breakfast. I was on my way to fetch you. How was the stream, not too muddy I hope?"

"It was great thanks," said Toby happily.

"Just muddy enough," answered Ben with a huge grin as they walked up the road chatting.

"Hold up. Let's have a look at your new boat. Oh yes she's a beauty. You've made a really good job of it."

"Thanks Granddad, we're well pleased with it. Oh, by the way, I spotted something called an enlarger in the loft yesterday, I wondered if you would show it to us sometime?"

"Oh yes, my old photographic enlarger. I never got around to buying a new one, or to fixing that one when the wiring went up in smoke. I'll see if I can repair it while you're with us, then if you want I'll show you how we used to do our photos before the days of computers."

"Yes please, that would be really interesting."

... ...

Chapter Eighteen

"Shall we go for a three now then?" Ben held up the small stone dice.

"Yep go for it," replied Toby.

"Come on then, let's set it up."

They were well practised now. In hardly any time at all they had Sandy topped up with sand and running quietly inside the locked chest with their mousetrap alarm set at the ready. Ben put the dice down with the number 'Three' uppermost and its plain companion next to it. Toby switched on the small torch and then watched the back of the slab he was holding. The grey surface became smoky as before and then began to form letters.

'Open eyes stare hard at me
Your size shall soon become like me
Stare again then roll those eyes
Then once more your head will rise'

"What do you make of that Toby?"

"It sounds almost as if it might shrink us?"

"That's what I was thinking and I suppose the bit about *'Your head will rise'* means growing again? This all sounds so unreal, yet I've thought that from the beginning. I guess we can only experiment again."

"Yep I guess so, but I might just watch this time Ben. I'm small enough already thanks and I can't see the point in being smaller still."

"I must admit I can't see much *use* for it, but I'm sure we soon will and in any case I'm dead curious to see what happens, so here goes."

Ben held the mirror and stared at it and his reflection stared back.

Toby had begun to say, "Is this really a good idea?" but before he had finished Ben had disappeared. He had started to turn around to look for him when he was stopped in his tracks by a tiny shrieking shout from Ben.

"Don't move or you'll tread on me. Look down. I'm right next to your feet. Whatever you do stay right where you are."

Toby, eyes wide looked down at his feet and found it extremely hard to accept his 'big' brother was at his feet, no more than around five centimetres high. He was incredibly tiny.

"Wow! It really is weird to see you down there."

"Ah! My ears! Stop shouting! You think it's weird. You should be down here, you're like a giant. You're the tallest moving creature I've ever seen, I feel very vulnerable down here. I'm coming back up or at least I hope I am? Phew! Thank goodness for that. Oh Toby, that was the scariest yet. Hey wait a minute, there's something wrong. I've come back bigger - a lot bigger, I'm way above your head now" Panic began to set in. "How can I ever explain this to anyone? Oh, you idiot, Toby."

Toby had suddenly become taller, back to his original height in fact.

"Sorry Ben, I had just squatted down a little to have a closer look at you when you looked in the mirror and came back. I never meant to frighten you."

Ben took a deep breath at the relief of it all.

137

"Oh God, for a moment there I thought I was going to be some kind of freak."

"You *thought* you were going to be?"

"Why you little - I'll get you for that." Ben wrestled Toby to the floor and began tickling him.

"No-he-he, no--please no more Ben. Listen, I've just had an idea. Do you think if we both shrunk, we would be small enough to ride on Grandad's trains?"

"Great idea already," said Ben releasing him. "And neither of us thought we would use it! Come on, let's go and see."

They were just about to shrink when there was a sudden 'BANG', immediately stopping Sandy and near frightening them out of their skins. The new alarm was working. Their mother was on her way up again.

On the bottom rung Cassie paused, asking, "Boys, is this ladder safe? Something made a loud bang as soon as I stepped on it."

"Yes it's fine Mum," said Ben hanging his head and shoulders down through the loft entrance. "It does that most times anyone comes up."

"That's alright then. It's probably just that I hadn't noticed it before. Nan and Grandad are still busy down the garage and said I can take you for a spin in the car for an hour or two. I would love to show you a few of my old haunts while we are over here."

"That will be great. We'll clear away our stuff and be with you in a few minutes."

Cassie had been longing to do this. Firstly she headed towards Morden to show them the old house, a pretty little mid-terraced place with a black and white frontage which had been her Nan's home before she had recently moved into her flat. This was where her Mum and Aunt and Uncle had lived during their childhood. As a small child, she too, had spent many happy times there. She parked the car and walked them round the back alley to show them the garden she used to play in, then took them along the virtually unchanged local streets to get to the run of shops nearby.

"To think I was younger than you are when I used to walk along here with Mum or my Nan," she said.

She showed them various places as she drove round telling them about her life as a child. Her first and second schools, the doctors and dentists, where her best friend had lived and the greens and parks where they used to play.

The place she would really have liked to have shown her sons, was the drama club which she and later, her sister Anna, had spent so much wonderful time at. She had made so many lasting friendships at the club, dancing, singing and rehearsing. It brought tears to her eyes now to think about all those lovely times. Not long after she moved to Australia however, the old clubhouse had been demolished to make room for a new supermarket.

She then drove the boys across Epsom Downs and through the Headley countryside to the top of Box Hill. Once they had walked across to the viewing place there, Cassie pointed out all the places she could remember.

"How do you know so much about it Mum?" Toby queried.

"When I was young our family often came here for picnics. We had no car then so we all used to clamber on the train, ride to Box Hill and walk from the station. Then we had to climb all the way up the side of the hill to get here. It was a real adventure and a wonderful day out. In later years your Dad and I used to drive up here."

Meanwhile Toby had spotted something of interest. A large coin-operated telescope. He swiftly borrowed all Cassie's loose change to look through it towards Dorking, Reigate, Leith Hill and the various other local landmarks his mother had pointed out.

"This is wicked! Did I hear you say earlier that we might see Brighton through here?"

"Yes, on a very clear day, you can just about make out the sea if you look in the right direction," Cassie explained while pointing. "Somewhere over there."

"Wow! This must be a really good telescope. So I should be able to see the 'Rialto' easily? That's ever such a tall building."

Ben and his mother spluttered with laughter.

"I never meant you would be able to make out the sea at Brighton in *Australia*. I meant Brighton in *England*."

"Oh, I'm not putting any more of my money in that old thing then," Toby exclaimed. "I would rather find somewhere that sells ice cream."

"What do you mean *your* money? Come on you little tightwad," Cassie said chuckling. "I'll take you where *you* can buy *all three of us* an ice cream."

It was evening by the time Cassie finally drove the car around the back alley to the garage. During their meal the boys told Nan and Grandad about their drive and what their Mum had shown them. Then, while the three adults got into a talk about the old drama club, the boys sloped away and whizzed off back to the loft.

"If we are quick we might get that train ride yet," said Ben. After switching on the lights above the train layout, they chose their grandfather's biggest engine and hooked a carriage on to the back of it. Ben checked the tracks and altered some of the points to ensure that if the idea worked out, they would get a good long interesting ride.

The two of them then held hands and Ben stared into the mirror. Instantly they were standing next to a very real looking engine and carriage on standby. But it was soon obvious to the boys that this grand idea was not going to work. Even though they were now only about four and five centimetres tall, they were still much too big to be able to get aboard it.

"Oh well," Toby sighed. "It seemed a good idea at the time, I was quite looking forward to it."

"So was I," said Ben. "We can still have some fun though, being tiny. In fact" he said looking down at the mirror in his hand. "I wonder-"

"What's that?"

"Well, although we have become small, so has the mirror. What is there to stop us using it again to become even smaller? If we can do that we might get our train ride yet."

"I don't know, we might disappear altogether?"

"No I am sure we'll be okay. No matter how small we become, the mirror will still remain the same relative size to us, so we should be able to use it to return as usual."

"If you *say* so, Prof but I sure hope you're right."

Once again although a little more nervously, the brothers held hands while Ben stared into the mirror for the second time.

The train engine and carriage were suddenly life-size.

"This shrinking seems very strange," said Ben.

"But I never felt anything happening to me at all," exclaimed Toby, "and it worked!"

"No that's exactly it, neither did I. It's as if everything got bigger rather than us getting smaller. It really is a weird sensation."

On looking round, the boys could have been standing on the platform of a real station. They climbed aboard the engine ready for some fun but then were forced to acknowledge the awful truth, the train was not about to go anywhere after all. All the controls that operated the engines were in the control area now some distance away, and were all full-size. The boys had no means of starting or running the engines whilst aboard the train.

"I somehow knew it was all going too well for us," Ben sighed.

"Hold up what's that strange noise? Listen."

There was an awfully loud growling noise which seemed to make everything vibrate and appeared to be getting louder all the time.

"What on earth? Oh no I think it might be Mum calling for us. It's because we are so small, I expect. Quick Toby give me your hand. No hold up again! We have to get out of this engine first or something is going to get damaged when we get big again. It could be us!"

The boys clambered out as fast as they could and grabbed each other's hands again. Ben performed a very rapid double eye-roll in the mirror and Toby kissed the stone.

"Yes Mum?" He called out quickly.

"Come along you two it's your bedtime. Why do you have to make me come all the way up the stairs before you answer me?"

"Sorry Mum, we never heard you. It must have been the noise of the trains running. We're coming. We just have to switch everything off."

"We've had a good week so far, what with invisibility, sailing our new boat, seeing Great-Nanny Flo, managing to get our alarm fixed up *and* getting out with Mum to Box Hill and everything," said Ben climbing into his bed. "Pity we never got our train ride though. Maybe if we"- then he realised he was talking to himself. Toby was already fast asleep.

Not quite ready for sleep himself, Ben picked up the small handmade book about his great grandmother's life and began to read.

··· ··· ···

Chapter Nineteen

Peaceful dreams came to an abrupt end the next morning, firstly by the noise of the bedroom curtains being pulled and then the wake-up call.

"Come on you two, time to get up," said their Mum. "It's a beautiful day and we are going into town early to have a look around. Nanny and Grandad have to go out on their own today as they are visiting an old friend who is not well. They have offered to drop us off in the High Street at ten o'clock and will hope to pick us up at around three on their way back. We will take a few sandwiches with us and once we have had a good look around the shops, we can go and find the park your Grandad has told me about. What do you think?"

"The park and the sandwiches sound good, Mum."

"Yep, perhaps give the shops a miss though, eh Ben?"

"Oh you two, what are you like? Come on, just get on with it," she said, chuckling as she pulled the bed-covers off them both. "Oh by the way, your Grandad *also* said there is a small stream running through that park. He thought you might take your new boat with you"

"Oh now you're talking, yes that would be good. Oh Mum, I'd best pop up into the loft quickly first. I just want to make sure we left everything tidy up there last night."

"Honestly you and that loft. I think I shall have to ask your Dad if we can move to a house with a loft so you can play in your own."

"Now that sounds a really cool idea," Toby murmured thoughtfully.

"Is it okay then, Mum?"

"Yes of course. You must always make sure it's left tidy. It's good of him to let you spend so much time up there."

"Yes it is, Mum."

"Don't be too long about it though, Nan and Grandad have to be out soon and we mustn't keep them waiting."

"This is all so different from the last time I was here" she remarked as they entered the shopping centre. "They had just started building this then but look at it now, it's fantastic! Lots of good shops and all under cover, I love it."

"Can we have a look in that music shop? I would like to see if they have any of our Aussie hits on the go?"

"Of course I'll take a look myself."

"Oh great, they have games in here too. Look, Ben, Play Station, Gameboy, Nintendo, they are all here."

"Cool. I wonder if they have games *we* don't." He leaned close to Toby and whispered, "There's one thing for sure, they won't have anything so good as we have, our Sandy!"

They spent quite some time browsing through audio titles and various game listings. But even though sorely tempted by some of their finds, it was decided they would be better buying them once they were home.

Other than when Cassie looked around a couple of the fashion shops, the boys were fairly happy with the shopping experience, especially the glass fronted lifts which glided up and down between the various floors. One of the supermarket stores had a huge sandwich and rolls showcase, which of course reminded them of their own food they had been carrying.

"Perhaps it's time to go and find that park we were told about," suggested Cassie.

"Good idea, Mum, I'm more than ready for our picnic.

"Me too," agreed Toby. "I'm starving! I expect it's because we've seen so much food around."

"Okay you win. Let's go find it."

"Why did you call it Grandad's Park, Mum?"

"Apparently it was the park he played in when he was a boy. He and his friends lived nearby and had their own shortcut to it through a ditch at the back of their house. They had some real good times there from the sound of it. He said for us to go to the top of the High Street and follow the road leading under the bridge. The entrance to the park is apparently on the right at the start of the hill."

It took them just a few minutes to get to the park and a couple more to find the enclosed play area. The two boys immediately started off in the direction of the slides but were soon called back by Cassie.

"Hey hold on you two, I seem to remember you saying you were starving. So, before you go, I suggest we eat this food I've been carting around with me all morning. We can sit on that bench over there. I made sure to bring a book with me, so after we have eaten you can go and play to your heart's content while I enjoy a read. But when you do, take care, okay?"

"Okay," the boys chorused. "We'll be fine, honest."

Once they had seen off their food the boys announced, "Let's go and have a slide or a swing or two, then we'll try and find the stream Grandad told Mum about."

"How long do you reckon we've been away from Nan's house?" Ben asked, as they neared the play area.

"Nearly two hours I suppose. Why?"

"While I was in the loft this morning I made sure to start Sandy, but he may have run out of sand by now if we've been out for that length of time."

"Neat idea, but he's too far away now to find out," Toby replied looking puzzled.

"We can easily find out if he's still running," Ben said. "But we'd best be seen playing first, as Mum is bound to keep an eye on us for a little while."

As soon as they had spent a few minutes in the play area, they went to look for the stream. Sure enough, it wound its way all along the park edge between the tree line and the park perimeter fence. Ben stopped as soon as they were out of sight of their mother.

"Okay, I'll leave you on your own for a short time. What I'm hoping to do is to go back and refill Sandy. Of course, if he *has* stopped, I won't be going anywhere."

"Ah now I can see what you meant, but it's a bit risky. If Mum should come over here to see what we're up to and you're not here, what then?"

"I'll have a look and make sure she is still reading. If she is, then with the speed of this magic travel of ours I should be back by the time she could walk over here anyway."

"I don't know. It was quick before, but that was only to and from the park near the house"

"Yes that's true I suppose but"-- he glanced across at where their Mum was still sitting, "I'll risk it anyway." He kissed the stone slab and disappeared.

"That's amazing, Sandy still running after all that time. Ben tweaking the sand valve that time to slow Sandy seems to have worked." Toby suddenly realised he was talking to himself and quickly checked again to see if his mother was still reading. "Come on, Ben, please don't be away too long," he worriedly muttered

147

to himself. He tried to stop thinking about the time ticking away by busying himself getting the boat from the carrier bag. He sat down with the boat and started to straighten out a crease in it that had been caused by the journey to the park, then jumped violently when a voice right next to him exclaimed, "There, that didn't take long did it?"

Ben was back and grinning. "I was there just in time, as the sand pot was almost empty. So in future, we do at least know we have around two hours running time on a full pot."

Toby immediately extracted his notebook and pencil from his pocket and faithfully scribbled in this latest piece of information.

"I put the full pot up quickly, started him again and then locked him in the chest with the alarm re-set. That works really well by the way. I went down to the bathroom for a pee while I was there and forgot all about the alarm. Of course the minute I stepped on the ladder, the mousetrap went bang and Sandy stopped. I jumped so much I nearly fell off. Then of course I had to reset it all again."

"You were hardly any time at all, Ben, amazingly. What worried me the most was which park Sandy might decide to send you back to?

"Yes I must admit I worried about that too, so I cheated a little."

"How do mean cheated?"

"I asked to be taken back to the park I had just left and it worked. It's all well worth knowing."

"Great, then let's go sailing. Here's the boat. I was getting her ready when you came back. Do you think we ought to name her before the launch?"

"Yes, good idea but what shall we call her? With the big funnel we put on her, she looks a bit like the

Titanic. But we won't call her that because the Titanic sank on its maiden voyage and we don't want to tempt fate. We ought to use a name from our own country really. Come on Brains, any ideas?"

"How about we call her, 'The Dingo', or 'The Roo'? No, better still, how about 'The River Boat?"

"Yes I like that idea. Perhaps we could name her after our own local river in Melbourne and call her 'The Yarrow River Boat'?"

"Cool! I'll write it on her side now with the pencil."

"Okay, providing she doesn't sink or anything on her first trial, we'll borrow that silver nail-varnish again when we get home and paint her name on properly."

The stream was more than a metre wide and looked to be ten to twenty centimetres deep at the most. The banks varied along the stretch nearest them but were mostly well above the water level. The boys found a shallow spot and launched their little boat with a gentle push. She floated beautifully, then gradually turned into the current and began moving off downstream while the boys walked the grass alongside her admiring their work. Then they found they had to trot to keep up with her as she gathered speed over the length of the park.

"She sails good," exclaimed Toby. "It must be wonderful to own a *real* boat."

"I'll bet," replied Ben. "I'll catch her now and bring her out. The bank is beginning to get a bit wild with stinging nettles and stuff up front and we may have trouble getting at her otherwise."

Ben ran ahead and quickly dropped down on the bank, then with out-stretched arms over the water managed to grab the little boat as she was about to sail past.

"Got you," he said as he scrambled to his feet again. "Now," he said as they walked back to the launch site,

"The reason I went back to Sandy was to make sure we would have enough time to try a real adventure. You were just saying how it would be great to own a boat. We do! 'The Yarrow River Boat'. If we use the mirror and shrink twice as we did the other day, our boat will seem as big as the real thing. We should be able to sail the entire length of the park on her, which at our shrunken size will seem like miles."

"But she's only made from paper? What about our weight on her?"

"I'm sure she'll be fine. Once we have shrunk to that size we are not going to weigh much anyway."

"I don't think we'll need to worry about Mum, by the way," Toby said. "She has obviously nodded off, her book is lying on the grass."

The boys put the boat back in the stream where the bank sloped gently down to the waters' edge and carefully wedged the stern in the mud to stop the current from moving her until they were ready.

"That should stay firm until we're both aboard," Ben calculated. "Then, if we walk towards the bow our combined weight should lift the back end out of the mud and free her."

"That sounds a good plan, Prof, but once we've shrunk, will we be able to get across the gap and on to her?"

"Mmm. Just as well you thought of that, Toby. That *is* going to be difficult."

After mulling over the problem the boys had a search around the path area nearby and found some discarded ice-lolly sticks. One of these they put on deck while the other was very carefully placed across the gap between the bank and the stern of the boat.

"*Now* we're ready to go," Ben said. "Have another quick look at Mum while I check the footpath for anyone else who might be heading in our direction."

"All is well," Toby duly reported.

While holding hands they instantly shrank. Ben stared into the mirror a second time and the world around them became immense. Carefully tucking the mirror and pouch in his pocket he turned to face the stream to find the huge 'Yarrow River Boat' rocking gently on the small lapping waves of a big river.

"Wow." Ben exclaimed. "That's impressive."

"Did we *really* make that, it's wicked," Toby gasped standing by his side admiring it.

"Your paint-work looks good, Toby and that lolly stick really looks the part."

The former stick they had placed between the bank and the boat was now the size of a real boarding plank.

"Time to go. Let's sail."

Toby was a little slow to answer. "Sorry, Ben, I'm beginning to have that strange feeling of danger again. I expect it's just the worry about walking across that plank. It doesn't look very safe to me."

"It's probably your dislike for heights. I'll go first if you like," Ben stepped on to the plank and tested it for give. It moved slightly as it settled into the grass but it was fine and he calmly walked across it and on to the boat. "I'll just test the deck as I'm a little curious *myself* to see how firm this paper is going to be?" He stepped out across it then cautiously jumped up and down on it a few times. "It's good," he cried happily. "You'll find it hard to tell the difference between this and the real thing. Come on over, Toby".

As he turned to encourage his brother across the plank, Ben's life seemed to freeze in shock and sheer disbelief. As if from nowhere a huge monstrous, black creature was silently moving up behind Toby almost overshadowing him. Moving on a number of legs but with the bulk of its body upright the creature was absolutely hideous. Two long antennae sprouted from above a massive blob of independently working eyes on its head which seemed mostly directed at the small boy, whilst a dark cavernous hole below its eyes that could loosely be described as a mouth was slobbering with saliva as if looking forward to a tasty meal.

Unknowingly, Toby was standing there nervously contemplating crossing the plank as the monster drew nearer. Horrific claws began to protrude at the ends of long tentacles which grew bizarrely from the lower side of its head and from around its huge belly and these began to stretch out for him.

Ben suddenly found his voice and screamed, "Toby! Look straight in front of you and get over here—*now*!"

Whether it was the shock of Ben's unexpected harsh order or just that he had finally made his mind up to cross the plank and get it over with as quickly as possible, Ben never found out. Whatever it was, Toby literally ran across the plank as if it was an everyday occurrence. If he had as much as glanced around behind him at that stage, things may have ended up very differently.

However, as he was stepping from the plank on to the boat he felt it wobble and automatically turned to see what was happening. His exultant expression instantly changed to extreme horror as he saw the huge creature first-footing the plank.

"Aaarghh! What the hell is that?"

By now the monster had begun to squeal excitedly as it thought it had its victim cornered.

"Quick," Ben shouted urgently. "We have to dislodge the plank or else we're in trouble."

Toby, still in shock, seemed unable to move. "That evil laughter again," he cried as if in a daze.

"Toby," Ben screamed out again. "Don't listen to it. You have to help, I can't move this on my own."

Luckily, Toby snapped out of it and quickly got a hold on his side of the plank. But by now the loudly squealing horror had moved completely onto the bank end of the plank and no matter how they struggled to move it, the weight was too much for them. The creature was waving its claws about in the air as it slowly started to move along the plank towards the deck, its eyes focussed directly on the boys.

"Toby get to the back of the boat-- Now!"

They dashed either side of the funnel to the stern. "Now hang on to the back and jump at the same time as me. Jump! And again, jump!"

At the second jump together, the boat began to rock in the water. The next jump made the boat rock so violently that she gradually slithered from the mud-shelf. The gang-plank together with its huge gruesome passenger gradually tipped at an angle until it eventually slid from the bow of the boat flinging the screaming creature into the river. Although it still had a hold on the plank with some its claws, it was caught by the current and swiftly swept downstream.

"Yes-s, result!" The loud exuberant cheers of the brothers overwhelmed the screams and squeals from the creature as it gradually diminished into the distance.

Still quivering with fright, Toby gasped, "That thing was grotesque! What the hell do you think it was?"

"I have no idea," Ben admitted. "It was like something alien, absolutely horrific." Then not wishing to further frighten his brother he added, "But at our present size I suppose it may have just been an ant or something as small as that. Nevertheless, we were lucky to get rid of it. It proves how careful we'll have to be from now on while we are in shrink-size."

He had been about to say how amazing he thought Toby's danger warning sense had been again, but thought he had best not risk raising the worrying subject of the evil laughter.

In the meantime, now free of the mud, the boat headed towards the middle of the river and then gradually turning with the current began to travel slowly downstream. The sheer joy of being on their boat, on the river, and now on the move, soon overcame all their recent frights and fear as their excitement grew for this new found adventure.

"How do we steer her?"

"I don't think we'll have to. We can let the current take us. But perhaps we ought to grab one of those oars each, just in case we have to push ourselves away from the bank or anything."

Ben experimented with one of the oars slipped over the stern of the boat and after a little practice found he could influence the general direction of travel from one bank towards the other.

"This is amazing. We know this stream is only small, yet at this size it seems huge. I suppose we ought to try on those life belts we've made. You never know when we might need them."

Toby glanced at Ben. "Do you really think we will?"

"I doubt it, it's just that real sailors have life belts for safety don't they? So we may as well play the part."

Both boys put on a life belt and they placed one of the coiled string ropes nearby for extra safety.

"The river seems to run fairly straight ahead so we may as well sit back in comfort and enjoy the ride."

Sitting on the deck with their backs against the funnel they began to relish the gentle movement of the boat as it became one with the stream, slipping past the spangled splashes of sunlight and bright blue sky showing through the foliage on overhanging branches.

"This is just wonderful," Ben commented, stretching his legs out and getting comfortable.

"Look out," Toby screamed abruptly. "We're under attack," suddenly throwing himself flat to the deck closely followed by his brother.

A massive sparrow curious of this bright flashing scarlet object floating down the river, firstly dived toward the boat, then performed a low-level fly-over. The sheer draft of wind the bird created took their breath away for a second or two.

"Wow! That bird was enormous. It was like a 'Jumbo' coming in to land right over the top of us. I hope it won't decide on a return trip."

From then on, Toby kept a very wary eye on their surroundings. "You'll need to steer to the right soon as there is a big green rock ahead on our left."

Ben glanced in front and began to steer the boat off course to clear it. As they slid past the rock they both screamed when it suddenly moved and two enormous eyes opened and stared unblinkingly at them.

"Jeeze! It's a frog," Ben laughed much relieved. "I don't know who was the most scared, us or him?"

As the laughter subsided the boat suddenly slowed, swinging abruptly to one side before coming to a stop.

"What's happening? Have we run aground?" Ben ran to the side of the boat and peered over. A floating piece of wood struck the side of the boat with a bang as it drifted past, making the hairs on his neck bristle when he remembered their earlier escapade with the monster.

"No," Toby answered. "Our funnel seems to have been snagged by a long rope high across the river."

Looking up, Ben could see the rope stretching from bank to bank, its ends somehow fixed in amongst the trees.

"Why on earth would anyone-?" As Ben began to ask he saw a dark movement in the trees on the far bank and realisation quickly set in. "It's part of a spider's web," he shouted. "Hurry, Toby, bring your oar. We'd best get free of this as quickly as possible in case it should think it has caught something tasty."

The boys had barely positioned their oars on the funnel close to the web rope when they saw its length over the river begin to tremble. They hastily began to try and push the web up towards the top of the funnel.

"It's coming," Toby shouted with a new terrified urgency as he saw the spider's legs beginning to emerge from the tree foliage and on to its web.

"We'll have to push harder," Ben answered. "The web is sticking fast to the funnel."

With a concentrated effort they eventually managed to slide the web over the top of the funnel and release it, but not before the huge spider had begun a rapid scrabble along its web at high speed with its eyes glistening expectantly.

Now freed, the boat began to veer around back on course as the current caught her and together with some desperate mighty oar strokes from the boys she leaped away from beneath the rope leaving the spider vainly reaching out with long scary legs.

"Phew! That was a close one," Ben said.

Now moving back towards the front of the boat, Toby said "Oh Ben, look at these," pointing ahead.

They were nearing the massive bank full of nettles they had seen earlier when recovering their boat.

"Strewth!" Ben replied. "Now I can see why getting brushed by stinging nettles is so damn painful. They are absolutely covered with needle-like spears."

"Yes, but no," Toby said, pointing again, "*Those* are what I meant."

At the far end of the nettles were twenty or more beautiful Peacock butterflies, gently fluttering their wings while basking in the sun.

"Wow! They are beautiful, just look at those colours. Their wings are probably taller than we are at present. Granddad was only telling me the other day that several kinds of our best butterflies including these and Red Admirals lay their eggs on nettles for protection, so that grazing animals don't destroy them."

A few of the butterflies decided the boat was a very attractive colour and flew closer to investigate, but seemed to lose interest in it once they realised there was no beautiful scent or nectar to be found. Nevertheless the boys were treated to an extremely wonderful air show as the beautiful creatures flew past the boat. Toby was absolutely fascinated with them.

"Do you know I've always thought their fluttering looked so light and easy," he said staring at them thoughtfully. "But seeing anything when at this size puts a new slant on life. They really have to work hard to fly at all and seem to drop the second they stop flapping their wings. I suppose they are not able to glide as birds do, which makes their flight always look so erratic."

Before long the river started to get wider and Ben could see they were nearing the bottom end of the park.

"Get the oars ready and we'll try and steer her into the bank."

They moved the oars and ropes to the stern. Ben lashed one of the ropes to the funnel and placed the remainder of the coil on the starboard deck of the vessel ready for mooring. Then they both manned an oar each and attempted to steer the boat in towards the bank. With some effort the boat came out of the main flow and gradually began to slow, but they were heading towards a huge rock directly in front of them. They desperately tried to steer back out again but were a little too late. Managing to clear the rock with the bow, the stern end clipped the rock hard causing Toby to catapult headlong into the river.

"No-oo," Ben shrieked. He grabbed up the tethered rope and stared into the water desperately searching for his little brother. Just as he feared the worst a small figure wearing a scarlet lifebelt and a face coloured to match it, popped out of the deep like a champagne cork, coughing and spluttering. The boat had now entered a small whirlpool of water formed by the current as it hit the rock and she turned off-course almost around the bobbing figure of Toby. Ben whirled the loose end of the rope above his head and threw with all his might. To his extreme credit or most likely sheer luck, the end of the rope snaked out and dropped in the water not far from his brother's shoulders. Toby saw the splash and after several stretching, gurgling attempts, managed to grab hold of it.

"Thank God for that," Ben muttered to himself with a huge sigh of relief.

But their problems were far from over. A long dark shape suddenly appeared in the water upstream. Moving towards Toby, it circled as if checking out this small moving thing that had appeared unexpectedly in its own private stretch of the river.

"Shark! Get me out of here," Toby screamed.

Ben wasted no time in answering or even wondering about it. He started hauling Toby in, hand over hand on the rope as fast as he could. The huge fish, on completing its appraisal of this brightly coloured object, broke surface slightly and flicked its tail to change direction. As it headed upstream again they both thought it had lost interest. But Ben's hope was short-lived and he redoubled his effort to bring Toby in as he watched the fish turning back in the direction of his brother.

"Toby! It's coming back towards you," he shouted. "Slap the water with the palms of your hands. Scream and make as much noise as you can."

It was pandemonium; Toby screaming and yelling as loudly as he could while slapping at the water surface, Ben also shouting and yelling whilst frantically attempting to haul his brother nearer the boat as the big fish gathered speed just a few metres away. Knowing he would not get Toby aboard before the fish achieved its target, he had to act fast. Dropping the rope and keeping a foot on it, he picked up the oar lying on the deck next to him. As soon as the fish was in striking distance, he lifted and swung the oar down hard at it. He completely missed the fish but he achieved the desired effect. The creature immediately swung round in an arc and disappeared off upstream.

Taking no chance of another attack, Ben instantly picked up the rope and resumed hauling Toby in. Following much effort, a small, very wet and slippery Toby was soon back aboard.

"Toby, are you okay?"

"Yep, I'm good—*now*," replied Toby, "Thanks for getting me away from that shark. He was enormous. I thought I was about to become fish food for a moment."

"It was your rope that saved you. I tied it to the funnel and luckily you'd made a good job of fixing that with glue. I'm proud of you."

The next second there was an enormous jarring thud which all but threw *both* boys overboard. Now completely out of control, the boat had rammed straight into the bank.

"Quick, Toby, if you have your breath back, let's go. This might be our chance to get off."

The boys dashed to the side of the boat and after a very quick glance threw themselves off. They landed safely on their backsides, but right in the middle of the mud on the side of the bank. With their weight gone from the boat, she slowly slithered from the mud bank and began to edge back toward the main current of the stream.

"Let's get out of here."

"I would but I can't move," exclaimed Toby, "This mud is like a swamp, my legs are stuck solid."

"Yeah, so are mine and it feels as if I'm slowly sinking in further. The only way out of this is the mirror—but I can't get my hand in my jacket pocket to get it –my arm is stuck too."

"Hang on, Ben, maybe I can reach your pocket. Yes, I think I've got it, here it is."

Abruptly two normal sized boys found themselves half-in the water and the mud bank. Struggling to get to their feet, they helped each other up on to the grass.

"Oh no just look at the state we are in. Hey, you have something scarlet in your hair? Here hold still while I take a look."

Ben pulled something out of Toby's hair. They both stared at it. "It's my life-belt," Toby cried and then slipped back into the mud giggling.

Ben was looking around at the stream. "Where's the boat gone? Oh look, there she goes."

The now tiny paper boat was beginning to speed up with the current.

"Quick let's go and grab it. We can't lose it now."

The two filthy muddy boys ran along the bank of the ditch constantly slipping, sliding and falling over each other amongst peals of laughter in the process of retrieving their beloved boat.

They had finally sat on the grass between the bank and the ditch to recover their breath and were checking the boat over for damage when their *real* trouble began. This time with no sensed warning signs of danger, from Toby, their mother had arrived at the scene.

She stared completely speechless but only for a second or two. "It *is* you!" she shouted in slow recognition. "What in hell's name have you both been doing? You are absolutely filthy and I just heard you laughing about it. I thought you were old enough by now to play on your own without getting into such a damned awful mess." She stopped for a brief second to draw breath, "Your Grandad won't want you in his car in that state and I don't blame him. We can't inflict the bus company with it either, we'll have to *walk* home. You can be expected to be grounded and don't even ask for how long. No, I want no excuses either. I shall have to put all your clothes through Nanny's washing machine. My God, I am so annoyed with the pair of you!"

··· ··· ···

Chapter Twenty

Although the boys had thoroughly enjoyed their time on the riverboat, the adventure had to remain a secret, so they had no explanations to offer for their seemingly terrible behaviour, or the mess they had got themselves into as a result. Their mother, still mad at them for being so irresponsible had enforced her 'grounding' rule, whereby they had to be somewhere within her sight for an unspecified period of time, which meant that even the loft was placed out of bounds for the time being.

For the first day the boys had to pass their time reading, watching television and making general conversation. Luckily the repercussions of the event began to fade and the family were soon again enjoying each other's company with trips out to the coast, castles and cinemas and to see relatives and friends.

One such day the family decided to take a walk into the neighbouring village. Cassie especially wanted to do this as it was something she had not done in many years.

Walking down the hill their Nan pointed out the Veterinary Surgery where Biggles was taken if ever he had any problems.

"Does he like it there?" Toby asked.

"It's more a case of him *having* to like it," answered Nan. "He's usually much happier though when he's safely on his way home. I don't know *why*, as the vets are really good and very kind to both animals and their owners. Nevertheless it is funny to watch their antics on arrival at times. Once the animals recognise where they are they seem to pretend they have lost the use of their legs. We have often seen people having to *carry* their dogs in, not always the small ones either."

"Do you have any trouble getting Biggles in?"

"Providing we manage to keep it a secret from him we are usually alright," his grandfather told him. "I get his cage in from the garage and open it out of his sight in our hall. Then I pick him up, make a big fuss of him and plonk him in quick and shut the lid before he gets to know what's happening."

"Does he behave himself once he's in the clinic?"

"Oh yes," said Nan. "He's nearly always on his best behaviour, very meek and mild. The funniest part is that as much as he hates that cage and being in it, the second he knows the vet has finished his check-up he can't wait to jump back into it."

The footpath the family used, generally followed an old millstream that made its way through the village. At one point their grandfather led the boys on a slight detour past the old mill there, while explaining that it had been in use to make gunpowder during the late 1700's. The two boys showed great interest in this until they were told it had since been converted into an office block.

As the rest of the family had gone ahead, Ben said, "Grandad, while you are talking of things from earlier times, can I ask you something about Sandy?"

"What was it you wanted to know Ben?"

"Well, as Sandy was made almost entirely from wood all that time ago and has no metal bearings in place as there would be these days, it just seems impossible that his moving points haven't worn away How can that be?"

"You are perfectly right. A machine like that would probably have stopped working centuries ago except for the fact that wood being a living tissue can absorb the power of magic as a protection from wear. Some types of wood are better than others and you can be assured Sandy's inventor would have chosen the best. That's why the machine keeps as new."

"Oh, that's brilliant, but there is still something else that bugs me. Surely the written language used in the riddles doesn't reflect the believed age of the machine?"

His grandad chuckled. "I'm pleased to see you are putting a lot of thought into this, Ben. You are right once again. You see in some respects, Sandy is not unlike a computer and has to be updated for the new generations of children who might use him. I have never seen the *original* words used in the riddles as they were changed *long* before my time, but the guardians *are* responsible for various changes now and then in order to ensure that children having access to the machine over the years will have every chance of understanding its messages. Obviously the guardian that has to make such an important change has to be well experienced in the ways of magic."

Toby by now was beside himself with impatience to ask a question. "Have you had to make many changes to Sandy yourself, Grandad?"

"Fortunately no. So far the only similar task I've had was to point out to you that the old torch fixings that had once been on Sandy had burnt away, but could easily be replaced by using a battery torch. You might both be interested to learn however, that the riddle wording was last changed by my great grandfather."

"Wow!" Toby stood very still for several seconds thinking about this and counting out something on his fingers. "Cool. So our great, great, great, great-grandfather must have been a wizard," he asked excitedly.

"In that respect I can only say that anyone constantly using a machine of *any* kind is likely to become something of an expert. For instance, I am sure both of you far exceed me in the knowledge of computers. But while we might refer to you as 'Whiz-kids', I doubt if we would call you wizards, not just yet at any rate."

"I rather like that," Toby said with a chuckle, "Whiz-kids--wizards."

Their grandfather seemed about to say more but then paused before saying, "We had best get back to our earlier conversation now as I can sense the others are just around the corner waiting for us."

Surprisingly, the rest of the family *were* indeed waiting for them just around the corner, waiting to cross at the roadside. The footpath the other side of the road led to the biggest of the lakes in the village which had its own island serving as a small nature reserve for the wild fowl that frequented it. Swans, Canadian geese, Grebe, Moorhens and ducks of various breeds and origins all existed side by side there and enjoyed being fed by visitors to the park.

"The birds love it here," their grandad told them. "As the various connecting lakes here are close together, some of the birds obviously like to visit the other waters. The Canadian Geese, possibly because of their size and the amount of obstructions such as trees and lamp-posts on route in their flight-path, seem to prefer to *walk* the short distance involved. Now and then one particular old chap will act like a school lollipop lady and hold up the traffic to allow his family to cross safely to the other lake. He made the front page of the local newspaper on one occasion."

"I'd love to see that. Do you think he'll do it today?"

"It's unlikely, Toby. But you could be lucky."

"Grandad," Ben asked. "If the stream we walked along connects the lakes, where does all the water come from in the first place?"

"I've been told the stream stems from an underground spring."

"So what exactly *is* a spring?" Ben asked, showing a keen interest.

"You've really dug yourself a big hole now, Tom," Maggie said with a laugh.

"I have indeed," he said with a chuckle. "I am not a geologist as you hope to be one day, Ben, so you will likely come back in a year or two and put me to rights, but I'll explain as best I can.

To begin with," he said, "those big hills nearby that we walked across the other day consist largely of chalk which is very absorbent. So instead of rivers running off the surface of the hills as in most other places, the bulk of our rainwater soaks through the chalk. Once the water reaches a foundation layer of rock, it will form an underground well or stream until it breaks out onto the surface somewhere at a lower level.

I can remember my Dad as a fireman telling me about an underground stream that used to flow beneath the cinema we used when we were young. Sometimes such an underground stream will eventually reach a low or weak spot in the clay or rock layer above and with the pressure of the water, will pop up above ground level forming a spring. Most times it will just gurgle out of a hole in the ground, or perhaps underwater in a lake like this. If the pressure is high, say after a heavy rainfall, and the hole or crack in the rock is only small, it can even produce a fountain."

Cassie gave him a clap. "I think you scored eleven out of ten there, Tom."

"Thank you Cassie. Now as I said, Ben, that's only *my* version of what happens. If you are really interested then you should look it up. Never be afraid of questioning anything you are told, or anything you may read. There is so much more scientific equipment to hand in our modern world that sometimes things that have been established for many years are overturned by new research."

"Thanks Grandad," said Ben, readily absorbing this information.

"Perhaps that's the spring, that huge fountain," Toby said, pointing towards the lake.

"Ah, there may well have been one similar to that a long, long time ago but these days, a lot of the underground water is pumped away for use by our much larger towns and populations," their grandfather explained. "I believe they balance it out now, so that we still have the lakes and the streams, but the fountain you are looking at is probably power-pumped simply for attraction."

Following a brief interesting tour of the local museum and a walk around the centre of the lovely old village, they headed for the small cafe recently installed opposite the post-office. This had become quite a popular local stopping place with its seats out in the sun Parisian-style on the broad pavement. After a brief respite with sandwiches and a well-deserved glass of lemonade they took a steady walk home.

"Time for a nice cup of tea now I think," Cassie suggested, filling the kettle.

"The best idea yet," her stepfather agreed.

The boys both thanked their grandparents for the village tour and said how much they'd enjoyed it.

"I would like to have another look at the museum sometime if we get the chance," remarked Ben. "There is some really interesting stuff in there."

"Alright, we'll have to see what we can do," Nan said.

Ben then stretched to full height saying, "My legs are tired. I'm going up to the bedroom to read some more of Grandad's comics. Are you coming up, Toby?"

"Yes, good idea, I'll join you."

The boy's legs miraculously seemed to lose their tiredness as they both chased up the stairs.

"Boys will be boys," laughed their Mum. "Don't you want to be with them, Tom?"

But Tom had not heard any of this. He had settled himself in the armchair with Biggles on his lap and the two of them had already dozed off.

··· ··· ···

Chapter Twenty-One

There was an unusually awkward silence between the boys in the bedroom as both attempted to read their comics. Toby finally broke it.

"Don't you want to go up in the loft anymore, Ben?"

"Yes sure I do, once we are allowed. But it wouldn't be the same without you."

"What do you mean without me?"

"Well after all the trouble we got into on the last adventure I didn't think you'd want to risk it again. After all, some of our adventures *have* been a bit dodgy. You could easily have drowned during the last one and that would have been my fault for getting you on the boat in the first place."

"Rubbish!"

"What?"

"I said rubbish. How do you know I don't want to do it again? And as for it being your fault that's complete nonsense." Toby pulled himself up to his full small height and stood with his hands on his hips. "Before you mention it, I can tell you I'd have bashed that shark right on the nose if it had got any nearer." Then looking slightly embarrassed on thinking about it, he added, "Even though at real size it was probably only a stickleback!"

Ben had to admire his little brother's show of nerve and honesty, but in truth felt very relieved. He had convinced himself that with the shock Toby had suffered and the trouble they had been in over the state of their clothes, especially as they couldn't properly explain it to anyone, he wouldn't want to know about any further adventures, *ever*.

"You really mean that don't you?" Ben said.

"Yep, you bet I do. Despite the trouble we got into, I loved that last adventure and I'm so glad we managed to get the boat back. I'm going to borrow Nanny's nail varnish again to paint the name on properly, then when we get back home it's going to sit on my bedroom shelf to remind us of our adventure sailing it."

"Oh Toby, that's great, it really is!"

"There's only one thing."

"What's that?"

"Would you answer me honestly if I ask you something?"

"Yes of course, ask away?"

"Well, do you-" He seemed to having trouble forming the question. "That evil laughter I heard. Do you perhaps think I imagined it or am going a bit mad?" he blurted out.

"Completely crazy, I've no doubt," Ben joked "But mad, absolutely not. You've proved beyond all doubt that you have an amazing ability to warn us of danger. Just because I don't have your gift of sixth sense and neither sensed nor heard anything strange, doesn't mean that you're going mad, Toby, far from it. Grandad once told us when he first introduced us to magic, that there is a reason for everything. The laughter you sometimes hear is probably *another* warning of some kind and there must be a reason for it. All we have to do is find out what it's about. We will, given time."

Toby looked very relieved. "Thanks Ben," he said. "Sandy is an awesome machine. I'm still having trouble believing the incredible things he's allowing us to do."

"You're right," Ben agreed. "I woke up last night thinking about that house fire. We still don't know how we got there to *start with* and there are so many other odd things about that adventure. We were there so long that the light was failing while we were in the tree and dark by the time we reached the fireman's house. Yet when we got back here to the loft it was still light outside."

"Yes it was come to think of it. Mum and the others got back from shopping just afterwards and I doubt if they'd been more than a couple of hours. How could that be?"

"I wish I knew. Come to think about it, how did we get back to the loft anyway? I don't remember any of that. I think I must have fallen asleep in the fireman's house?"

"I suppose I did too, although I do seem to remember the lady taking the pouch from around Luke's neck."

"Strewth! I never noticed he had it with him. So we could have used it when we were in the tree? Perhaps he brought it with him but had forgotten how to use it. Whoa, hang on a minute, it was around *my* neck when we got back to the loft and I never had it to start with? I guess the lady must have put it there. But how would she have known? This gets stranger and stranger. That reminds me of something else too. She knew our names and she seemed to know Luke as well. She said something really odd to him but I can't remember now what it was."

"I couldn't hear much above the crackling of their lovely fire from where I was sitting," Toby commented. "But I'm quite *glad* we never knew that Luke had the pouch in the tree with him."

"Why do you say that?"

"Well, we'd have been straight back to the loft without our ride in the fire engine and we would never have been rescued by the fireman *or* met his nice lady."

171

"Yes you're right. They were both lovely people. In fact it was all one terrific adventure, even if it was dangerous. Then what about Luke's age? He only seemed a little older than me when he rescued us. What on earth could have caused that? We must get to ask Luke soon what he remembers of it."

"Why don't we telephone him *now* and find out?" Toby asked.

"No. We would have to use Nan and Grandad's telephone. It might prove difficult to talk about it in front of them and in any case ringing America might cost them a lot of money. We had best leave it until we are back home in Melbourne, then we can have a long chat with him on our cheap phone package, or perhaps on Skype if he uses it?"

... ...

Chapter Twenty-Two

Do you think we'd be allowed to go over to the stream with the boat yet?" Toby queried.

"No. I think we'd better give that a miss for a little while yet," Ben answered, "or else we'll be back in Mum's bad books. But it has been a day or two since we were grounded, so perhaps we'll give it a try for the loft once tea is over."

They left it until tea had been cleared away before asking. Following a firm reminder that there were to be no repeats of their disgusting recent performances, they were then given the all-clear. It was not long before they had Sandy running and a train on the track as a cover.

"It's great to be allowed up here again even if it *is* early evening. I would like to see what a 'Four' might do for us but I think we'd best settle for a short outing this time. What would *you* like to do, Toby?"

"I'd like another look at the park we sailed in. That big slide there looked really good. That's if Sandy will take us there?"

Ben set the alarm, "Okay, we'll give it a go. Oh heck I never realised I'd got this in such a mess last time we used it," he said looking at the mirror and cleaning some of the mud from its surface with his fingers. "The same mud that got us into so much trouble before."

"Don't worry. I wasn't planning going anywhere near that. We'll stick to the path and the play-area this time."

"Just as well too. Remind me to give this mirror a good clean tomorrow in case Grandad should see it.

We're supposed to be keeping everything spick and span." He grabbed his brother's hand and looked down into the mirror.

"The path in the park where we sailed please," he asked and winked.

They were instantly standing on a path somewhere, but the light there was already beginning to fade.

"Here we go, something odd already. It was light outside when we went upstairs to the loft and that was only a few minutes ago."

Toby was busy looking along the side of the path in the poor light and testing with one of his feet. "The grass here feels very soft, we had best stick to the path as we don't dare take mud back on our boots tonight. We seem to be near the bottom corner of the park, I can just see the trees that surround the play area over there." The path turned either left or right a little way ahead. As they approached the junction they both suddenly stiffened as they became aware of a shadowy figure of a man standing in amongst the bushes to the left as if watching their approach.

"I don't like the look of him," Ben said quietly. "It might be a good thing we are not going in his direction. When we get to the bottom don't hesitate, just turn right and keep walking as if we haven't seen him. If he says anything ignore him and keep moving."

They reached the bottom corner and started walking up the path in the direction of the play area. The shrubs along the border were overgrown and making it very dark along the path in places. The boys had not gone far when they heard a strange noise just behind them.

"What's that," Toby whispered nervously.

"Don't look round, I think it's that bloke walking behind us. He seems to be wearing squeaky shoes."

"Oh God, is he following us?"

"I expect it's just coincidence, but we'll soon find out. Start walking a little faster."

As soon as they speeded up so did the noisy footsteps.

"Slow down a bit now." Once again the noises matched their pace. Following a second variation of their walking speed with a similar result, Toby was becoming very nervous and Ben was getting annoyed.

"Let's try something else. On the count of three stop dead, but be ready to run like hell towards the park should we need to. Ready? One, two, three!"

On stopping, there was an utter silence behind them. On looking round it was too dark along the shrub-lined path to see anyone, but they knew he was there somewhere as they could hear him breathing.

"I don't like this," Toby whispered. "He's really scaring me. What are we going to do now?"

"He's scaring me too, Toby, but I think it's time he had some of his *own* treatment. Give me your hand."

Ben quickly made them both invisible. "Now it's our turn to have some fun."

"But Ben we are supposed to keep this all a secret?"

"It will be okay. He's unlikely to tell anyone what he's about to see because he would have to explain what he was up to himself. Do you have the torch in your pocket?"

"Yep, here you go. I feel a lot safer now he can't see us. What do you have in mind?"

"You stay here and make a few weird howling noises, you're good at that. It will not only help but I shall know where you are. Give me about ten seconds first."

Toby waited and listened for a short time. The man was moving around a little as if wondering where they had gone. There was a sudden rustling noise and a startled gasp of alarm from the man as some of the bushes near him waved about as if alive. A beam of light appeared on high with no sign of a torch or of anyone holding it and began steering itself ever nearer the shadowy figure. The light went off for a few seconds and then on again and something white and fluttery appeared in it. As the thing fluttered down to the ground with the light following, it disappeared entirely. The light then went out again. The breathing sound seemed to abruptly stop as if the man was holding his breath. The bushes moved again and the light reappeared, spinning around until it was pointing directly into the man's eyes. He put his hand up in fear as if trying to ward off an evil spirit. This was the ideal cue for Toby. Making an unearthly howling noise he scuttled forward towards the man, purposely dragging his feet through the loose gravel and groaning horribly for maximum effect. The man's frightened eyes immediately swung in the direction of the noise. The light followed to show the gravel on the path moving as if something was heading fast in his direction, yet there was nothing visible to explain it.

It all proved too much. The man gave a terrified yell and crashing out through the bushes took flight. All the boys could hear was the frenzied squeaking of his shoes disappearing into the distance at high speed.

Their own fear now spent, the boys collapsed together in laughter.

"That was wicked. The moving bushes and light looked eerie enough but that white thing was really scary. How did you manage that?"

"I threw my handkerchief in the air and kept the torch shining on it as it fluttered down, then I picked it up from the path the second it landed so that it disappeared again. But what finally cracked him were those howls and groans you made. I turned the torch in your direction and that gravel shifting effect as you dragged your feet was so frightening you almost had *me* running off alongside him."

"We worked well together there, Ben"

"We sure did! Well, I suppose we'd best get off to the slides now or else it will be too dark to see what we're doing. We'll stay invisible until we get there."

They headed on towards the large trees they had seen from the bottom path but as they approached them, Ben began to see that all was not quite as they had expected.

"That looks more like a forest than the play area."

Toby was strangely silent.

"I'm beginning to wonder just where Sandy might have brought us."

There was still no answer.

"Toby? Where are you?"

On getting no reply Ben immediately used the mirror to regain their visibility. He could just make out Toby standing motionless in the gloom several metres back down the path and hurried back to him. "I'm sorry Toby, I didn't realise you had stopped. I was chatting away to you and it was only when you never answered"- he paused and asked, "are you okay?"

"Yes, except I'm having one of those things again. I can sense danger?"

"But it's all over now."

"No, strangely enough that didn't affect me like this. This is something else, *real* danger, and so close I can almost smell it."

He was interrupted by a loud unearthly squeal from somewhere amidst the trees ahead of them.

"Oh no! That sounded just like that monster thing from our boat adventure."

Peering through the gloom they could just make out a dark shape moving through the trees off to their left.

"Yes, it certainly sounded like it, but from what we can see of it, that has to be too big to be the same monster because we are not shrunk this time. Yet it did seem to have a similar effect on you. Let's be invisible again, so it won't be able to see us, then perhaps we can follow it and find out what it is and where it comes from."

With some reluctance Toby agreed. They quietly made their way over to the edge of the wood while making sure to keep the dark shape in sight but well ahead of them.

"It's heading out of the park towards that big gate over there. It seems to be dragging a big black bag full of something?"

"I don't remember seeing a gate there when we were here before? There seems to be a light the other side of it, yet I don't remember any houses being there either."

"Oh my God the gate is opening all by itself! I can see a little more now. The gate seems to lead directly into a tunnel?"

"Ben! It *is* that horrible thing again, it's just a lot bigger. I can see it more clearly now in the light of that entrance."

"Yes you're right. Oh hell! Look at that light. It's one of those old torches burning that Grandad told us they used long ago. Whatever is going on here?"

"Ben, it's that evil laughter again, it seems to be coming from inside the tunnel."

This time, Ben listened intently for a second or two, his own face beginning to show fear in the poor flickering light from the distant torch. Ben snapped his thoughts back to Toby and found him cringing and bent double with a white face and hands pressed over his ears. He decided his brother had had enough.

"Okay I know, hold on Toby." He pulled the stone from the pouch and kissed it.

Instantly they were back in the safe environment of the loft.

"It's alright, it's gone." He put a hand on his brother's shoulder. "We're back safe in the loft. Everything is alright now."

"Thanks, Ben. I'm so sorry. It was even louder this time."

"I know, I heard it too."

"You did?" His little face lit up with relief.

"Yes, I did, really," Ben nodded. "And I agree with you, it really *is* a horrible evil sound."

"I don't know what to say. I'm so sorry you had to hear it at all, yet I'm so glad you did. I really began to think I was going nuts."

"But I told you I believed you."

"I know but I thought you were just being kind."

"Silly sod, don't you remember, I said you were completely crazy."

They looked at each other and began to grin.

"That's more like it, "Ben said.

"So what on earth do you think caused all that," Toby asked. "Day became night and even the park seemed different. I'm afraid the monster and everything else was just too much for me. But now, knowing you heard it too, makes it seem much easier somehow."

"I don't know for sure but I'm wondering if some of that might have been my fault for not cleaning the mirror properly before I used it," Ben admitted. "I think the reflection may have been distorted because of the mud. I did only wipe it with my fingers. We were told we would find the reasons for keeping it all clean as we went along, but I never dreamed that the reason might turn out to be quite so ghastly. My fault I guess. I'm sorry bro'."

"No worries. I would have done just the same. At least we know not to go over that side of the park again, especially while it's dark."

"The trouble is we're not even sure that *was* the same park." Ben walked over to the loft entrance and looked down at the stairwell window. "It's still light outside even now," he said. "We obviously have a lot more to learn in the use of Sandy including finding out about that creature and the evil laughter too. I really don't think the monster part of it had anything to do with a dirty mirror because we had trouble with that before."

"Yeah fine, but not tonight thanks. I don't even want to talk about it or else I shall be having nightmares. Let's do something different."

"We don't have much time left now and I have to give the mirror a clean before we dare use it again. Throw a 'Four' if you like, so that we can see what that will bring us."

"Yes, let's do that, though I can't imagine what it might be. We can already wish to go to other places, become invisible, or shrink ourselves. What else can there possibly be?"

"If I could tell you I would, but Sandy never seems to fail in surprising us, does he?"

"You're right, he's wicked."

"Come on then, let's find out what the four does. Here, I'll let you throw the dice."

"Thanks, right here goes. It's a two. No, I'll throw again It's a one."

For once it was Ben who began making a show of looking at his watch.

"Okay," Toby said. "I'll have to *place* a four I guess. It might be a while before I manage to throw one."

He carefully laid the die down with the number four uppermost next to the plain one then took a step back to watch the stone slab react. Words gradually formed.

'Look through me up to the sky
Soon you shall be near as high
Look to me and make a frown
I shall see you safely down.'

Toby's face immediately brightened. "That sounds as if we are going to be able to fly."

"Exactly what I was thinking. That's awesome! We shall have to try it straightaway."

"Oh Heck! I guess it's down to me to say it this time then."

Ben looked up, "Pardon?"

"Dinosaurs!" His cheeky little face glowed in the poor light. "Shouldn't we clean the mirror first?"

"Oh geeps, well called! I was just about to use it again wasn't I? Okay, I think that's a good sign for us to pack in tonight and go downstairs. I think we've both probably had enough for one night anyway."

... ...

Chapter Twenty-Three

Another day passed before they had the chance to follow up on their latest clue. Holiday time took over in the morning with a day trip out to the New Forest, the boys thoroughly enjoying ball games and picnics amongst the trees and watching the groups of small wild ponies living there together with the occasional sighting of deer. Here and there they came across lizards sunning themselves on rocks and once recoiled at the sight of a snake disappearing rapidly as they approached a clearing. All in all they thoroughly revelled in their day out but although dropping into their beds with exhaustion when they got back that night, they still managed to get into the loft fairly early the following morning to experiment with their latest findings, despite there being another family outing booked for the afternoon.

Toby set the machine up and running while Ben gave the mirror and all the pouch contents a good clean. Then without a word to Toby he looked into the mirror past his own reflection and up to the inside of the loft roof. With a huge rush of disbelief and excitement he instantly found himself hovering, or floating like a weightless man in space at the top of the roof interior.

"Hey, how about this?"

"Wow Prof, that's wicked. What does it feel like being up there?"

"Really weird," gasped Ben. "Largely because there's nothing visible holding me up. I keep expecting to drop like a brick but so far so good. Keep clear in case I do fall, I'm going to see if I can manage to move about."

Toby thought it highly amusing when Ben first started waving his arms and legs about. He looked like some huge ungainly bird that had been placed in the air before being taught how to use its wings. At first he flapped his arms up and down but to little or no effect. Then he gave the appearance of a swimmer doing the breaststroke, but the progress achieved was nothing compared to the huge effort put in. After a time however, he did at least manage to turn himself completely around to head in the opposite direction.

"It's alright for you to laugh," Ben said between puffs of exertion. "You haven't tried it yet. It's not as easy as you might think. Watch out, I'm going to come down now and I don't know how this is going to work." Extremely worried he looked into the mirror again and creased his forehead into a frown. Immediately he began to gently float down to the loft floor, not unlike a big leaf in the autumn.

"Wow," he said on landing, still slightly breathless. "That descent was really something. I didn't know what to expect, but at least it didn't just drop me."

"That looked really wicked. I'm looking forward to having a go at that," Toby said excitedly.

"With practice we might even be able to fly," Ben said, "but I have my doubts. Here's the mirror if you want to have a go, then it'll be my turn for a laugh."

Toby was quickly up in the roof space and floating, but for some reason he was floating on his back and looking at the roof above him.

"Oh heck," he cried. "Whatever's going on?" He tried to turn himself over and found Ben was right. It was not as easy as he had expected.

Ben below, was already in stitches laughing at his little brothers' antics. Toby with his usual impatience was furious with himself because he was still the wrong way up. In desperation he grabbed hold of one of the roof joists that appeared to be getting in his way and gave it an enormous shove. The joist went nowhere of course, but Toby *did*. He not only shot backwards but turned over and over like a big propeller. He drifted the whole length of the loft still slowly turning the way a man in space might but luckily managing to slow and stop before crashing into the wall at the other end.

"Do it again," laughed Ben, "that was hilarious".

By now Toby had had enough and was trying his best to imitate a discarded feather fluttering down.

"That was horrible," he complained. "I was up the wrong way most of the time and couldn't see anything except the roof and I wasn't able do a thing about it. Why was that, Ben? *You* were the right way up."

"I don't know. We must have used the mirror at different angles I suppose. We'll need to experiment more. Maybe we'll find it easier *outside*, especially if we shrink first. I guess we'd probably need to be invisible as well."

"Oh wicked, three magical things at the same time. Can we do it now?"

"No, we won't risk upsetting the apple cart. We might be out there longer than intended and then Mum will be looking for us. We're supposed to be going out this afternoon. I guess our flight will have to wait until tomorrow."

"Okay tomorrow then," Toby agreed, but looking a little puzzled. "What was that you were you on about before, Ben? '*Upsetting the apple cart?*'"

"Sorry, it's an old saying that Grandad uses at times. In this instance it just means we shouldn't chance wrecking the peace with Mum yet."

"You English and your weird sayings," Toby said with a grin and a shrug.

When they came back from their outing that evening the boys were really excited at their morning flight prospect and they volunteered for an early night. Cassie was so surprised she felt their foreheads for high temperatures in case they were coming down with colds or something worse.

Partly because of their early night but largely due to excitement, the boys were up at the crack of dawn the following morning and could hardly get into the loft quick enough. Toby gathered the necessary items to take with them, while Ben saw to Sandy and carefully placed him running inside the chest again and locked. The morning appeared to be working out well for them as their Grandparents had driven off early to the nearest supermarket to do the weeks shopping whilst leaving their Mum busy catching up with the washing.

"I'm ready when you are, Ben".

"I'll be right with you."

"What are we going to do first, shrink or disappear?"

"As there's only Mum to get past, I suppose we could just shrink. But there is one problem with that. We won't know where Biggles might be this morning."

"Why are you worrying about Biggles?"

"Well he might be getting old, but I don't fancy having him thinking we're mice or something. He can still be pretty fast when he likes. A lot faster than us I'll bet, especially once we've shrunk."

"Oh, I never thought of him chasing us. Invisibility is a must then."

"I agree. So we'll- no, wait a minute, we're doing it again. We only have to speak the place and we'll *be* there. We won't have to worry about getting past Mum or Biggles. We'll still shrink first though, twice in fact, in case there is anyone in the park when we arrive. Oh and talking of mice reminds me. I haven't set the alarm yet and there is no way I'm going near *that* thing once I've shrunk."

He quickly set up the alarm.

"Ready, Toby?"

"Yep," said Toby grabbing his hand.

Ben stared into the mirror once and then again. The loft instantly became vast around them. "It's just as well we have decided to *wish* ourselves to the park. I don't think we could have managed the ladder *or* the stairs at this size," he said.

Then still holding Toby by the hand, he again looked at the mirror and asked, "The park at the bottom of the garden please," and winked at it. Instantly they found themselves amongst a dense thicket of very strange bright green trees unlike any they had ever seen before, having no barked trunks or branches and all of which were waving about alarmingly in the breeze.

"What on earth did you do, where are we?" gasped Toby. "We can't seem to get anything right anymore. Whatever has gone wrong this time?"

"I'm not sure," answered his brother. "I asked for the park, you must have heard me, but this is more like taking part in an animated film. Whatever *else* might be going on, at least I know our equipment is clean this time." He took a closer look at some of the trees. "Oh of course, these are not trees, it's grass. It's because we

186

are so tiny. Perhaps it's time we were invisible, there's no telling what creatures there may be in this lot."

"Not more of those weird monster things?" Toby asked and shuddered at the thought.

"If that *was* some kind of huge insect, then almost certainly, but I don't think we'll need to worry so long as they can't see us."

Ben fished around quickly and pulled something from his trouser pocket. "I've brought a long piece of Nan's thread with me today. At our present size it will make quite a useful rope. We'll both tie an end to our belts then we won't lose track of each other once we're invisible up there," he said pointing to the few clouds above them. "It will also mean less noise shouting to check each other's whereabouts. There's one good thing, we know that if I were to go back using the stone, you would come too from wherever you are, okay?"

"Yep, no worries, Ben."

After grabbing Toby by the hand, Ben immediately lifted the mirror and looked into it, blinked once and then again. As he opened his eye from the second blink, Toby had disappeared, then he realised *he* had too. It was so strange he thought, this going invisible thing. He always expected to *feel* it happen but never did. Then because you are looking out from yourself he thought, until you actually take a look down at your legs or at an arm, you don't realise you *are* invisible. It really was quite fantastic. He touched himself on the leg to make sure it was there, then felt a complete idiot for doing such a stupid thing. Toby was there too because he felt the string move, probably because he was checking *himself* out.

This was going to be a little nerve-wracking, the possibility of floating or flying in an unrestricted space for the first time ever, especially when shrunk and invisible. A whole new experience and one of the many since they had been introduced to the adventure machine. He began to marvel at all the things they *had* done recently but his thoughts were abruptly interrupted by a small voice nearby.

"Ben, are you there?"

"Yes I'm here, I was just thinking how cool this is."

"Yep, I agree. What do we do now?"

"Let's go for a float to start with and try and get the hang of that first. We'll have to be extremely careful because we don't have a roof above us to limit our movement this time, so anything might happen. But at least we won't be seen."

"Cor," Toby said, using his recently acquired 'comic' language. "Can you imagine the trouble it might cause if we *were* seen?"

"Yes. I expect they'd have the police or even the army out looking for aliens and UFO's."

"That could be great fun."

"Yes, it would for us but it could frighten the hell out of a lot of people. Our biggest worry though, would be having Sandy taken away from us if we were found out and we certainly don't want that to happen."

"No fear. Not now we're beginning to see what's possible when using him."

"Hey what are we doing? Here are we, invisible and about a centimetre tall in a strange grass forest and we're wasting time talking. Give me your hand again and let's go for it."

Ben lifted his other invisible hand wondering how he was to aim the two of them into the sky with an invisible mirror. But once again he need not have worried. The mirror was invisible but amazingly its reflective face was hovering in front of him where he knew he held it.

He angled the reflection high up into the sky. There was no sensation of speed or moving, they simply found themselves floating on their backs way above the park and the *real* trees and much higher than all the houses.

"Wowee," Ben shouted. "This is terrific, we can see for miles up here."

"Er yes," answered Toby nervously. "I've never been so high, especially with nothing underneath me to hold me up. As for seeing for miles, all I can see is down there and *that* really looks like miles. I don't like it a lot, Ben."

"Sorry Toby, I didn't know you were feeling that way. No worries, we'll go down again straightaway, and gently," he added hopefully as he heard his brother moan. "Like we did in the loft yesterday."

He frowned at the mirror reflection breathing a sigh of relief as his words proved to be true and they slowly began to lose height.

"Look there's Biggles in the back garden", said Ben, trying to ease his brother's fear.

"Oh yes I can see him. He's chasing something, a butterfly I think."

Toby temporarily forgot his altitude worries watching the old cat running around and performing huge leaps into the air. "It looks almost as if he is trying to be up here with *us*," he said. Very soon they landed amongst the grass again as lightly as a pair of leaves falling from a tree.

"There you go, that wasn't so bad was it?"

"No," admitted Toby. "Actually it was good. I think because I was the other way up in the loft yesterday I never got to see below me until today and then it was really frightening. Now I know how wicked it is on the way down I could go up again and enjoy it."

189

Ben looked at him in surprise. "You really want to go up again?"

"Yes really," answered Toby. "It was just my nerves more than anything."

"No worries, it's new to both of us I suppose. It's the same as going on one of those dangerous looking rides in an amusement park. Once you've braved it the first time you can't wait to have another go. Come on then, let's go."

But they suddenly froze in their tracks at a loud noise that sounded like a war zone opening up all around them. First there was an ear-drum shattering sound like a machine gun being fired, followed by a deafening air-rushing noise that ended with a ground shaking thump almost next to them.

"What the heck--?"

A chattering Magpie seeming to them as big as a double-decker bus, had swooped down out of the sky and landed after spotting something moving in the grass. The bird grabbed the exposed end of the worm and with its huge beak proceeded to pull it out of the turf. It was an awesome spectacle for the boys. The bird spread its feet well apart to steady itself, while it gradually raised its head and neck, slowly but surely extracting the worm inch by inch. The worm, fighting for its very life while being stretched almost to breaking point, still somehow managed to plump itself up in its hole in the ground to try and hold on and make a battle of it.

"That poor worm," was all that Toby said and not altogether loudly at that.

The Magpie immediately stopped pulling at the worm and its eyes swivelled round to stare in Toby's direction. Even though it could not see him, it had definitely heard him. It let the worm go and the worm gratefully slid back into its hole and disappeared as quickly as possible.

Luckily Toby had noticed he had alerted the bird and hardly dared breathe. The bird instantly knew there was something there in the long grass that might mean an even tastier meal than the relinquished worm. It stood very still gently cocking its head from side to side while listening intently, eyes checking every blade of grass, its huge yellow beak parted slightly as if ready to grab anything that moved. Ben stealthily put his hand down and got hold of the string he had tied to his belt. He pulled the string gently until it was almost taut, and then moved his other hand along it to find Toby. He all but let out a gasp of shock as his hand encountered something cold and clammy moving along the string towards him.

It was his brother's hand. Toby had apparently had a similar idea. Ben immediately grabbed a hold on it and began to bring the mirror up to his face. Right at that very instant however, the bird, still aware of something there it could not yet see, decided on a new strategy to flush it out into the open. It flapped its huge wings and jumped into the air about fifty centimetres high, then purposely came back to ground with another huge thump. The draught from the bird's wings coupled with the sway of the long grass it caused, completely felled the two boys, leaving them lying on their backs unable to move as the bird started a fresh search for its new interesting victim.

As they laid there desperately still, trying not to give their position away, the huge beak came closer and closer to one of Ben's feet. Ben had breathed in some dust when he fell over and could sense a sneeze coming on. He had to chance a quick movement to find his brother's hand again and as the bird lifted its head to look directly at him he eased the mirror up to his eyes and rapidly glanced at the reflection of the sky above them. Instantly they found themselves in the air much higher than they had been before, but safe from the Magpie.

Ben's sneeze duly arrived and the effect of it pushed him back through the air for some distance taking Toby along as well because of the rope between them.

"Wicked, now we have *powered* flight," Toby said while Ben was recovering. The two of them simply lay there thankfully in the air for a few minutes to get over the fright.

"Now I know how you felt when that shark nearly got you Toby."

"You're telling me. Thank goodness you had the mirror. If it hadn't been for that I'm sure that bird would have pulled us apart."

"Yes, but on the other hand I suppose, without the mirror we wouldn't have been there in the first place."

"True Ben, but life's a heck of a lot more interesting with it, even if it is scary sometimes. So don't ever think about leaving me out of it anymore because I'm really enjoying this, all of it. So what shall we do now?"

"Let's see if we can fly or at least move while we're up here?"

"Geeps, I'd got so comfortable I'd forgotten where we were. It's like lying on an invisible bed"

"No more worries about the height then?"

"Nope, no worries and I love using this all-clear vision up here."

"All-clear vision, oh you mean not seeing your nose or anything because we are invisible?"

"Yes that's it, scary to think about, but fantastic."

The boys, now in a much lighter mood, began waving their arms and found much to their surprise they were able to propel themselves through the air to some extent.

"This is wonderful. Perhaps with practice we could actually *fly*?"

"Wheeee," was all Toby said as he gave his arms a big pull and moved away until the rope between them almost took Ben with him. This convinced Ben their shrunken form must be the reason for their improved ease of movement. Seeing that the rope might hamper their varied flying techniques he quickly untied it, warning Toby to keep in contact now and then by calling out.

"As we're so small and high up I don't suppose anyone down there would hear us anyway."

The boys practised flying for the next fifteen minutes or so, trying to find the most effective method before pausing for a breather.

"Phew, I feel as if I have been practising for a channel swim," Ben said. "I must be well unfit. You know when you think about it the wizard or whoever he was that invented Sandy was really good. If he hadn't thought to return us to the loft when Sandy stopped we would really be in trouble if someone set off our alarm. The magic would stop and we would drop like stones."

"Thanks a lot, Ben. I *was* beginning to feel quite comfortable up here."

"Sorry Toby, I never meant to scare you. Let's go back now for a while. Thinking of our alarm I expect Mum will be checking us out before long. How do you want to do it? It's your call this time."

"I quite fancy being a leaf again, but I'd sooner not chance that Magpie still being around. Beam me back, Benny," he decided.

"Okay here we--are!" exclaimed Ben. He'd kissed the stone slab and they were instantly in the loft. "Wow, that is so fast!"

"Hey we're not floating any more either."

"No and we're normal size and visible again. Using the stone seems to cancel out most things. That's well-worth knowing."

"It doesn't look as if we've been missed yet. Maybe we could carry on a bit longer?"

Ben quickly looked in the pouch. "Okay then, what shall we do now?"

"Let's use the dice again and see what happens with the 'Five'?" Toby was once again full of anticipation.

"Yes 'Five' it is then," Ben replied. He picked up the dice and placed them down again with the number five showing. As usual, the surface of the stone slab gradually formed a new message.

> *'Cut a form from my new wood*
> *Wish or place to make it good*
> *Return when done do store it well*
> *Another change another spell'*

Toby pulled a carving from the chest. "It sounds as if this has to be something to do with these Ben, but I wonder what it means when it says *'to make it good'?"*

"I really don't know, Toby. There are certainly a lot of them in the chest so there must be a good reason for keeping them. The clue seems to suggest they can be stored for some other time, so we should be able to use one of these at first instead of carving our own. Choose one and we'll see what happens."

"Righto." Toby made a quick selection. It was the beautifully sculptured lion they had seen when they first went through the contents of the chest.

"I love this one," he said. "What do you think we should do with it?"

"Your guess is as good as mine," said Ben. "Put it down over there next to Sandy and the dice. The clue says 'Wish or place'. The dice are already placed on five and nothing is happening, maybe because we have just used them to give us the clue. Perhaps I should place them a second time."

Leaving the blank cube in position he picked up the carved die and then carefully placed it down again with the five showing on top.

"Nope, still nothing," Toby remarked.

Then they became aware of a strange noise opposite them. When their eyes followed the direction of the noise they instantly froze. A life-sized lion was sitting a metre or so away from them busily cleaning the claws on its huge feet.

... ...

Chapter Twenty-Four

"Oh my God!" exclaimed Ben softly. "What have we done this time?"

"More importantly, what do we do now," whispered Toby his face drained of colour. "I'd sooner have to cope with the Magpie any day."

Ben had little chance to answer. The lion stood up on all fours and casually walked across to him and licked him on the cheek with its huge rough tongue, then sat down beside him purring almost like his own cat. Without a thought Ben automatically stroked the huge cat and it responded by rolling over on its back as if asking for more.

At that precise moment their alarm mousetrap went off with a loud bang. The boys, already in a state of fear almost flipped into full panic expecting to see someone coming up the ladder. Their heads turned and minds raced as to what might happen when they were seen to have a lion in the loft. Luckily there was no-one there. Neither when they looked again was the lion, he had become a harmless wooden carving once more.

"Wh-what happened?" Ben stammered from the shock of it all.

"I'm glad it *did*, whatever it was," remarked Toby. "It was almost as if the lion was frightened off by our mousetrap. Phew I loved that old cat as a carving, but I'm not so sure about being so close to the real thing. How did you have the nerve to stroke it?"

"It was more out of habit than nerve. When it licked me and sat down purring, it was so much like our own cat I stroked it without putting much thought to it."

"It was massive. What would we have done if it had attacked us?"

"Somehow I don't think it would. After all we did ask it to come because of the carving. I know we might not have chosen the lion if we'd known what was going to happen, but someone must have carved it for a reason and kept it, so it's probably a friendly lion?"

"Wow! Imagine us having a friendly lion of our very own. He'd soon frighten off any enemies we ever made. I'm beginning to like him much more already."

"It's strange though that he became a carving again?" Then on looking around Ben said, "Ah, now I can see why. The lion must have nudged Sandy and set the alarm off when he rolled over on his back."

Toby was pleased to hear Ben's solution but soon excitedly said, "Hey, thinking about it, this must mean any of those carvings in the chest can become real when we want."

"Yes I guess it does. It looks as if we're going to be really busy. There will be even more if we manage to carve anything ourselves from those blanks in the chest." Ben glanced at his watch. "We'll have to select a more harmless carving once lunch is over and see what happens then."

After lunch they began removing other carvings from the chest.

"We'll leave the blank blocks there and perhaps the transport carvings for now."

"Oh why? I love the look of that little car and the aeroplane."

"They look good to me too, but we need to find out what we're doing first and be very careful in what we choose. Let's face it, the lion was big enough. I think we could do without a real car or aeroplane here in the

197

loft and after what happened earlier I think we'll have to give most of the animals a miss too. Most of them would be far too big or dangerous to be in the loft."

"Too right, how about we try something a little safer then, like the rope perhaps?"

"Okay, that sounds to be a good choice."

On starting Sandy he placed the rope carving close by and turned the small dice over to read five. The coil of rope instantly became real and of a very useable size. Other than that everything appeared to be as before. Ben picked up the rope thoughtfully.

"This seems a strange thing to carve from a chunk of wood, though I suppose it could be quite a convenient way to carry a rope if we needed one. In fact any of these carvings would fit into our jacket pockets easily. Now we have to figure out how to get the rope back into a carving again. I don't think the clue told us that."

"We got the lion back alright, Ben."

"Yes, but only because Sandy stopped."

"That's true. How about kissing the stone then?"

"That might work fine for us here but if we were out on an adventure somewhere and wanted to return anything to its carving, we already know that kissing the stone would end our adventure as well. No, there has to be another way."

"How about kissing the dice instead? The dice bring the carvings to life after all and I seem to remember that was what I did by chance at the time of the dinosaurs?"

"That sounds worth a try," Ben said as he picked them up. He tried kissing the numbered die but nothing happened. But the second he put the plain cube to his lips the rope became a carving again.

"Oh well thought out, Toby. So it seems that's what the plain one is for. We're learning all the time. We'll try one or two other things just to make sure."

"I'll tell you something, Ben."

"What's that?"

"This could be quite handy for you. You could turn all your girl-friends into carvings with those magic lips if you're not careful," he said.

"Cheeky devil. I don't have any girl-friends. Well not yet anyway, though I intend working on it. What do you mean by 'handy'?"

"You'd be able to keep them all to yourself in your pocket," laughed Toby, "or bring them back to the loft and change them for a kiss and cuddle."

"Mmm, sounds a great idea, but leave it out, I've enough problems as it is," he replied with a chuckle.

They experimented with changing various weapon and tool carvings and found the plain die returned them to their former wooden state easily.

"I suppose we ought to play safe and try the same with one of the animals now," said Ben. " What do we have Toby?"

"Let's see. We have an elephant, a horse, a cheetah, and an eagle, for starters. Oh and of course our friend the lion."

"Oo-er, The thought of changing any of those in the loft is a little worrying."

"The elephant would probably be the *slowest* mover," said Toby, "and possibly the friendliest."

"That's true and I've an idea how I might use him."

"How?"

"I'll go invisible and wish myself to the park with the elephant carving. We'll set our watches first to read the same." He chuckled at what he had said. "That's you and me of course, not the elephant," he corrected. "As soon as I'm there I'll make the elephant real and then I'll kiss the dice to return him to a carving. I'll get you to stay here just in case it doesn't work. Give me two minutes, then stop Sandy if I am not back. That will certainly return the elephant back to his carving and me to the loft. Are you okay with that?"

"Yep sure, that seems a good plan."

They synchronised their watches.

Toby looked at Ben and asked, "How about making the elephant *invisible* too, so no-one can see him?"

"I would prefer to but the trouble is *I* wouldn't be able to see him either. You're right about the elephant likely being the slowest mover but he might still amble off. If he's invisible I won't know where he has ambled off *to*."

"Oh I see. Okay then Prof, I'm ready when you are."

Ben picked up the elephant carving and the dice and made himself invisible. "Right," his voice said. "I'm off-- *now*."

Toby started counting off the seconds.

There was no one in sight in the park so Ben put the elephant carving down on the grass where it instantly became visible. He had forgotten everything with him would be invisible. This included the dice he had in his hand so he could not see the numbers or even which cube was which. He placed them down next to the carving so that they *were* visible and looked at the carved one. Needless to say the five was not in sight. Assuming it was on the underside he picked the die up to turn it over and between his fingers it instantly became invisible again. Fumbling with the unseen die he convinced himself he had the five on top and placed it back on the grass. But he had turned it too far and the five was now on its side. This was infuriating as he knew his precious time was ticking away. With another attempt he finally managed to get the die in the right position and was instantly joined in the park by a massive visible elephant, just a metre or so away.

Only *now* did he see how foolish he had been in his choice of this enormous creature. It could only be made *invisible* if he had a hold on it. Right now anyone around, even if at the other side of the park, would likely see it. Knowing his time was rapidly running out he made a quick grab for the dice in order to kiss them but dropped them again in fright when the elephant suddenly trumpeted.

"Shush, keep quiet for God's sake," he said to the elephant. Now he was in real trouble and dropped to his knees desperately searching amongst the long grass for the dice. His biggest problem - *other* than the elephant - was that as soon as his fingers as much as brushed against one of the hidden dice it became instantly invisible making it more difficult to find again. Now as if he didn't have *enough* trouble to cope with, he was shocked to hear a loud groaning nearby.

"Oh no, not elephants!"

It came from a scruffy bearded old man holding a near empty Gin bottle in his hand. He must have been asleep in the long grass which was why Ben had not noticed him before. The old man now sat bolt upright waving the bottle in one hand, intermittently staring wide-eyed at the elephant, then closing his eyes and rubbing them with his other hand. "Oh no. Oh no, not elephants," he repeated over and over again.

Ben's fingers finally curled around the dice but before he could get them to his lips he found himself visible and back in the loft. Toby had stopped Sandy at the end of the allotted one hundred and twenty seconds.

"Oh thank you, Toby. Strewth! I can't believe those two minutes could have turned into such a nightmare."

"Why, what happened?"

"There was someone asleep in the long grass over the park. I didn't see him at first but when the elephant trumpeted"--

"Oh heck, the elephant *trumpeted*?"

"Yes, that's what I thought. The noise woke the old guy up and caused me to drop the dice in the long grass."

"Oh no!"

"That's what the old man kept saying, 'Oh no, not elephants,' over and over. He looked like an old wino and was well drunk I believe. I expect he thought he was seeing things because of the booze. At least our elephant wasn't pink but I don't suppose the old guy even realised that. Hopefully he'll never drink again, so some good may have come of it."

Toby laughed and spluttered, "That all sounds so funny. Did it work?"

"Did what work? Oh hell what an idiot. I never had the chance to try it and now I don't have the carving *or* the elephant. Quick Toby, start Sandy again. I'll have to go back. The elephant might still be roaming around in the park for all I know. Give me another sixty seconds. I'm off."

This time he had hardly disappeared before he was back again and tightly clutching the elephant carving.

"Phewee! Thank goodness for that," he sighed, slumping to the floor in relief. "At least the elephant *had* returned to his carving. It was right where I'd left it thank goodness. I could see that old wino right over the other side of the park that time. It looked as if he couldn't get out of it fast enough. The elephant disappearing must have really seen him off. The best part of it all is that no-one will ever believe him if he tells anyone what he has seen, so all is well."

"Not quite Ben. We still don't know if kissing the blank one will work for the animals?"

"You're right we don't. *You* brought me back and changed the elephant to a carving by stopping Sandy. But I'll tell you this much, I'm not ready to repeat the performance again yet, certainly not with the elephant anyway."

"Why don't we shrink him first? We could tie some string around his neck then like a lead."

"Good idea. You're definitely the brains of the outfit, well on this occasion at any rate," he added. "You're right, perhaps we should use the elephant *after* all. He is the most placid, friendly looking animal of the whole bunch. If we were to shrink him at least twice, a string lead should work well."

"How are we going to shrink him?"

"Ah good question, I was wondering that myself. Perhaps if I hold his trunk or an ear it might do the trick. We'll need to experiment with something. But wait a minute, before we can shrink him, we first have to change him from a carving. Having seen him for real, we certainly can't do that here in the loft, his weight would probably take him straight through the floor and into our bedroom below."

"No way then," remarked Toby, shocked and horrified at the thought.

"Heck! What do we do? Let's think this out again. We can't have live animals in the loft, largely because of their size. If we change them outside, the police might be called in to investigate and then we'd really be in trouble. If they are invisible we stand the chance of losing them and that might cause an even worse problem. There must be a way or else there is no point in having the carvings. We've either got this all wrong or we are missing something. Come on 'Brains'," he said looking at his little brother. "What have we missed?"

"Don't look at me I don't have a clue. I think when you shrunk me on the train that time my brain must have *remained* shrunk."

"That sounds likely for both of us," countered Ben. "But joking aside we'll have to keep our heads together on this one."

They both came up with various ideas while they were doing other things during the course of the day but still went to bed that night with the problem unresolved.

Sometimes sleep itself can be a means of obtaining an answer to a difficult problem, though normally not in a very direct fashion.

... ...

Chapter Twenty-Five

Ben woke with a start and switched on the bedside lamp. Glancing at his watch he saw it was just after three in the morning. Then he began to remember the dream he had woken from.

He had been riding along what seemed to be a path through a jungle, seeing strange animals and vegetation unlike anything he had ever seen before. His mount had jumped over an obstruction in its path making Ben hold on to the reins more tightly. Then abruptly, he knew it was *not* reins he was holding on by but thick fur of some kind. The next worry that came to him slowly was that he had never ridden a horse before and then that this was obviously *not* a horse. As he had looked past his handhold, the creature he was riding on had turned its head to look back at him. It was none other than the lion! He had a firm grip on part of the lion's mane and it had been taking him deep into the jungle.

Ben was now instantly wide-awake. So much so he decided to wake Toby.

"Wha–what's up, what's happening Ben?"

"I've been having a dream I must tell you about."

"Oh alright," Toby said beginning to settle back comfortably. "What was her name?"

"It wasn't a 'her' at all, but that doesn't matter."

"What do you mean it doesn't matter. Of course it matters. You've woken me up and I need to know these things."

"Toby, please shut-up and listen. I dreamt I was riding through a jungle and of all things it turned out to be a lion I was riding on. I'm fairly sure it was *our* lion."

"Oh, I see. I'm sorry Ben," Toby said, but still part asleep and perhaps not altogether interested.

"I'm sorry I woke you but I just had to tell you. I was riding on his back holding on by his fur and he seemed to be very friendly. He even looked back at me as if to make sure I was okay. I woke up from the dream when he had to jump over something in his path."

"That sounds one heck of a dream, one worth waking up for."

"Yes it was. But more importantly, it reminded me of the clue for changing carvings. The clue says '***Wish or place to make it good***'. If '***make it good***' means 'make it real' then it could be that there is a choice of how we do it. So far with everything we've changed we have 'placed' the carving and dice on the floor or on grass. When we 'wish' ourselves anywhere we always have the mirror and stuff in our hands. Maybe if we are *holding* the carving and dice in our hands we will go to wherever the animal lives."

"Sick! So it looks as if we wasted our time yesterday with the elephant and everything?"

"Yes it looks that way. But never mind, if we are right then we've learnt a lot too. All we have to do is to prove it."

"What do you reckon we should do now?"

Giving a huge yawn Ben checked his watch again.

"Oh cripes, it's not half-past three yet! Sleep now I reckon. But later today we'll give it all a try."

Early morning found the boys prepared for their new experiment.

"I've just had a look at Grandad's shed from the bedroom window here and can see that it's not locked. We could try the lion carving in there. Hopefully if I'm right, he'll take us with him to his jungle. If not he'll only be confined to the shed for the very short time it will take me to turn him back into a carving and no-one will ever know. What do you think?"

"Excellent. If, as you said the other day, I'm the 'Brains', then you must be the 'Master Planner'. It sounds like another wicked idea, Ben."

"Mmm, thanks for your faith. I just hope it turns out better than my elephant plan--that was a near disaster."

"Thinking about it, it's just as well you decided on the lion this time."

Ben looked a little puzzled. "Why?"

Toby grinned. "Can you imagine the state of the shed if we were to change the elephant carving for real *inside* it?"

"Geeps! I never thought of that. It's only a tiny shed. The elephant would be wearing it like a waistcoat. How would we ever explain that to Grandad?"

"Worse still, how would we ever explain it to Nan?"

Once they were ready, he looked into the mirror and requested, "Grandad's shed in the garden please."

"What's next?" Toby asked looking around the inside of the shed. "Cripes! I hope you're right with your theory about us going with *him*, else things are likely to be a little cramped in here, Ben."

"Well this is where we find out for sure. Grab a hold, Toby."

Ben took the lion carving from his pocket and holding it and the plain cube on the flat of one hand, placed the die with the five showing on top next to it. The shed interior instantly disappeared, to be replaced with a mass of leafy vegetation overhead and a tract of jungle stretching out all around them.

"Yes," said Ben happily. "Result! I don't suppose we'll ever forget now but make a quick note in your book please, Toby. If we want the real things to come to us, we need to put the carving and dice on the floor or ground near us. If we want to be taken to where the animal actually lives, then we hold the carving and dice in our hands."

Toby took his notebook out and faithfully scribbled it in.

The lion was stretched out on his belly a little way in front of them. Toby gave a sharp intake of breath at seeing the big creature so close to them again.

"Don't worry, Toby," Ben whispered. "I'm sure this is going to be okay but just in case of trouble, I have the stone in my hand. I only have to kiss it and we're all out of here."

The lion looked up and seemed to recognise Ben. He gave a low growling kind of purr and rolled over on his back. Ben plucked up courage and carefully moved nearer. With one hand firmly clutching the stone he stretched out the other and stroked the lion. The huge old cat nuzzled his head against Ben's hand and purred again. Watching this, Toby overcame his fear and helped Ben make a huge fuss of the lovely old animal.

"You're right he is lovely and surprisingly soft," Toby muttered quietly. "Now what should we do I wonder?"

As if in answer the lion gently rolled over again and slowly stood up on all fours turning his head round until looking at his own broad back as if trying to tell them something.

"This is going to be so like my dream," exclaimed Ben. "I do believe he wants us to climb on his back. I'm going for it."

"I'm not so sure. Be careful, Ben."

"I shall be, don't worry. I still have the stone in my hand."

The old lion stood very still as if waiting. Ben approached and patted him on his back. The lion purred again. Ben then got a hold on the big cat's fur, swung a leg over and settled himself on the creature's broad back. Toby was rooted to the spot with fear for his brother. The lion then looked at him and as if helping him come to a decision, moved slowly over and stood alongside him offering his back. He then nuzzled him very gently.

"It's okay, Toby. He wants you on his back too. It'll be alright, really."

Once again Toby eventually overcame his fear. Grabbing a hold of his brother he swung his right leg over the lion's back and sat astride the animal behind Ben.

"Okay then, I'm on."

The next minute they were both swaying side to side in unison as the big old lion started off with them into the jungle.

"Ben suddenly chuckled to himself and asked, "Do you remember those old 'Doctor Who' episodes we watched on the television recently?"

"Do you mean that strange guy in that old phone-box thingy?"

"Yes that's it. Whenever I hear that music in the future I shall think of Grandad's shed being like that from now on. You know small outside and vast with a jungle inside it."

"Grandad's Tardis!"

The boys had been in various rain forests back home in Australia and found them really exciting. The sound of water trickling over natural rock amongst huge ferns and old gnarled tree trunks covered with moss, lichen and creepers all to a wonderful backdrop of birdsong, had been completely different from anything else they had ever experienced and altogether quite beautiful.

But this was something different again. They found themselves travelling not along a man-made board-walk as they may have been back home but simply following a light animal track weaving through the surrounding vegetation, possibly formed by the regular use of their friend the lion himself.

The boys sitting high on the creature's back, found themselves having to continually dodge or push aside all manner of branches, leaves and hanging fronds as they moved through growth that was unusual to them. The noise from the jungle was incredible. There was much bird noise, but other than the familiar raucous squawks of parrots, none they recognised, and even this largely drowned out by other noise. Strange scuttling and snuffling sounds as unknown creatures moved about sniffing for food or for each other, in the dense undergrowth. Loud screeching and whooping noises as animals, presumably mostly monkeys and chimpanzees called or threatened others. Occasionally they would sight a small animal or a brightly coloured parrot, even a snake here and there. Luckily the latter made an exit as soon as their lion put in an appearance.

Until now, Ben and Toby had seemingly lost the art of conversation. Fear and surprise at times, but mostly sheer delight had temporarily stilled their tongues. Toby regained his speech first.

"I'm really beginning to enjoy this."

"So am I, it's utterly fantastic. This old chap is so comfortable to ride on, too. But the best part I think is because he's the king of the jungle the other animals keep well out of his way and are hardly likely to even notice us."

"Oh of course, that's why that snake disappeared so quickly. I was getting ready to jump off and run for it."

"Yes it was a bit scary. I thought you hadn't seen it, as you never mentioned it."

"I was too scared to talk," Toby admitted.

"As the lion's now our friend, we ought to give him a name, something special to remember him by. Any ideas, Toby?"

Still nervous and unable to think properly, Toby replied, "I can't come up with much other than Rover, or Bonzo."

The lion as if he had taken in every word gave a low growl, as if in serious disapproval.

"It's you who should be called Bonzo, after a suggestion like that," Ben said. "Never mind old friend," he said, patting the lion's back. "There's no way we're going to call you that. I think as we already know you're the king of the jungle, we should call you King."

"Oh nice one, Ben, and I'm sorry King, I didn't mean it," Toby apologised nervously. "I was only joking."

King abruptly stopped, put his head up high sniffing the air and gave a huge roar. The boys started to laugh, at first thinking the lion was happy with his new name, but their laughing was cut short by an answering roar from very close by. The boys' heads turned at a disturbance to their right to see a huge lioness emerging from the undergrowth.

"Trust me to think nothing will bother us while we're with King," Ben muttered worriedly, "I never thought of another lion."

King stood stock still, but nowhere near as still as the boys on his back when the lioness approached them growling and snarling with her huge sharp teeth bared.

At first she stared directly and threateningly, at the boys. Ben felt Toby's arms tighten round him seeking protection and found himself wishing he had someone human to cling to. As the lioness drew closer she seemed to dismiss the two boys as no threat to herself and switched to glaring and snarling directly at King instead. King stood his ground, waiting. As soon as she was in range, King brought up his left paw so swiftly the boys hardly saw it move and clouted the jaw of the lioness really hard, but apparently with his massive claws withdrawn. She let out a terrific roar but backed off and dropped down in a crouch as if as in submission. King suddenly stood up on his rear legs causing both boys to slide off his back into an untidy heap behind him on the jungle track. The stone flew out of Ben's hand and landed in amongst the greenery at the side of the track a metre or so away. For a moment it seemed as if the lioness was about to spring on top of them, but King positioned himself between her and the boys and growled threateningly. Much to the surprise and huge relief of the boys, she now rolled over on her back and let King nuzzle her.

Ben seized the seemingly safe moment and very cautiously slithered over on his belly towards where he believed the stone had gone, having to leave a terrified Toby laying like a titbit a keeper may have thrown to his enormous pets. While groping around with one hand in the undergrowth, Ben felt extremely vulnerable himself as he noticed the huge eyes of the lioness were watching his every movement. His nerve almost left him as his hand briefly encountered something alive and on the move, then thankfully his fingers found and grasped the familiar shape of the stone.

"Phew!" whispered Ben as he edged back alongside his brother. "That was lucky. I began to think King had brought us to his home for lunch and we were going to be it," he whispered nervously. "This lioness is probably his wife in our terms. He's brought us along to meet her and she isn't too keen on the idea. We'll just have to hope he convinces her that we are okay."

"I sure hope he does a good job of it. I don't think my legs are up to running far *or* fast yet. King's back is so broad I feel as if I have frog's legs now after riding on him for that distance."

"You *could* be better off with frog's legs, Toby, if we did need to make a quick exit. Frogs are pretty good jumpers and move very fast when they need to," Ben joked, trying to make light of it all. "But we'll be okay," he added when he saw alarm returning to his brother's face. "I have the stone again now just in case."

The lioness seemed to have completely forgotten the boys. She had got back to her feet and was making a big fuss of King as if he might have been away from her for a long, time.

"What was that?" Toby turned his head drawn to a new noise in the undergrowth quite close to them.

Before Ben had a chance to answer there was a movement in the low-lying vegetation along the side of the track and a small furry round head with bright yellow-green eyes and long whiskers stared out at them, curiously.

"It's a lion cub," whispered Ben. The two boys watched in amazement and delight as the tiny animal ignored them and stealthily crept out towards the lion and his mate. Then, even more delight as a second cub followed the first. The two small furry youngsters crept stealthily across the clearing, low down on their bellies, then suddenly pounced on their parents. Real pranksters, the two small cats were soon thoroughly enjoying themselves making mock attacks on their

213

father, then hanging on their mother's ears and tail. Finally, once she decided enough was enough, their mother picked up one of them by the scruff of the neck and stalked off into the undergrowth.

King caught the other cub by placing one massive paw on its back and by grabbing him around the neck in his huge mouth. He then surprised it *and* the boys by bringing it to where they were still sitting on the track and gently dropping it right in front of them. The boys and the small lion cub, all shocked, just sat and stared at one another for several seconds. Seemingly determined they should become friends, King nudged his small cub until it was almost on Ben's legs.

Beginning to see what was going on, Ben stretched out his hand carefully, so as not to alarm the small creature and gently stroked it. The cub seemed to like this and edged nearer. Once it knew it was safe, it suddenly bounded onto Ben's lap just like a kitten. For several minutes the cub played with the boys, all three of them rolling over together in a big untidy heap, laughing, chuckling, purring and mewing. The small lion cub was wonderfully soft and cuddly and full of fun. It was so fast at times it seemed it must have more than four legs as they were just a blur of movement. King stood close, proudly watching as if they were all his children and making sure there were no real up-sets or arguments.

When finally he decided they had all had enough rough and tumble, he reached into the pile of writhing bodies, picked up the young lion cub by the neck and despite all their protests walked off following the same direction as the rest of his family.

The boys now at a loss to know what to do, followed. After about a hundred metres in varying directions, they entered a small clearing which appeared to be the lion's home patch. The lioness was already there stretched out sleeping with the other cub moulded alongside her beneath a big tree. It was a beautifully peaceful spot with a river running right alongside and most of the area screened off by dense jungle. King dropped the cub near its mother and walked over to the river for a drink. When he returned, he too, stretched out amongst his family for a sleep.

"Maybe it's time for us to go home?" Ben suggested. "My watch seems to have stopped but we must have been here for ages. Although at least this time we know that if anyone had looked for us, our alarm would have taken us back."

"Oh Ben, what a great time we've had. I don't want to leave them now but I suppose we have to. Okay," he said making up his mind. "Let's get back."

... ...

Chapter Twenty-Six

"That was an amazing day yesterday, Ben. I would have liked to have brought that lion cub back with us. I loved him."

"Yes he was lovely. Now we know how to do it we'll have to pay the jungle another visit soon and see them again. I think King would like that, too. It seemed to me, he thought we were his sons the way he looked after us, the lovely old creature."

"I noticed that too, it reminded me of Dad. I am so missing him, Ben."

"So am I. In fact I've been thinking about Sandy and Melbourne again. Where do you suppose we were yesterday?"

"I know we were in a jungle but I hadn't thought about where the jungle *was*. Africa I suppose? Is that what you mean?"

"That's it exactly. Now, if we had asked to go to Africa, would Sandy have been able to get us there?"

"But he already did."

"No, the lion carving took us there."

"Yes, but Sandy made it possible. I don't quite follow you, Ben?"

"Well, when we wink-wished for Australia that time, Sandy couldn't oblige. What I'm wondering is, if a lion carving can take us to Africa, why don't we try an animal from Australia?"

"Wow. Do you really think that would take us there?" Toby asked excitedly.

"Don't get your hopes too high, Toby, but I reckon it's possible. I can't begin to imagine how we get to places we ask for at all. Over the park, Grandad's shed, the bathroom. None of those things would have existed in the inventor's time. Mostly, it's as if the magic acts on our *own* knowledge or imagination of such things. But when it comes to other countries, Sandy was built so long ago that maybe his inventor didn't know of their existence and we're no help in that respect. Other than hopping on a plane I couldn't *imagine* how to get to Australia, could you?"

"No, I wish I could."

"Perhaps with a carving like the lion, he's able to take us to where the real thing lives or is normally found. The magic is so fast, too. If that was an African jungle we were in, it took us no longer to get there than it did to Grandad's shed. Magic's a very strange commodity. We are very lucky to have been allowed the use of it, so we need to try new ideas and learn as much as we can. I suppose it's like being an apprentice really, where the lore or knowledge is all there for the taking and it's up to us to make the most of it. Maybe this time we should try carving our own Aussie animal and see if that will work?"

"Do you think we could?"

"We can but try. We'll have to borrow some tools first, from Grandad. Mind you, I'm not sure if we'll be able to carve anything remotely like an animal when neither of us has tried before."

Toby sighed. "If it's left to me we'd probably end up in monster land."

"Exactly," Ben said laughing. "I think that goes for me too, but we won't know until we have a go."

"Why don't we carve something fairly easy? Like one of our parrots for instance?"

"What do you mean, *easy?*" I think carving a parrot from a block of wood might turn out to be quite a task.

But in any case I think parrots are off the menu, so to speak, as there are wild parrots everywhere these days, even here in Surrey and East London. In the meantime let's concentrate on slowing Sandy as much as possible and time him on a full pot of sand so that we'll be able to keep some check on the time when we're out on an adventure. That's going to be extremely important for the trip to Melbourne. If we do manage it we'll need as much time as possible just to get there and back."

Toby had a look through his notes. "So far, the best run we've had was just over two hours from full. That was after you partially closed the sand valve. That seemed a very good result."

"Yes, it was, but if we can stretch it a little more, all the better."

"Ben, you said something just now about 'the lore'. What did you mean, exactly?"

"Sorry Toby, I never meant to confuse you. Lore is the old word for the knowledge of a certain subject, in our case now, magic. In the same way as folklore, a knowledge or belief of people in the old days."

"Oh right, thanks Ben, that makes sense now."

Ben lifted the machine from the chest and sat it firmly on the loft floor while he bent low and shone the torch on the pot slides hoping to find a way of slowing Sandy even further.

Toby peered over Ben's shoulders. "We still don't know what those signs are for. We were far too busy trying to get him up and running at first to worry about them."

"You're right. Originally we put the pots in the 'Sun' position. The wheel ran forward and appeared to use the sand quite fast. Then I found I could slow it to some extent by not fully opening the sand valve. I remember marking the top pot at a low-level with your pencil once. What results did we get from that, Toby?"

Toby flipped through the pages of his notepad again.

"Ah, here we are. Lowest mark-about a quarter full, or three quarters empty."

Ben laughed. "Did you really put that in as an entry?"

"Of course I did. It's what you told me and I like to be accurate."

"But I was just mucking around at the time. I didn't expect you to write it in."

"Oh, I see, and there was I thinking it was vital information. Anyway I suppose the important part was the time. It says we were gone for nearly half an hour."

"That's great, Toby. I'm only kidding you on. It's good you bother to write it in at all and it has certainly proved to be very useful. We still need to discover what those 'moon' positions are for. We did once move the pots there, remember? The wheel ran backwards but never appeared to make very much difference, other than possibly having given us two quite frightening adventures? We've not tried it in reverse since changing it back."

Toby never had the chance to comment. The mousetrap sprung and Sandy stopped. Someone was climbing the loft-ladder. They barely had time to get in front of the machine before their grandfather stuck his head through the entrance, and said, "I thought I might find you here, fellers."

He climbed into the loft. "I came up to give you something I made a few days ago. Knowing you are missing your Dad and Australia, I thought it might help. I never expected you to have a use for it this soon but knowing now how quick and inventive you two guys are then I guess you might after all. If you have no need for it or don't yet know what I'm on about, then please put it in the chest for me with the others for another time, lads." He handed them something wrapped in an old piece of cloth.

Ben uncovered it. It was one of Sandy's blocks carved into a Kangaroo.

The two boys were overcome with joy.

"Grandad, how did you know? You couldn't have given us anything more special."

Their grandfather sighed with relief. "That's alright then. I wasn't at all sure you'd know what I was talking about, or why I should give you a Kangaroo above all things, but your reactions tell me all I need to know. You guys have obviously made great progress in your adventures and haven't needed to ask me anything, which is really good *and* quite amazing. But I'm glad, because it's so much more fun for you and more exciting to find out for yourselves as you go along. You've been very secretive too and I'm very proud of you both for that. I'm sure you'll agree by now, this is a pretty good machine?"

"*Good*, it's *fantastic*. We can't thank you enough for letting us use it."

"It's your right and you're more than welcome, lads."

"Thanks for the Roo, Grandad," said Toby grinning from ear to ear with glee. "It's wicked, just like the real thing. You're very good at carving."

"As an old adventurer myself I've had plenty of practice," he explained, chuckling as he retreated back down the ladder.

"That was truly amazing, Toby. Grandad turning up with the very thing we needed. Now we know for sure we're on the right track."

"So we can give it a shot soon?"

"I reckon so, yes. Just one more quick time trial. We'll close the valve down to a trickle of sand on a quarter full pot and see if we can gain another half-hour or so."

While Ben made the adjustments, Toby made a hastily scribbled addition to his notes. After making sure their alarm was set and their watches synchronised, they wink-wished themselves to the park.

But their timing experiment was doomed to failure. After what seemed about ten minutes, Ben having just come down the big slide to a rough landing, checked his watch to find it had stopped. He was about to ask Toby the time when they heard a commotion of some sort coming from the other side of the park pavilion. There was the noise of several feet running, some sort of scuffle, then a woman's voice shouting, "Go away and leave me alone! Get off! Help somebody. Help!"

The two boys immediately jumped off the swings and ran towards the pavilion.

"Hang on and let's see what's going on first," Ben cautioned as he peered round the corner of the building. "It's two guys, about eighteen or twenty, trying to steal a woman's handbag. We'll have to help her somehow. Grab my hand first, Toby, and at least we can be invisible."

This they did, then both ran at top speed towards the incident. The taller of the two men was attempting to hold the lady still, while the other was trying to pull the handbag away from her. Although her size and age was against her the lady was determined to hold on and was shouting as loudly as she was able. "Help, get off me. Help."

"Go for the short one Toby. Use the old school leg collapsing trick, but don't just push him in the back of his knees, kick him hard and get him down if you can. Let's go. Now!"

The bag-snatcher suddenly collapsed on to his knees with a yelp of pain and shock. The woman took her chance and swung her leg out and kicked him and he went over in a heap. The taller man surprised at his friend collapsing for no apparent reason automatically let go of the lady and moved to go and pull his companion to his feet. It was a bad mistake. Ben saw where he was heading and dropped in a low crouch right in front of him. It worked like a dream. The man fell headlong over the top of the invisible Ben and right on top of the first who had just been struggling to his feet. The woman, keeping her wits about her once she was free, ran off as fast as she could still clutching her handbag and screaming for "Help."

"Quick, Toby, help me to keep these guys down," Ben whispered. "I have the rope carving in my pocket."

Toby managed to keep the men busy for the split-seconds Ben needed to change the rope carving. Being invisible it was surprisingly easy for the boys to keep kicking the mugger's feet away from them, or charging them bodily to keep them on the ground. Ben managed to tie one foot to another and with Toby's help, an arm and so on, until eventually the two men lay completely trussed up facing each other on the ground. Both were yelling and shouting at the top of their voices as they had no idea what on earth was happening to them, or how. They were even more confused and terrified, both showing wide frightened eyes, when the rope visibly materialised as Ben and Toby stepped away.

Within the space of a few more seconds there was another commotion. The noise of a siren as a police car came screaming up the small drive leading to the pavilion. It pulled to a stop close to the two roped up wriggling figures. Two policemen accompanied by the lady that had been attacked got out and hurried over to the reclining figures.

"That's them," she pointed. "They attacked me and tried to snatch my handbag. They didn't reckon on me fighting back."

"Crikey, Missis, they certainly went for the wrong person this time," said one of the policemen. "We could find a job for you on the force."

"Yes, that we could!" the other officer exclaimed. "How the devil did you manage to tie them up like that?"

"She's an old witch, that's how," said the nastier of the two from his horizontal position on the ground.

"Well, well. Look what we have here. Hello Johnny, my friend. Oh, and you too, Mick," said the first policeman. "What a wonderful day this is turning out to be. I've been longing to look in at you two at your work. It appears we've got you dead to rights this time my friends. Perhaps we should call your solicitor now, and see how he'll explain this one. Let's see, perhaps a UFO abducted you but they didn't like the smell so they tied you up and threw you back. I certainly would have had I been the Alien," he laughed.

"Even if your solicitor could manage for once to admit the truth for you, it's not going to do much for your credit in the *Nick*, when your chums hear about this little tale. How this little old lady you both *bravely* decided to rob, not only sorted you out but left you both tied up with a rope while she came and got us," laughed the other policeman.

Oddly enough, there were no more clever remarks from the two criminals. They just had to lie there and admit defeat.

After a little effort and possibly a little purely accidental rough handling, the policemen managed to get them into the car still roped together.

"Are you taking them straight to prison now?" The old lady asked. "They deserve it."

"They do and they will eventually go. But first, we'll get them locked away in a nice comfortable cell at the Police Station while we get all the paperwork sorted out. If you let us have your address we'll come back for you shortly, as we will need you to sign the arrest details. We'll make you a cuppa while we do that, then bring you back in style afterwards."

"You're going to be quite a celebrity with our colleagues at the station for collecting these two for us, I can tell you," the other policeman commented. "You can rest assured they are not going to wriggle out of this one."

"I'd love to come along and have a cuppa please and meet your colleagues to sign a statement or whatever it is I have to do. But please I must confess, I only in your words, 'Sorted' them. I never tied them up. I can only assume someone else must have seen what happened and came along with a rope right after I had run to get you. They made a jolly good job of it too."

"Never mind, my love, you did the right thing. Hopefully the person or persons will come along and tell us all about it soon, then they can have their rope back. If they don't show up over the next day or two, we'll pop a note in the station window to tell them where they can collect."

"Oh good. Here's my address, I'll toddle off home now then and wait for you," she said as she walked off.

With that, the policemen climbed back in the car and sped off leaving the two real heroes of the day standing unseen in the park.

"Are you okay, Toby?"

"I'm fine Ben. I loved getting the better of those two creeps. If we hadn't been here for that poor lady, they would have had her bag for sure. Are you okay?"

"Yep, I'm good. This invisibility thing is fantastic. I doubt we would have done much to help her without it. I expect I shall have a bit of a bruise on my thigh later. That tall bloke caught me with his foot as he fell over the top of me, but I'll bet it's nothing compared with their bruises. Oh well, we'd better get back I suppose."

"But Ben, we were going to wait until Sandy stopped and *took* us back to the loft so that we could time him"

"Heck yes, we were too. With all the excitement I'd forgotten all about that. As it happened it's just as well he *didn't* stop! What is the time?" He looked at his watch. "Oh of course, it's not working. I think I must have knocked it coming down the slide in the park. What time do you make it, Toby?"

"Ten past eleven - no hang on, I'm sure that was the time when we left the loft." He pulled his notebook from his pocket. "Yes, I thought so. I wrote it in so that I could time the sand flow without forgetting. My watch must have stopped too."

"That's odd," Ben exclaimed. "My watch reads the same, but we must have been here for almost an hour? Sandy should surely have stopped long before now."

"I'm finding it all a bit puzzling, Ben, what do you want to do?"

"We'll have to go back and try and find out what's going on. I'll use the stone Toby."

As usual they were back in the loft in a blink of an eye. Ben lifted the lid from the sand pot and peered inside it. "That's odd, we can't have been out as long as we thought we had, Sandy seems to have only used a few grains of sand."

"I'll go downstairs and check the time," Toby suggested.

"Okay," Ben replied deep in thought. Abruptly he jumped at a loud bang behind him, then Sandy stopped. The mousetrap alarm mechanism had operated the instant Toby had grabbed the ladder and gone down it. Within a few seconds he came rattling back up somewhat breathless, partly due to exertion but more because of excitement.

"You're not going to believe this, Ben. The time *is* just after ten past eleven."

"You're right, I *don't* believe it. Which clock did you look at?"

"I knew you'd ask that. I didn't believe it either, so I checked all three and they all say the same. Just after ten past eleven."

"Are we going mad or what? Did all that really happen in that short time? Hey, my watch is going again now but it's still only reading just after ten past eleven."

Toby stared at his own watch with eyes widening. "So is mine, this is getting really spooky. Whatever is going on?"

"It has to be something to do with us slowing Sandy right down. Both our watches started again once he stopped. Wait a minute, what did that clue about the signs say, Toby?"

Toby got his notebook out again and nervously fingered through the pages. "Here it is, '***The sun be on - the moon be back***."

"Mmm I thought that was it. I'm beginning to wonder if by slowing Sandy almost to a stop, we have somehow made our *time* slow or stop too. I feel completely stupid even suggesting such a thing but time has been strange before when we've been using him. Remember that fire adventure? That was almost as if we had all gone *back* in time."

"The fire." Toby flipped through his notes. "We had Sandy in the *reverse* position *then*," Toby commented.

"Oh my God! Then it must be that the moon setting makes time slow even further or go backwards somehow. That has to be it! *'The moon be back'.*"

"But hang on, Sandy was on the Sun position this time?"

"Yes but the sand was set at just a trickle, almost to a stop."

"So you think that's why all that we did only took a few seconds?"

"I think it must be. This is incredible. Is there nothing we can't do when we have Sandy? It seems he is a time travel machine as well. That might begin to explain some of our previous odd happenings too. Now I can see why we have to keep him such a very close secret."

Toby suddenly looked extremely excited. "Hey, this is awesome, if we leave Sandy's settings as they are at the moment we should be able to get to see Dad easily,"

"Yes you're right. We ought to be able to get to Australia with no worries at all," Ben agreed happily.

Despite all the wonder, excitement and pure magic being available to the boys, getting to see their Dad for a few minutes was still of prime importance even though the end of their holiday in England was rapidly approaching.

"Let's go now," Toby suggested hopping up and down with glee at the prospect.

"Oh Toby," Ben said putting an arm around his little brother's shoulders. "I'm so sorry to dampen your enthusiasm yet again, but I'm afraid we have something even more important to do first. We have to get our rope back somehow."

"But the police have it. How are we going to get it back without telling them everything?"

"The way I see it we've done them a big favour. I expect they would gladly give it back to us if we asked, but then as you say, they would have to know *exactly* what happened and we can't tell them. It's *our* rope and we'll have to *take* it back. It won't be stealing because it was ours in the first place. The only problem we have is, will Sandy take us there? We'll give them an hour or so to allow them to get back to the police station with the lady and then we'll see what we can do."

••• ••• •••

Chapter Twenty-Seven

Once mid-day had passed the boys used invisibility again, then asked the mirror to take them to collect the rope. They found themselves standing just outside the door of the police station. Pushing it open, they walked through into a kind of waiting room having a long counter top and a policeman standing behind it. There was another door that appeared to lead into an office behind the counter. The duty policeman was having a word with someone in the office situated to the side of him.

"-then according to our blokes they found 'em there just where she'd left 'em. Oh hang on a minute Bob, there must be a strong wind getting up out outside. The door just blew open. I'll pop over and shut it."

The man on duty slid a small catch somewhere under the counter and folded back a hinged part of it to walk through and go and shut the door. Afterwards, while he was replacing the counter trap-door, the man in the office called out.

"Come on, Fred, I'm still waiting to hear the rest of the story. Why were they still there?"

"Alright I'm just coming. Well, that's the funny part of it," he continued, "They were both lying there tied up tight together with a rope when our lads arrived. The little lady said she'd sorted the pair of them out but quite how she could even get free of them is surprising, especially *those* two as they're both nasty little pieces of work." He chuckled then, telling his colleague, "They both tried to tell us she must be a witch the way they were man-handled."

"They *would*, those two. They'd say anything rather than admit some poor old dear got the better of them."

"Actually, she did admit she hadn't tied 'em up, so someone else *must* have been involved. It's just a pity we don't know who it was. I'd like to shake 'em by the hand for a job well done."

"Oh well, the main thing is someone did and now we've got them. Nice to know there's someone out there on our side. It's just a shame it doesn't happen more often. Where is the lady? I'd like to thank her myself."

"She's gone now. She came in and signed a statement and as you can imagine we all made a big fuss of her. She stopped for a cup of cocoa and Sid gave her one of his sandwiches, then the lads drove her home. She was a nice little lady, she reminded me of my old Mum."

"I didn't think you ever had one," laughed the other man.

"Cheeky devil," Fred muttered. "Oh by the way, the rope that was used is out here under the counter in case anyone claims it. If there is a claimant, we obviously need to know a lot more about the incident, who they are, you know, all the usual witness stuff. I thought I'd better tell you, Bob, just in case they should come in while I'm on my lunch break or something."

"Okay I'll look after it."

"That's good, now we know where to look," Ben whispered. "Stay here and count slowly to ten to give me time to get up onto the counter. When you've finished counting, open the door and hold it open wide for a few seconds and wait outside for me."

"Yep, will do, Ben."

Ben carefully climbed on to the counter right in front of the policeman who at the time was standing stock still with wide eyes looking all around the room. Ben waited. The door suddenly opened wide and stayed open. The officer looked up fully expecting to see someone come in but there was no one in sight.

"Blast the door," he muttered to himself. "That's the second time. I shall have to get the catch looked at. I'm sure I shut it properly before." Once again he had to lift the counter top and go through to close the door.

As soon as he was away from the counter, Ben jumped down on the other side and quickly grabbed the rope. He just made it out through the open counter gap before the officer returned. Ben opened the door yet again and walked calmly through it nearly falling over the invisible Toby waiting for him outside. Almost immediately afterwards the door was slammed shut again behind him with a bang by the irate officer inside. The two boys outside giggled mischievously. Ben coiled the rope neatly and was about to get them back to the loft when the door flew open yet again. On this occasion it was the other officer who opened it. He stepped through and looked up and down the road several times.

"No, not a soul in sight, Fred. You must be imagining things."

"I don't know what's going on here," remarked Fred, appearing outside, while shaking and scratching his head. "At one stage I thought I heard someone whispering. Then the door seemed to develop a mind of its own and now would you believe it, that damned rope has disappeared."

"Perhaps there really is some witchcraft going on around here," the other officer muttered to himself.

"What was that you said?"

"I said you'll be telling me in a minute, there really is witchcraft going on around here," he said laughing.

"You don't think--?"

The boys never heard the rest of the conversation. They had already returned to the loft with the rope carving safely in Ben's Pocket.

"Phew! It's a relief to be over that rope problem. It was lucky that the policemen were talking about the incident when we arrived, otherwise we would have had no idea where to look for it."

"Yes they were really helpful," Toby agreed.

"Boys!" Cassie called from the stairwell. "We have to go into town for shopping and various reasons and are likely to be there for best part of the afternoon. You are welcome to come with us or if you prefer to stay, the lady next door says for you to go to her if you have any problems. Which is it to be?"

"We'll stay please, Mum."

"I rather expected that would be your answer. That's fine. I'll tell the lady to keep an ear open for you."

"Thanks Mum. Take care, see you later."

"Wow! I think today will have to be the day!"

Toby's eyes gleamed in anticipation. "You mean-?"

"Yes! Australia!"

"Definitely go and see Dad?"

"It can't get much more definite, especially now we know more about the time thing, Toby. Grandad has even carved us a Kangaroo, so he must be expecting us to give it a go."

"Do you think he might ever have used Sandy to go to Australia himself, Ben?"

"No. If he had, then there would already be an Aussie animal in the chest and he's only just carved this one."

"Wow! So we're going to do something that even Grandad has never done before."

"Even better than that, it's something that *no one* has ever done before. There are no Aussie animals in the chest—right?"

"Oh yes of course, that's really awesome." Then his impatience began to rear. "So let's go then, Ben, right now," he pleaded.

"Okay 'Dinosaur'." Ben looked at Toby and grinned. "But we still have to think carefully about what we're doing before we jump into a big adventure such as this".

"Alright, Ben, point taken. But really, what is there to think *about*? Everyone else is out of the house for most of the afternoon so we won't even be missed."

"Well firstly, we have to refill Sandy, and set him on slowest trickle again."

"Oh yes, of course."

"Then we have to set our alarm system and make sure we have everything we need with us for the trip."

"Yes I suppose there is that, too."

"Then we have to get some warmer clothes on. A jumper and a coat for instance."

"What do we need those for, Ben?"

"Because its winter time back home in Melbourne"

"Oh! I hadn't thought about that."

"Then we have the time difference to think about. We're eleven hours behind Melbourne, so if we were to go now, Dad will probably be in bed asleep."

"I'm sorry, Ben, you're quite right, *again*. There *is* a lot to think about first. I guess I was getting far too excited at the thought of the trip and seeing him."

"That's okay, Toby, I am too. Come to think about it, we'll be best seeing Dad while he's asleep anyway. We won't be able to talk to him or even give him a hug because we have to keep the visit a complete secret."

233

"It will still be wicked to see him and check that his leg is getting better, anyway. I must admit I'm glad *you're* planning it, Ben. We'd have been in real big trouble if I'd had my way."

"I sometimes feel rotten to you as I always seem to be putting your brakes on."

"It's just as well you do most of the time. So, what now?" he asked, still just a little impatiently.

Ben grinned. "Well, having thought it out, we'll get on and do those few things, then we'll go."

"Yeeesss," shouted Toby, punching the air with his fist. "Result at last!"

... ...

Chapter Twenty-Eight

Using their new carving together with the correctly positioned dice, the boys experienced a few seconds of dream-like unreality before wide-eyed awareness set in.

As Ben had expected, they had arrived at night-time. The only light came from the star-studded night sky above them. They appeared to be somewhere far out in the middle of the country having no buildings or artificial light anywhere in sight. Could this *really* be Australia? It was certainly not the Australia they were accustomed to. They huddled together for several more seconds while experiencing a mixture of fear and wonderment until startled by a large shuffling dark shadow slowly heading in their direction from the depths of gloomy blackness. Was this another of the squealing monsters they had seen before? It was certainly large enough and moving in the predictable upright stance. With an intense effort they both remained in absolute silence while dreading to hear its horrible squeal or the almost expected evil laughter that often seemed to accompany the weird creature.

Although terrified at the thought of exposing the nightmare as a reality Toby stealthily slid his hand into his pocket and grasped the small torch firmly. With one sure movement he swung it out of his pocket pointing it towards the moving black shape as he switched it on. With synchronised gasps of relief the boys at last realised it was simply their Kangaroo caught in the bright beam of light.

As in a previous adventure when their lion carving had not only taken them to its country but also helped

235

them with their adventure, now it seemed the new carving might also stick by them. The big old creature performed another small hop and shuffle and then stopped right alongside them.

"Phew!" Ben let out a long whistle of escaping fear. "Grandad's carving worked well, but I'm so glad we were able to see what it was before it got any closer."

"Thank goodness for the torch. I think I might have died of fright without it. Where are we, Ben? This could be Australia, but it sure doesn't look much like Melbourne."

"No you're dead right, Toby. I'm just hoping we *are* in Australia and not stuck in an animal park somewhere that has Kangaroos. No, that's just me, worrying myself stupid. The time change seems right and just look at those stars, I guess it has to be Aus."

"Yep, okay, but how do we find Melbourne and Dad? We seem to be miles from anywhere."

"I was wondering if our friend here would mind us hopping on his back for a lift like our old lion friend did in the jungle. The problem with that is, a big busy place like Melbourne would be the last place a 'Roo' would want to go, I expect. But as we are so far out in the country we'll just have to give it a try. At least he might take us somewhere a little *nearer* civilisation, then perhaps we can find out where we are."

The two boys turned and somewhat nervously approached the Kangaroo which stood head height above them and seemed to be taking its time in looking them over.

"Hi guy," Toby said. "Thanks for showing us the way over."

"Would you mind if we grab a lift towards the city, please," Ben asked.

The kangaroo stood quite patiently in acceptance while the two boys attempted to get up on its back, but as soon as they were in position and it reared up on hind legs and tail ready to move they both slid down again and landed on their backsides. Annoying as this was, it also proved to be very lucky. As Ben was getting to his feet he almost lost his balance and had to grab at the animal for support. That was when he discovered their mistake.

"Hey Toby this isn't a 'he' after all, it's a female 'Roo' with a pouch. If we shrink ourselves she might let us use it to travel in so long as she has no 'Joeys' (baby Roos) in residence."

"It sounds a good plan, Ben, providing we can convince the lady about it."

They linked hands and shrank. The kangaroo now towered high above them. Luckily, being so small, they were also light and she once again waited for them as they used her fur to climb all the way up to her pouch and slide inside.

"Wow, I thought it was dark *outside* but I can't see a thing in here," Toby exclaimed, attempting to feel his way around.

"There's no point in feeling for a light switch," Ben said jokingly. "We're lucky at least there are no Joey's in here to contend with. Try standing like this and holding on to the pouch edge, then you may be able to see over the top."

Toby followed Ben's idea and found he could just see over the top of the pouch, but had barely grabbed a hold when the kangaroo started to move. She began to hop using her strong back legs together with her huge tail causing boys to experience a new kind of travel. It was very like being on one of those old fairground clown cars that have out of shape almost square wheels.

"Are-you-okay,-Toby?" Ben asked between bounces. "I-can't- imag-ine-how-a-Joey-ever-surv-ives-this-treat-ment," he gasped.

There was a muffled answer from somewhere deep in the bottom of the pouch. Ben knew his little brother must have lost his grip on the edge and had slid down inside. He bent down and found Toby curled up on the bottom of the pouch.

"Are you okay?"

"Yes, I'm fine thanks," Toby answered a little drowsily. "It's lovely and warm down here."

Ben curled up on the bottom of the pouch himself to see what it was like.

"Mmm, it is, and a lot more comfortable too. Now I'm beginning to see why the Joeys always seem ready to climb back in after having a hop around. It's more of a rocking motion down here, not so bouncy. I think maybe we'll have to call our Kangaroo, Bouncy?"

There was a loud snore of approval from Toby.

"It really is quite nice down here,-it's---"

The two 'human Joeys' were soon both happily curled up and fast asleep in Bouncy's pouch, as she slowly but steadily hopped along on her journey towards an unknown destination.

The boys slept for nearly an hour before some inner urgency had them stirring again. For a second or two they wondered where they were, until realisation had them scrabbling to their feet and peering out of the pouch at the star-lit countryside.

It had changed quite dramatically while they had slept. There were hills around them now and the stars were reflected on the surface of a huge lake to their left. At the far extremes of the lake there were a few house lights visible. But oh joy, beyond the steep hills to their right was an enormous glow of light that spread for miles.

"That has to be Melbourne. Yippee," Toby shouted excitedly.

"I'm sorry if I sound to be an old misery," Ben said, a little more cautiously. "That's obviously a big city out there and I *hope* it's Melbourne. But it could be Sydney, Canberra, or even Perth. Our 'Roo' might have brought us to Aus., but there are Roos all over our country so we *could* be absolutely anywhere."

"I hate to admit it but you're right," Toby agreed suddenly losing most of his new excitement.

In the meantime, knowing the youngsters in her pouch were now awake, Bouncy had spotted a clump of fresh grass and stopped for a chew. The boys, seeing they were now not so far from ground level slipped out of the pouch and on to the grass to stretch their legs.

Ben stumbled at the strange sensation of having solid ground beneath his feet again after all that bouncing and had to put a hand down to steady himself. Something slithered from under his hand and he had the distinct impression of it turning rapidly towards him when he, together with Toby, were knocked flying by the Kangaroo's huge tail to end up in a heap about two metres away.

When they recovered they were amazed to see Bouncy performing some sort of hop-dance, turning around and around at high speed, slamming her feet to the ground on each revolution.

"What's happening?" Toby screamed. "Has she gone mad?"

Then just as suddenly, Bouncy ceased her dance and calmly resumed eating.

"Stay here, Toby. I'll approach her and check and see if she's okay."

Before moving, Ben decided to bring them both back to full size in case of trouble. He then very carefully walked over towards the Kangaroo half-expecting her to rear up to attack him, but after a quick glance in his direction she put her head down and carried on eating. By now Ben was walking across her 'Dance Floor' when he suddenly stopped in his tracks and stared down at the ground near his feet.

"Oh what?" He gave a low whistle. "Now I can see what she was up to. Bouncy has probably just saved my life, possibly yours too, Toby. There's a dead squashed snake here. That must have been what I put my hand on when I nearly fell over. She knocked us both flying to get us away from it, then squashed it with that funny little dance of hers. Oh, Bouncy, thanks girl, I love you," he shouted as he bounded over to her.

Toby was soon beside him hugging her too, with grateful tears running down his face at the thought of her saving his big brother's life. "Thank you Bouncy, thank you," he cried.

When their emotions had settled, they realised precious time was flitting past and they were making little or no progress in getting to Melbourne to see their Dad.

"I wonder if that *is* Melbourne over the hills there. Is there any way we can find out?"

"One thing's fairly certain, Toby, we won't be able to get there to see, not on dear old Bouncy, anyway. It would take her hours, even if we were able to persuade her to go there in the first place. I suppose we could try flying there but we're not that good at it yet and it does look an awfully long way."

Toby had to agree. The hills themselves looked many miles away from their present position and it was quite impossible for them to tell what distance lay past those to the spread of light beyond. Nevertheless they had to do something.

"Come on we'll shrink again and give flying a try. At least we'll be on our way. But first of all we must look after Bouncy."

He returned her to a carving and carefully placed her in his pocket, patting it lovingly.

"Okay then, Toby, hang on," he said extending his hand for his brother. He caused them to shrink, then said, "Here we go!" He angled the mirror so that he was looking at the sky and instantly they were there, floating high up above the ground in that beautiful star-laden sky. For a few seconds they simply laid there spellbound by the sight of it.

"I never knew there were so many stars," exclaimed Toby. "There are millions of them."

"They are really quite awesome," Ben was lying comfortably on his back seemingly almost amongst them. "I suppose they are there all the time, but light pollution usually prevents us from seeing them."

"Light pollution did you say, Prof? What's that?"

"Oh crumbs, how can I explain that one? You know if you look out of the bedroom window at night with the light on, you can't see much detail outside unless you first turn the light off inside?"

"Yep."

"Trying to see the stars when there is a lot of street and building lights on around you in a big city like London or Melbourne is the same, except that you can't simply switch the lights off. That's what's known as light pollution. That is why out here where it's really dark, we can see so many more stars. But this won't do, we are getting far too comfortable. Let's get going."

After a good twenty minutes of flying towards the pollution glow and steadily gaining altitude, they were now almost on a level with the distant hilltops and began to see the lights of the city itself more clearly in the distance.

"That looks so good," Toby said.

"It sure does but we need to be a lot nearer to be certain if it's actually Melbourne. That's going to take an awful lot of arm work yet and more importantly, a heck of a long time. Perhaps we could use *this* guy to help us?" He produced another carving from his pocket that he passed to his brother.

Toby gasped when he looked at it in his hands. "The Eagle, yes, he'd sure be able to help with those huge wings but that beak looks pretty mean, Ben. Those eyes don't look very friendly either."

"Now don't go upsetting him by talking about him like that before we meet him, Toby. I thought he might come in handy so I brought him along just in case. The other carvings have been friendly, so I'm sure this one won't be any different." Then he added a little uncertainly, "Will he?"

"I guess we'll have to trust him," Toby said bravely, but his frightened eyes revealed his innermost hidden feelings.

"Our only other option is to go back, as we're never going to fly that distance ourselves and we can't even be sure that we're heading towards the right city yet."

Toby came to an instant decision. "Okay Ben, we'll use the eagle. How shall we go about it though, go down to the ground first?"

"No, as he's a flyer we'll probably be best meeting with him up here. The only problem is our size. While I don't altogether fancy the idea, I'm afraid we'll have to shrink a second time, otherwise the two of us might be too heavy for him to carry for that kind of distance."

"Must we really?"

"Afraid so. Come on, let's do it."

"Okay then," Toby answered, though still somewhat reluctantly and immediately closing his eyes tight-shut in fearful anticipation.

Ben shrunk them once again which appeared to make very little difference to them while on high as they had nothing close to relate their size to. He then produced the dice and momentarily held them with the carved five uppermost next to the eagle carving. After a few seconds Toby gradually released one tightly closed eyelid, then the other.

"It hasn't worked Ben," he managed to utter sadly, but really trying to camouflage his relief. He had hardly said it when there was an ear-piercing screech and a 'Swoosh' of disturbed air immediately above them.

There were no introductions. They were simply and abruptly plucked out of their comfortable floating state by two gigantic feet and propelled through the air at a fantastic speed. Both boys screamed at the top of their voices and then again even louder as a massive beak came down towards them and a huge yellow eye either side of it stared at them, examining their every detail as if trying to decide which of them to eat first.

... ...

Chapter Twenty-Nine

Held in the iron grip of the huge talons on each of the giant bird's feet, the boys gradually began to calm down as they flew effortlessly with the eagle over the hills and across mountaintops. Ben never dared to raise the *new* worry that had just formed in his mind. He had easily recognized the bird as a 'Wedgie' or Australian Eagle because of its tail shape, but had his doubts as to how well it matched the extremely old carving in his hand. Was this actually *their* eagle?

"I'm sorry I got you into this, Toby. I thought that if we had a problem I'd soon get us out of it using the stone. I have it in my hand here but there's no way I can get it to my mouth, he's holding me far too tightly."

"It's not your fault, Ben. In any case I did agree to it."

"If we weren't worrying what he might do with us, this could be really wicked. Flying with this guy is something else. He rarely has to flap his wings as he's so good at finding thermals."

"Thermals, what on earth do you mean? He's not wearing thermals?"

"Ah! That hurts. Please don't make any more jokes, he's holding me too tightly," Ben said trying hard to stifle himself from laughing.

"I wasn't joking, I was just doing my best to get my mind on anything other than what's really happening to us. What did you mean then, about the thermals?"

"Oh! Perhaps I'd best explain. Thermals are not only warm clothing, they are also warm currents of air. You'll learn about them when you start science lessons at school. Heat rises from various sources, causing warm upward air currents known as thermals. Birds sense these and use them with wings fully spread to get lift and save energy. Now, thanks to you, I've got this image in my mind of birds flying around wearing thermal underpants."

The pair of them shook with laughter, much to Ben's discomfort again, causing the eagle to venture another close scrutiny of his strange travelling companions.

Ben eventually carried on. "That's where the birds of prey come into their own. They all have huge wing-spans and are able to make good use of the thermals for lift and to glide for extra-long periods while searching for small creatures below on the ground they can catch and eat."

"Urgh! Please don't talk about their eating habits right now, Ben."

"Sorry mate."

Their unusual mode of transport had now reached the last of the high ridges and the bird started to veer away from the city lights to follow the hill line back into the darkness, resulting in a mild panic attack from the boys.

"No-o-o," they shouted at the top of their voices.

"We have to go to Melbourne *plea-s-e*," Toby yelled.

The eagle's head came down again and looked at them sternly one after the other with its huge eyes. Then it lifted its head and veered around until it once again headed towards the lights and taking them several miles further on. Then after another peer at them with those frighteningly magnificent eyes, it released its tight grip allowing the boys to slide back into the free air above the lower hills fringing the city. They fell for a short time until flight levelled them out and they found themselves floating again. There was a sudden screech as their eagle circled once around them as if checking to see they were safe before heading off back into the darkness.

"Thank you friend," Ben shouted after it as he replaced the carving in his pocket

"Thanks Eagle," Toby added, now beginning to recover from his fears.

Once they had manoeuvred themselves back into a flight path they could see they were now quite close to their target.

"I think we are alright, Toby. I can just make out the sea which is possibly at Brighton beach just over the back of the city. Yes, that tall building there has to be the Rialto. Dad took us to the restaurant at the top once to show us the view, do you remember? Look there's the Yarrow River flowing through the city. It's Melbourne right enough. Hoorayyyy!"

"Result at last." Toby shouted with sudden renewed vigour. "Let's get flying. Melbourne, here we come."

As before, they seemed to make the best progress with a kind of swimming style breaststroke. It still took them a good ten minutes or so just to clear the last of the hilltops. Then they could see hundreds of houses and buildings below them and wonderfully a warm current of air caught and lifted them on high and into a light wind.

"So this is what you meant about the gerbils-- no, thermals wasn't it?" Toby corrected himself. "They certainly help don't they?"

"Yes they sure do. Even more than Gerbils might," Ben grinned to himself. "I think this wind is heading us in the right direction which is lucky. Undo your coat Toby and hold it open like a sail."

They both stretched out their coats and the wind blew them out like air-sacks vastly increasing their speed as they flew straight towards the city.

"This is great," Ben shouted. "Thanks to our Eagle we're really getting somewhere now. Flying like this I feel like Superman."

"I must be Captain Marvel then," Toby replied, remembering his grandfather's comics. "Wheee!"

"Use your coat and steer yourself over here, Captain Marvel and grab my hand. I think we'd best be invisible before we get too close to the lights in case we're seen. Better keep hold too while we're up here, to save losing track of each other."

Ben looked quickly in the mirror, blinked twice and the brothers blinked out of visible existence.

"I'm glad I have hold of your hand, Ben. It's a bit scary being right up here almost above the city, especially not being able to see you."

"Yes I feel the same. But no worries, we're doing good."

"Have you any idea which way is home when we get to the city, Ben?"

"I *think* I'll be able to find it alright, but we'll need to find something familiar to get our bearings on first and as quickly as we can."

"I'll be glad of that. It would be grim to lose our way in Melbourne now after all this."

"Too right it would. We'd best soon spot something we know though, this wind is starting to take us out towards Brighton Beach and the sea."

"Oh no," Toby groaned.

"It's okay, look, there's the Botanical gardens down there. We'll head for that. It's about as near home as we're likely to get flying with this cross-wind. I'm going to bring us up a size now," Ben said using the mirror. "That's better, our extra weight should slow us up a little so we won't overshoot the park. Let go of my hand and we'll use our coats to see if we can steer towards it. The park should be closed at this time of night, so once we're over it I'll make us visible again so we can see each other. Go for it," he shouted. "Now!"

The boys, chattering to each other all the while to stay in contact, gradually managed to drop height out of the main wind strength and angled themselves around until eventually they were streaking towards the park.

Abruptly they found they had company. They had flown straight into the flight path of some fruit bats, which had taken temporary residence in the park. The fruit bats, slightly larger than the boys in their still invisible shrunken form, sensed them with their radar-like squeaks and flew with them like a squadron of fighter planes on a sortie, curious as to what these other night flying creatures could be, or where they were heading. The boys considered this great fun. As soon as they were well over the park, they said farewell to their wing patrol and Ben restored their visibility, warning Toby he was about to drop them down to ground level.

"Get ready, here we go."

"Not in the pond, please Ben."

"I've a good mind to make *sure* of dropping you right in it, after that remark," Ben retorted. He held the mirror ready and as soon as he saw a likely landing place he went for it. They fluttered down slowly and landed as lightly as feathers together on the grass fairly near the park entrance.

"Wow" exclaimed Toby. "We've done it, we're actually here in Melbourne. Hooray."

"This *is* great but it's still a long way home on foot. It normally takes Mum and Dad about a quarter of an hour to *drive* us home from here."

"We could get a taxi, Ben?"

"We could, but we've no money to pay for it."

"Mum would pay him when we--ah, of course, Mum's

248

still in England. Sorry Ben, I'm getting tired and not thinking straight."

"I know, it crossed my mind too. *Dad's* here in Melbourne but of course we can't tell *him*, or anyone else come to that, that *we* are. After all our efforts to get here I'm beginning to think we're stuffed even now. We don't have the time or the energy to walk all that way. Even if we did, the police might pick us up for wandering the streets late at night. Crikey, can you imagine the fuss there would be? The whole family would hear about it and we'd never be able to explain how we got here. We would lose the use of Sandy for sure. In any case I'm tired like you and I doubt if Sandy can help us any more to get home."

"Pity we can't make a carving of Dad, then Sandy could help us," Toby remarked.

"That sounds comical, making a carving of Dad. Poor Dad, I expect we'd make a right mess of it if we tried. Shame, the idea sounds okay, except that Dad would then know all our secrets. If only we had something else to-- wait a minute," he said fishing in his coat pockets. "I brought the cat carving with me. The first time I saw this," he said producing the carving from his pocket, "I realised how much it was like our own cat, Cass. I've been missing him almost as much as Dad, that's why I've been carrying it about with me. Do you think it's worth a try?"

"It's a bit risky Ben, there's no telling where that cat might take us?"

"It can't be any more risky than our flight just now with Ed the eagle."

"That's true. I thought the eagle was going to eat us for sure. But he was good and that's a good name for him. Ed the eagle," he repeated. "I like that, it sounds familiar somehow."

"At least we have the usual get-out, Toby. If by using the cat it takes us somewhere completely different we can still use the stone to get us home." He was busy with his many pockets again. "Perhaps I should put my photo of Cass near the carving when we try it. It sounds a bit silly I know, but perhaps then Sandy will know which cat we need to go to. It's all down to magic after all. Who knows, it might work?"

"Yes, give it a try, Ben. I think we're at the stage now that anything's worth a go."

Ben told Toby to position the dice when they were both ready. Ben put the photograph of his cat flat on one hand and carefully placed the cat carving on one edge. Toby moved closer and placed the dice as requested. As he took a step back, he tripped on a cat and nearly fell backwards into a swimming pool. Cat he thought? Swimming pool? When they had a closer look around in the dark, they found it was their own swimming pool at the bottom of their garden. The cat he had tripped on *was* Cass who had now recognised Ben and was already making a huge fuss around his legs.

"Cass? It really is you and you've brought us home. I've had you in my pocket all the time, you could have probably brought us here straight from England."

"He would've too I bet," said Toby. "But then we'd have missed out on an awful lot of fun and adventure, especially that flight with the eagle"

The two boys had now forgotten their tiredness.

"We're here, we've done it," Toby cried out happily.

"Shush, Toby, or we'll wake the whole street up."

"Whoops, I'd forgotten it's late at night and we haven't seen Dad yet," Toby whispered.

"Come on, let's go see him now. He must be asleep as all the lights are out. We'll have to be very, very quiet and invisible too. If he should accidentally wake and see us we'd be in no end of trouble."

"Yep, okay."

The boys became invisible once again which strangely enough never seemed to have any effect on Cass at all. Nor did the cat seem to notice that he too had become invisible because of Ben carrying him. Ben put him down while he took the spare key for the back door from their special hiding place out in the back yard. Once they had let themselves in they crept up the stairs and peeped through their parent's bedroom door. There he was, their lovely Dad, in his bed fast asleep and snoring. They had missed him so much these last weeks. With tears welling up in their eyes they crept across the bedroom to take a closer look at him. They realised his leg problem must have improved as his walking stick was leaning against the wall near the door instead of being close to the bed. They both desperately wanted to give him a big hug and tell him all about their exciting trip to see him, but were sensible enough to know it was impossible. Instead they took it in turns to lean over him and gently kiss him goodnight and whisper their love for him. Feeling for his little brother, Ben then took him by the hand and led him gently towards the door.

Just as they were leaving the room their Dad suddenly sat up in his bed seeming to look directly at them and shouted "What the hell--? Oh it's you Cass! You silly damned cat, you frightened the life out of me." Apparently the cat, wondering what the boys were up to, had jumped on the bed to find out.

The two boys had to exit the house even more quietly than expected but as quickly as they could before they started laughing over the cat incident. This at least took some of the sadness away at the thought of returning to

England again without their Dad. Ben stroked the cat carving and replaced it in his coat pocket with the others before they both made a big fuss of their real cat who had followed them out through the yard door. Finally Ben whispered, "See you again soon, Cass. Take care of Dad."

Getting back to their grandparent's house was a doddle after all they had been through. By the poolside in Melbourne they simply grabbed hands, kissed the stone and abruptly found themselves back in the loft in England. Quite amazingly, everything seemed perfectly normal there. Sandy was obviously still running and they had not been missed.

The boys found it difficult that night to even consider sleeping. They were still full of excitement having finally reached Australia, yet knowing at the same time their holiday in England was almost at an end.

"This is still all so unbelievable," said Ben. "It's like the best dream ever and there always seems to be something more to do, more things to find out."

"More adventures," murmured Toby thoughtfully. "I'm so glad Grandad chose *us* for it."

"I keep expecting him to ask what we've managed to do with it, but I guess if he used it for a long time himself, he'll have a pretty good idea anyway."

"Yep I suppose he would, I never thought of that. Wonder what adventures *he* had"

"He said something the other day about having had plenty of practice at carving. I wonder how many of the carvings in the chest are his. Perhaps when we come again we'll be able to find out and hear about some of his adventures. We ought to try and get to have a long chat with our great Nanny Flo too, one of these days, about the things that happened to her long ago."

"Why, what happened to her, Ben?"

"Well, I've been reading that little book she has written. It's all about her life and about her relatives back in the early nineteen-hundreds. She had an uncle who was a tram-driver, one that made church organs, a grandfather who was a compositor in a newspaper print shop, and would you believe, she was actually kidnapped when she was a young girl."

"You're kidding."

"No. Apparently after losing both her parents she had to live with her Granny, who didn't look after her very well, so her uncles kidnapped her one day against her Granny's wishes to take her to live with *them*. Then later on she wrote quite a lot about her life during the last big war. It's all ever so interesting."

"Wow. I must have a read of that."

"Yes you really should. But you'll need to be quick as I have to give it back to her soon."

... ...

Chapter Thirty

The following morning to Toby's annoyance his mother decided he must have a hair-cut as he was due to start a new school on their return home to Australia.

"*Must* I have it done over here, Mum? I shall have three days at home before I start school."

"Yes I'm afraid you must. We'll probably all suffer from jet lag on the first day back and I shall have far too much else to worry about, getting clothes washed and shopping done before I go back to work myself. So come along, let's get it over and done with. Are you coming with us, Ben?"

"No mine's alright thanks, Mum. I had it cut just before the holiday."

"That's fine then. Hopefully we'll only be gone for an hour or so. Nan and Grandad will be back from the shops before then I expect. I think you are big and ugly enough to look after yourself for that short time," she joked, "So we'll leave you to it."

"Yes I'll be okay, Mum."

Once they had gone, Ben sat in the bedroom for a short time recalling all the fantastic things that had happened to them over the period of their holiday. When the dinosaur incident came to mind he was suddenly seized with a new urgency. What had he done with his old pair of trainers? 'Oh my God', he thought. 'They are still in the shoebox under the bed'.

Getting on his hands and knees he groped around underneath the low bed until he could feel and drag the box out. He began lifting the lid but closed it again extremely quickly—the stench that came from it was absolutely vile! This wasn't just the normal unpleasant smell of a pair of his well-worn trainers confined in a small place, this was from blood-soaked trainers that had been hidden in the box more than three weeks ago! Ben gagged at the smell and the realisation that they had been under his bed all this time. He had to get rid of them and the quicker the better. Rummaging around in the bedroom he found an old plastic carrier bag. In this he figured they would be less likely to be discovered amongst the rubbish at a random check than in the shoebox and after all, that would need to go into the cardboard recycling box for the following week's collection, providing of course it was not blood-stained.

Opening the bedroom window he took a deep breath of fresh air, removed the lid and without looking at it quickly dumped the contents of the box directly into the carrier bag, instantly tying the top of it as tightly as he could. Before breathing again he checked the inside of the box for staining. Luckily there was none obvious, so grabbing his deodorant spray he liberally treated both the inside of the box and the bedroom with a long squirt before starting off downstairs and breathing normally again with the gruesome bag clutched in one hand, yet unsure of what he was to do with it.

As if some unseen magic was at work to assist him, he heard loud ominous noises coming from outside in the road. He recognised that sound. The rubbish removal lorry was coming up the road and emptying the wheelie-bins. If he could only make it in time?

He dived down the remaining stairs and threw open the front door. Yes! Their bin was standing outside undisturbed. He flung open the gate, lifted the bin-lid and dropped his evil-smelling bag inside as the gloved hand of the bin-collection man reached for its handle.

"Cor, only just in time, mate," the man said.

"Yes, I did leave it a bit late," Ben replied cheerily as he closed the gate behind him.

Back indoors Ben began thinking how much they were going to miss the use of Sandy once they were home. As this was going to be all too soon now he decided to take a small adventure on his own for half an hour or so and wondered what he should do.

'I know,' he thought. 'The way that stream in the park appears from underground intrigues me. I've been going to suggest we have a closer look at it sometime. I think maybe *now* is the time.'

As he prepared to start Sandy he briefly wondered about the settings, but having already decided on only a brief adventure without wishing to get too involved with possible out-of-time problems, he quickly set the alarm, then the valve to a normal running position.

After picking up the pouch and the torch he wink-wished himself to the park and made his way straight over to where the little stream ran from the tunnel into the bright sunlight. Climbing down to the ledge where they had stored their shoes while sailing their boat recently, he peered under the arch of the tunnel. There was a metal grille fixed there, probably to prevent the danger of children entering and possibly getting stuck inside. Over the years the grille had been damaged or had eroded away leaving a hole a little bigger than an adult male hand-size towards the top. Feeling adventurous and having checked to make sure no one was about he simply stared into his mirror, shrank, and then switching on the torch, climbed through the hole.

Once inside, the torchlight revealed the tunnel had been constructed by the bolting of huge old flanged metal pipe sections together at some time in the past. In his now shrunken form he was small and light enough to carefully walk along the tunnel on the flat crusted area at the sides of the running water formed by mud and crud over the years.

At first he found himself counting his paces as he moved along the tunnel, until the thought amused him that by now he was possibly walking below some of the neighbouring houses along his grandparents' road and wondered what would go through the minds of the people living there if they were to know.

He stopped for a second or two to shine his torch around. His grandparents had once told him that when they had been children the whole estate had been built on farmland which had a small stream running across it. Presumably, to save the possibility of flooding in the future, this part of the stream had been specially piped to retain the natural land drainage before the local roads and housing had been installed. Ben had a developing interest in English history and felt quite honoured to think he might be seeing something no-one had set eyes on since the old farm had existed, seventy or more years ago. He realised he was only seeing it *now* because of his privileged use of Sandy, then immediately felt selfish for not at least sharing this adventure with his brother. But then, this was a chance for an adventure at the end of their holiday he could not afford to miss.

After walking for several minutes the light of the torch beam showed the tunnel ahead veering slightly to the left. Having had the chance to explore the local area and footpaths these last few weeks, he imagined the stream would likely have come all the way underground from the big park situated the other side of the main London Road.

"That would be really good," he said to himself excitedly. "I could probably walk the entire length of this and come out the other side of the estate and into that park. Toby and I could probably use this as our own secret footpath at some time in the future."

Without warning, part of the hardened sediment he was walking on gave way. His foot slid dangerously, following the inside curve of the pipe until the water was past his ankle almost causing him to fall headlong into the stream. "Oh damn," he swore to himself as he strove to recover his balance.

Once he was back on a firm footing, he switched off the torch putting it inside his pocket, then leaned back against the wall of the tube while he slipped off his right trainer and emptied it of water. The noise from the emptying water as it dribbled back into the silent stream echoed loudly and eerily along the old metal drainpipe in the darkness. Now holding his sodden trainer under one armpit and managing somehow to retain his balance he removed and wrung the water from his sock. His eyes were becoming more used now to the almost no-light condition, so he paused in his actions for a second or two while looking back towards the entrance. He found he could just make out the dim reflection of light on the water coming from around the slight set in the tunnel and was quite surprised to see how much distance he had already covered. As he struggled in the poor light, balancing on one leg trying to get his wet sock back on his foot, he considered his current position should he be above ground.

It was possible he might by now be nearing the main London Road. Wondering if he would hear the noise of the traffic above should he happen to be that close, he stood very quietly for a while once he had his shoe back on, listening. But instead of the sound of distant traffic coming from above he heard a gentle splashing noise from somewhere behind him in the tunnel. Whatever *is* that? He had not passed any dripping water or anything else that he had been aware of to create a noise like that. While listening intently, the noise stopped at times for a while, but each time he heard it again it seemed as if it had moved a little nearer.

Something was moving back there and to his concern it could only be heading in his direction. Ben knew that it couldn't be human because of the tunnel size and the small hole in the grating. Somewhat nervously, it occurred to him that when there was a silence, it was either pausing to listen, or to sniff for his scent along the silted crusty stream edges where he had been walking. His normal calmness began to desert him. He felt a strange prickling up his spine and his heart began to quicken while hastily fumbling in his pocket to retrieve the torch. He paused on the brink of flicking on the switch. Would the light of the torch assist his pursuer in its hunt? He could do nothing else. He needed that light if he were to move on along the tunnel in an attempt to stay ahead of whatever it was. Switching it on but without even daring to flash the light behind him in case it should show him something he would rather not see, he hurriedly recommenced his walk.

He had at first been under the impression the tunnel would lead him to the other park. Now he began to worry as to whether there might also be a grille at that end of the tunnel. There might not be a hole there he would be able to escape through. Then a really worrying thought struck him, it was quite possible that the contained stream might follow the old land contours underground for a long, long way before he was likely *to find* another end to the tunnel.

'Oh God, what have I done? I haven't told a soul what I am doing. I could be in real trouble in here and no-one would ever know,' he fretted himself. 'If something bad did happen to me I might never be seen again.'

He began to speed up his pace, but this was not easy inside a pipe with water running along it. He desperately wanted to run but knew that would be inviting disaster as it was so slippery underfoot. He glanced back again. What little reflected light there was now seemed to flicker as his pursuer moved steadily nearer. He looked ahead again and risked switching off the torch briefly in the hope of seeing light from the far end, but there was only an intense blackness. Worse still, when he switched the torch on again the already dimmed beam began to flutter as if the batteries were about to give up altogether. Abruptly he rallied and decided to turn and face his unseen follower while there was still some life in the batteries. Whatever it should turn out to be, he had no intention of letting it leap on him from behind without even knowing what he was up against. Then, just as abruptly a far better idea came to him.

"Enough is enough," he muttered to himself, "I'm out of here."

His hand already on the pouch around his neck calmly went for the stone. The next second he was fumbling frenziedly through the pouch, then his pockets. The stone was not there. His mind flashed back. Toby sometimes carried it when they were out together. Foolishly, Ben had not checked the pouch before starting out on his solitary adventure.

By now his pounding heart was making so much noise inside his chest he could no longer hear the stealthy approach of his pursuer. Ben considered invisibility but in this instance it was unlikely to help him. The thing apparently following him seemed to have little need of light for direction and might just as easily find him by scent alone. He had no carvings with him to change for assistance. In his near panic, his brain was sluggish. The only answer he could come up with was to shrink again in the hope the creature might yet pass him by.

Ensuring he had both feet firmly set on the crusty silt edge before changing size he swiftly brought the mirror up to his face while shining the last glimmers of the torch on it to ensure he had the mirror the right way round. But as he did so he must have held the mirror slightly off angle and instantly screamed at the reflection the weak torch light revealed. It was not his own face he saw reflected in the mirror, nor that of his unseen pursuer which was still somewhere in front of him, it was the evil yellow eyes and vicious teeth of a massive rat towering immediately behind him.

An awful lot happened in the next few seconds. Somehow, Ben managed to keep his nerve, move the mirror slightly and shrink again. As the torch and mirror swung away from his face he saw a massive dark shape launching itself in his direction. But the dark shape flew straight over his head at the enormous rat behind him. He could only cower below the two huge fearsome creatures and cover his ears to protect them from the horrendous noise of battle raging above him. A battle that he could only imagine would end with him as the prize.

At his now tiny size, any one of the huge clawed feet scrabbling around in the death fight so close to him could either knock him flying into the now deep water to drown, or at the least, could permanently flatten him. An enormous roar and horrifying crunching sound accompanied by an awful abruptly cut off piercing shriek, signalled the end of the battle. Then nothing--

other than a long period of extreme silence which seemed to put more strain on Ben's ears than the previous battle noise.

All too soon, Ben became aware of something huge moving towards him, sniffing the settling air. He cowered to make himself as small as possible with his arms protectively over his head as if in an attempt to hide, while fervently wishing he could physically disappear altogether, when there was a sudden rumbling, deafening "Per-r-row-w-w!"

Ben all but collapsed with the relief at recognising the sound of his pursuer. It was his old friend Biggles who must obviously have squeezed through the hole in the grating and followed his scent all the way along the tunnel.

In the following still seconds of sheer relief, Ben sensed Biggles stiffen and turn as if listening to something further into the dark reaches of the tunnel. Then he heard it himself. It sounded as if a whole army of shrieking rats was on its way to avenge their fallen comrade. Without another thought Ben groped in the blackness and grabbed hold of his friend's fur and climbed for his life. As the horrible squealing noise grew louder he felt Biggles stiffen again as if wondering if he should take them on. Then abruptly with his decision taken, they were off, streaking along the old pipe at top speed, seemingly regardless of the water and general crud. Ben was quite sure they were going to lose this horrific race as the noise from the rats began to gain on them. But luck was with them. Many of the leading rats paused at the smell of blood having reached the scene of the previous battle, causing congestion in the tunnel and giving Biggles a much needed advantage. The relief of sudden bright daylight filtering through the metal grille welcomed them at the end of the pipe. The old cat squeezed through the damaged grille with a tiny Ben hanging on for dear life and then pelted through the park, over the fence and home. The rats on reaching the light of day simply gave up the chase.

Biggles found his favourite spot under the apple tree and sat down to have a clean-up. Ben gently slid from the cat's back and restored himself to normal. He made a huge fuss of the old cat, before shakily making his way indoors. Once indoors he felt quite surprised that other than one wet foot and somewhat damaged nerves, he was still intact. He cleaned himself up, switched off everything in the loft, then went into the kitchen and poured the cream off a new pint of milk into a dish. Out in the garden Ben placed the cream down in front of his rescuer.

"Here you are old friend, and you can expect more of these from now until I have to leave you. I shall never know how or why you knew to follow me, but I owe you big time. He gave Biggles a thorough check over, which Biggles never protested to at all, to find luckily that the old cat had come through his fight completely unscathed. Thank you Bigsy," he said giving him another stroke and a cuddle. "I've always loved you."

When the others came home from the shops and the barbers they found Ben and his old beloved Biggles all cuddled up and fast asleep under the apple tree.

··· ··· ···

Chapter Thirty-One

It was the last evening of their holiday. During the afternoon their grandparents had driven them around to say goodbye to most of their relatives and friends in the local area, all very nice but quite sad.

Ben and Toby had made a special visit to their Great Nan to return her little book and tell her how impressed they were with it and to talk about some of the happenings during the many years of her life that had been so vastly different and interesting from their own.

Now back at the house, tired from the driving and conversation, the adults were having a quiet doze, which meant the boys could creep up the stairs to have one last look at the loft. They knew it was doubtful they would get the chance in the morning as they would all be busy preparing for the trip to the airport.

After making sure they had left the trains as their Grandad would want them, they refilled and started the old sand machine for the last time, marvelling yet again as the big wheel and fan blade spun effortlessly. After a few minutes of quiet watching each with their own thoughts, Ben said, "We'd best turn Sandy off now, Toby. We must get him back in the chest and tidy things up."

Toby leant forward and said, "Goodbye old friend," and turned off the sand valve. They both watched in silence as the wheel slowed and came to a stop.

"It's good that Grandad says we don't have to take him apart. We'll just take off the sand pots and lock him back in the chest, ready for the next time we come over and see him."

Ben carefully lowered Sandy into the chest watching yet again as the old machine shrank to fit the space while Toby dismantled their mouse trap security alarm and added it to the rest of the contents. Ben checked through the pouch making sure to include the stone slab before locking it all away inside the old chest and whispering "Goodbye and thank you, Sandy."

Once everything in the loft was safely switched off they went down the ladder closing the trap-door behind them.

"I am so looking forward to being with Dad and Cass again, yet I'm dreading the thought of saying goodbye to Nan and Grandad tomorrow and leaving Sandy and all our adventures behind," Ben said sadly.

"So am I, Ben. We've sure had some good fun with them all haven't we?"

"It's been a fantastic holiday. The hardest part of all is that we can't tell anyone about our magical adventures, but even discounting those it's still been one heck of a wicked holiday. I've loved every minute of it."

"I wonder how long it will be before we can come again," Toby mused.

"A couple of years at *least* I expect, Toby. There's one bright side to it though, Grandad said Sandy was ours to use for a good few years yet, so we'll just have to work on getting back here as soon and as often as we possibly can. We've hardly begun to find out what we *can* do with Sandy's help yet."

"Which has been your favourite adventure so far, Ben?"

"Oh, that's a hard one. I loved them all, especially getting to Dad. But despite the danger we were in, I think my favourite was the fire and our rescue from that old house. It's largely the mystery of it all that intrigues me. There is still so much we can't easily explain about that event. What was your favourite, Toby?"

"I must admit I really enjoyed that fire adventure too, even though I was terrified at the time. I was glad to be able to prove to myself that my warnings of danger can be right, too. But *my* best adventure was with King and his family. We must try to get to see them again sometime."

"Yes, I loved our old lion friend and his cubs myself. Hey, talking about our adventures, I thought about the dinosaur one earlier and suddenly remembered my old trainers were still in the box under the bed."

"Oh no! That could have been disastrous!"

"It's okay, I've dealt with them." Ben related his story to Toby. "I've just got to put the box in the recycling collection now."

"Are you sure it's alright now for recycling?"

"Yes of course," Ben replied, picking up the box and lifting off the lid. "Here," he said thrusting the box towards Toby's nose. "Have a smell."

"Er yuck, no thanks!" Toby moved well clear. "I wouldn't want to smell *that* if it had only had your *normal* smelly trainers in it, but I wonder what will happen with those trainers now?"

"How do you mean?"

"Well, suppose they should cut open that bag and see the blood on them. They might think they've found a clue to a murder or something?"

"I doubt they *would* cut it open, it will probably just get buried. But even if the blood *was* found they wouldn't be able to tie it to anyone. In fact if some poor scientist *was* given the task to identify it, he would be altogether at a loss to explain it. Fairly fresh blood from a long extinct dinosaur!"

Toby giggled. "It's not surprising it smelt so bad when you think about how old it must have been."

"Ugh, let's change the subject shall we?"

"Best idea yet," Toby agreed.

In their bedroom, they found their mum starting to pack their clothes and bits in the suitcases ready for the morning departure. She knew this was the last evening they would all spend together for some time and was suffering very mixed feelings. She dearly wanted to be home with Jack again but dreaded the thought of having to say goodbye to her parents and to England for such a long time.

"Come on boys, you can help me with this. Put all the clothes and stuff to one side that you'll need tomorrow, and I'll pack the rest. This is awfully sad to have to do this but the sooner it's done, the better. It will save us a lot of time and worry tomorrow."

Once they had finished, Ben and Toby wandered out in the garden for a last look around. Their grandfather followed them out.

"Hey! I want a word with you two."

"What's up, Grandad?" Ben asked.

"I was just having a word with an old friend of mine. He was walking his dog and stopped for a chat at the front gate. He was telling me about some strange goings on down at the station a little while ago. He's a policeman you see."

The colour instantly drained from the boy's faces.

"It seems there was an attempted mugging of a little old lady a few days ago near our park pavilion. Apparently the old lady not only fought off the two thugs but somehow managed to get them both on the ground, produce a rope and tie them up securely before going to fetch the police. It was a feat quite beyond her, according to Fred. The muggers themselves apparently said they thought it was witchcraft. Then to top it all, the rope used for this incredible event mysteriously disappeared from the police station almost from under the policemen's noses. Fred said it was a most peculiar day, as even the station doors kept opening and closing all of their own accord."

Their grandad stopped and stared at them, first one, then the other, reminding them somewhat of a similar recent occasion with the Eagle.

"I suppose this wouldn't have anything to do with you two boys, now would it?"

Ben looked at Toby while raising his eyebrows and shrugging his shoulders.

"Grandad, we have to own up, it *was* us. We're really sorry, we never meant to cause any trouble but when we saw those two attacking the old lady we had to do something. We did our best to help without giving our secret away, but when we--"

Ben was interrupted by their Grandad grabbing the two of them together and giving them a huge bear hug.

"I just knew it had to be something to do with you guys as soon as old Fred told me about it. Very well done lads, I never dared to dream you'd be able to put the machine to such good use so quickly, that's absolutely brilliant."

"You mean you're not cross with us."

"Cross, of course not. I'm even more pleased than old Fred and his colleagues, and that's saying something.

They haven't a clue how it all came about but they are ecstatic to get those two behind bars at last. It seems they have been trying to catch them red-handed for several years. I just needed to make sure it *was* you guys that were responsible for the good deed and to thank you and say how proud I am of you both. I'm so glad old Fred came along before you had to go home. I only wish I could tell him about you and what really happened."

"Gosh thanks Grandad." The colour started to come back into Ben's face. "But it's you they have to thank, really. I doubt we would have been able to help her at all if you hadn't let us become adventurers."

"Yes thanks, Grandad," Toby said, now red-faced with happy embarrassment. "We've had some wicked adventures."

"Good, I'm so pleased," he answered. "I've no idea how you pulled that one off and it shall remain your secret for the time being. Sometime though, when you're a bit older, I'd love to hear all about your adventures. I might even get to tell you about some of my own."

"Oh yes, we'd love that," Toby admitted.

"Come on then fellers," their grandfather said putting an arm around their shoulders. "Let's go and see what the others are up to."

... ...

Chapter Thirty-Two

Air turbulence disturbed the boys' long seated sleep.

Toby pressed his pointing finger against the aircraft window. "Look! There's a Jumbo over there just like ours, it's probably on its way to England."

Ben leaned across his younger brother to peer into the distance. "Oh yes, I can see it. It looks so small from here it's hard to imagine so many people being in there. It's almost as if they've been shrunk by magic," he added quietly with a huge yawn.

"Yes, just like we were at times. I'm really going to miss our magic."

"Shush" Ben whispered, putting a finger to his lips. "I agree with you and I'm missing it too. This flight is so *slow* after Sandy travel that it's really boring but we have to keep very quiet about it," he added, looking at the sleeping passengers around them. "Sandy could have had us to Aus. and *back* again twice by now. Oh well, never mind, let's see how we are doing."

The boys turned on the small screens set in the seat-backs in front of them and checked the moving map lay-out to see which part of the world they had reached. Other than this device and the time duration, the fact they were thirty-thousand feet higher and travelling at least four hundred miles an hour faster, this trip did not *now* feel that much different from their usual daily ride on the school bus, bumpy road stretches included they thought, as the huge Jumbo-Jet went through another long patch of air turbulence.

They were at last nearing the end of the twenty-four hour flight home to Melbourne, Australia. The first part of the journey had been quite miserable after leaving their grandparents at the airport. But things had soon brightened up once they thought about home and their Dad who would soon be waiting for them at the other end of their flight.

"Right, we had best wake Mum now. Our coastline is just coming up on the map and I know she wants to see Uluru on the way in."

As he spoke a great cheer went up from some Aussie students clustered near the windows. Cassie was instantly awake at this and soon watching with the boys as the first signs of the Australian landmass came into view far below.

"There she is, the old beaut," shouted one of the Australians. A big cheer went up in which the family joined.

These were mostly students on their way home after several years of study at various universities, and 'backpackers,' youngsters travelling the world while they were able, with just a rucksack. Ben and Toby held them in admiration thinking, 'one of these days…'

Soon they were flying past the famous red mountain below named by the Australian Aboriginals as Uluru, yet it was still several hours before they finally descended and bumped to a stop on the Melbourne runway.

Once through customs they were absolutely delighted to see their Dad waiting for them. He was still using a stick for some support but he told them his doctor had said he would be back to normal within a few months.

He was delighted to have his little family back safe and sound and with him once more.

All three of them slept on until late the next morning when they finally woke to the smell of cooking sausages and bacon on the barbecue.

"I have some hot news to tell you guys," Jack said as he served out the food. "Firstly, with a note from our doctor I managed to get a full refund on the flight fare I never used."

"Oh well done," Cassie cried. "I must admit I was worried at the thought of losing all that money."

"Secondly, I've just heard the firm's insurance are going to pay me something out on the accident."

"So they should," Cassie said, "It was their faulty equipment that caused it."

"And thirdly," he said, "I'm in for a good yearly bonus soon. At least enough for a few weeks holiday in England. That's if you could stand another holiday over there of course," he said with a grin.

"Oh wonderful! How about we go for a Christmas," Cassie asked. "I'd love that. It seems ages since I've had a real winter Christmas."

"Suits me fine, I can't wait after missing out on the last holiday," he answered. "Providing of course the doc is happy with that. What about you two guys? Would you like to come along?"

The boys had been too busy with huge grins and thumbs up signals behind their parents' backs to comment until now.

"You try and stop us, Dad, you bet we're coming."

"I'll go and ring your Nanny and Grandad straightaway," said Cassie excitedly. "I'm sure they'll be over the moon."

"I don't think they'll like the idea at all," Jack said with a straight face.

"Why ever not?" Cassie's face registered some shock.

"Not at two o'clock in the morning over there, I'll bet," he said laughing.

"Oh my God, I hadn't dreamed about the time back in England with all the excitement."

"Talking of dreams," their Dad began, "I had one recently about you guys. I dreamed I was asleep in my bed and you three came all the way from England and kissed me on the cheek. I woke up suddenly to find the cat had jumped up on the bed and was licking my face."

"Oh, that's so funny," laughed Cassie.

"Yes that was, but then I thought I heard voices down the yard near the pool. So I slipped on my pants and grabbed the torch to see if someone had got in and was messing about."

"What happened?" Ben asked nervously glancing across quickly at Toby's reactions.

"Well there was no-one in sight, anywhere, but it was all a little spooky."

"What was?" Cassie looked a little puzzled.

"Knowing you were due home soon, I had been tidying up and had swept the yard that evening, but there was still a fine layer of dust around. When I had a look around with the torch, I came across two separate sets of small footprints near the pool which led to our door and then back again. But the strange thing was that there were no entry footprints to or from the yard. I know it sounds stupid, but it was almost as if whoever or whatever they were, they had been beamed down then back up again as they do in Star Trek. I had a job to get back to sleep that night I can tell you for thinking of aliens."

The boys could not contain themselves any longer. They both burst out laughing, with relief as much as anything else. They knew exactly what had happened and what their father had just said wasn't so far from the truth. But there was no way they could tell him.

Looking a little put-out, he asked, "What did I say that was so funny? It really was spooky," he objected.

"Sorry dad, it was the thought of you creeping about in your pants with a torch looking for aliens. You have to admit it does sound comical. It was probably just a Joey, anyway, they can jump quite a distance. You probably just didn't spot where it landed."

"Yes, I guess you're probably right, Ben, and it was dark, so that does seem a pretty good explanation."

"Dad, we haven't told you a thing yet about our holiday," Ben hastily got in as an attempt to move everyone's thoughts away from the unexplained visitation.

"When we first arrived over there, Grandad was already in the loft and he invited us up to show us his model railway------"

Later, when the boys had a chance to talk alone, Toby said, "Geeps Ben, that was dodgy, Dad hearing us when we were down by the pool."

"Yeah, poor old Dad. Finding something like that would have spooked *us,* especially a few weeks ago."

"Good job you came up with the Joey idea."

"Yes, but I felt so rotten though, it must have made him feel really silly."

"Yep, I'll bet it did, but what about his great news of our next holiday?"

"Oh yes, awesome! We'll be back for more adventures with Sandy sooner than we expected. In the meantime we'll have to get our heads together and try and raise some new ideas for adventures to experiment with."

"Come to think of it Ben, we haven't tried the number *six* on the dice yet. I wonder what new wonders that might open up for us?"

...The End (of Volume One)......

Next in the series-

Volume Two: Return to the Lore.

More than a year passes before the youngsters return to the UK. Slightly older and wiser, they are eager to increase their knowledge and experience in the use of the ancient skills allowed them. By delving into some of the mysteries previously experienced together with new abilities presented to them, they begin to meet with people, races and creatures they have only read or dreamed about in legendary tales or history. Both boys are slowly coming to realise they have only scratched the surface of their ultimate boundaries and are unaware of the hazards they will likely encounter should they continue......

Lightning Source UK Ltd.
Milton Keynes UK
UKOW03f1359191014

240301UK00002B/15/P